THE CLOUD
AND THE FIRE

THE CLOUD
AND THE FIRE

BOSTON TERAN

Copyright 2013 by Brutus Productions, Inc.

Library of Congress Control Number: 1-954903801.

ISBN: 978-1-56703-062-4

Published in the United States by High Top Publications LLC, Los Angeles, CA
and simultaneously in Canada by High Top Publications LLC

Cover design by brightspark
Interior design by Alan Barnett Design

Printed in the United States of America

ACKNOWLEDGMENTS

To Deirdre Stephanie and the late, great Brutarian…to G.G. and L.S…Mz. El and Roxomania…the kids…Natasha Kern…Janice Hussein, for her keen mind…And finally to my steadfast friend and ally, and a master at navigating the madness, Donald V. Allen.

This work is based on historical fact.

America is a cruel, cruel nation
but its cruelty is its beauty

American Flag *newspaper*
Matthew Christman
1862

• • •

And the Lord went before them by day
in a pillar of a cloud, to lead the way;
and by night in a pillar of fire,
to give them light;
to go by day and night

Exodus. 13.21

BOOK ONE

CHAPTER ONE

Along the eastern rim of the world, the Civil War began with a cannon shot after a century of hate. Each side would raise a prayer to God, then behind bands and flags its native sons would march along the dusty roads of fate. Each side had prophets and generals and governments pledged to their cause. Each side had songs. Each side believed in the will of means. Each side would end the war with lines of graves and fallen kings. Neither side would ever be the same.

Along the western rim of the world, a child was being born under the sign of the bear. From the port towns of Monterey and San Francisco, a generation with picks and axes was laying claims. They were carving out their history beneath a star cut from gold. There would be a war fought here too, but there would be no kings.

Outside Monterey, a road ran up from the bays, past stands of small farms then through the long, sloping waist-high grasslands to the coastal range that cut a line southeast across the state. At the Salinas River, the road began its ascent into the foothills.

Twenty miles of rutted disaster, chinked out by miners, carved along the edge of the mountains' stone facing. It was a treacherous road, a scar on nature's back. At most places no wider than the width of an ore wagon. At other points, so dangerously thin the ore wagon drivers carrying gold across the summit would disembark and walk in front of the horses, cursing and sweating, glancing down the sheer cliff face where their bones would rot if they should fall. All of this for a dollar a day and feed.

A morning fog drifted in from the ocean, heated and turned to haze along the flats, but as it climbed, got cold, and a runny mist began to settle in well up beyond the fall line leaving rows of dark clouds to cross the peaks. There was one road up, and one road down through Peneche Pass. The road beyond the eastern slope ran straight and flat across the wetlands to Tulare Lake and the scrap hut town, born under the shadow of the Whitehorse Mine.

A horse and rider had been traveling this road since dawn. By nightfall they were well up into the pass. There was no moon, or at least none to speak of. The clouds had seen to that. Good luck drifted past.

Horse and rider were silent. Like ghosts from some ancient myth they crawled along, cutting through the ground mist that seemed to give way as they passed. The only sounds were the short bursts of silvery wet from the horse's nose and mouth, and an occasional floating echo of bridle metal. In the dark the sound reminded the rider of the time of slaves, who'd spent their lives in leg irons cutting through the dusty fields along the Rio Colorado. Hobbling along, they'd hacked away the brush under the watchful eyes of the jefe's guards. The rider's legs were still scarred from those irons. The bones bent.

Horse and rider stopped. The ground mist had thickened. The road threaded around a huge outcropping of stone. Beyond was black. It was not hard for him to sense he was at the edge of the world. He rested his hands on the saddle horn and listened, picking through the wind for any sound that wasn't right. Each hand was missing an index finger.

His skin was dark like his ancestors whose blood, the blood of conquerors from Spain, mingled with the Indians of the western desert. A people born from rape, then bled down through the centuries till it had washed him ashore. His face was scarred, his eyes were black. And they missed nothing. They say he killed without remorse. That he hunted his prey with impunity and, like some biblical king, would never grieve. No one knew his face. The Whitehorse Mining Company had put out rewards. Each a promise, each unfulfilled. A line of graves had been his answer. They say his heart was black. It seemed he had been riding a thousand years.

He knew a mile ahead the road would reach the summit and in a small clearing cut from the woods, there was a cabin built as the mining company's relay station. He turned off the main road and began his ascent up the remains of a narrow path that led through broken rock and scrubby pines.

The incline became steeper, the trail more narrow, the rock more stubborn, the ground less giving. The horse was old but had not outlived its strength.

Sifting through the trees, faint traces of moonlight fell across the rider's coat: frock length, white, made from ancient African wool. Woven by Ethiopian slaves, this coat was a legacy from their time before the chains. Before their souls were stolen and shipped across the water to a nation of vagabonds.

On the back of the coat, in wools of red and black, was the face of a lion. The mantle a sign of its imperial past. The coat was yellowed and dirty brown. The dust and rain had scarred its face, but it still warmed. And there was a hole, a quarter's size, where the shoulder met the lung. Its edges singed black from powder smoke. The rider had survived even that. He knew he would wear that coat until he died.

Down a long hollow of black, a momentary wisp of yellow illuminated behind glass. He had come upon the relay station.

• • •

Along the valley floor the Ox River bent in a half-moon around Gull Hill. Lines of tents and huts ran up from the river bank to the Whitehorse Mine sitting just below the crest, its two story high founder shaft and sheds ringed by a penthouse held back the stone overhang.

Behind a row of tents near the shore a small group of men played Spanish Monte on a woolen horse blanket. They were killing time and drinking mescal from metal cans. Then, a Mex noticed a stalk of flames well up in Peneche Pass. The men turned to look and a grim silence settled in and you could hear the rushing well of water running through iron pipes from the mine to the river, poisoning it with rock and sludge. The flames got wind caught and yawed skyward.

"It's pretty high up," one remarked.

"The relay station," said another.

Within an hour a dozen men were climbing up through the pass on horses and mules, carrying torches to guide their way along that scratched out edge of road.

It was well past dawn when they reached the summit. The fog hadn't eased back yet, and they maneuvered in slow single file around the stone facing that opened to a clearing where the relay station was built.

The flames had burned down pretty low, leaving just scattered dots of reddish yellow guttering like fallen stars along the ground. The smoke drifted up thick and black. Where the roof had collapsed, a section of crossbeam was snapped off and bent up and it now stood just above the mist like St. Andrew's cross.

The men were given orders to fan out and begin the search. They would not find the ore, nor the wagon and horses. And the dead?

They would not find them either.

Nor their bones.

CHAPTER TWO

Like Rome, San Francisco was built on a ring of sacred hills. The town had been nothing more than a row of docks and half a dozen streets until the discovery of gold at Maxwell's Creek had brought a flood of argonauts who believed their dreams were in the ground to be dug up.

Beyond those few streets, the town had spread from Kerry Hill to Happy Valley. There were rows of shops, and warehouses made of brick with tin roofs, gambling halls and hotels all wedged up against each other and shacks, street after street of shacks, all thrown together with scrap wood, lining the outer rim of the districts. Beyond the shacks, tent cities made of canvas, burlap, and sections of mainsail dotted the hills.

The Christian horn of manifest destiny had blown. A Bible, pick and ax had replaced the Roman short sword. And preachers in wooden storefront hovels, with rows of benches under canvas roofs, divined the sacred principles of a land yet unfulfilled. Each man now was Adam.

• • •

The offices of the *American Flag* newspaper were on Sacramento Street, in a little clapboard rathole, where the road swept up and away from the harbor along a row of laborer shacks and mud lots. On the downslope behind the building was a dumping ground for trash and when the wind turned, you knew it.

The *Flag* was born of insurrection and crowned by some an influential voice of truth in the wilderness and by others branded a political manifesto that was a mouthpiece for deceit.

The editorials, of late, had aimed their vitriol at a clandestine group that was growing in quiet power in California and known as The Knights of the Golden Circle.

Sitting at his work desk in the shadows of the stairwell and writing by the light of a whale oil lamp was Matthew Christman. He was a brittle young man with a sallow complexion and thinning brown hair. There was a hint of faded aristocracy to him that some found offensive.

Matthew rummaged through his canvas satchel looking for tobacco and rolling paper. It was filled with notepads, pencils, two sets of spectacles, a notebook as thick as a Bible and just as important, and lastly, a honey colored bottle of laudanum. He rolled and lit a cigarette and looked over the editorial he was working on.

BEWARE OF HALOS

The Knights of the Golden Circle—the name conjures up a concept of Camelot in California, does it not? But was the idea of Camelot a secret citadel for the cutthroat notion of a California, bled of racial color? Purified of the bootstrap black, the illiterate greaser, the grinning grimy Chinese, the grim knife wielding Chilean, the grub brown Hawaiian. Because California is richer than the whole of America, it holds a special place in our pursestrings.

The Golden Circle is no halo, my friends, but a yellow flashburn of gunfire aimed at the very idea of the political overthrow of the most notoriously adventurous state in the mind of Americans...California. They want the state cut loose. They want it white. They want it now.

Bottles of lamp oil were flung through the *Flag* windows as Matthew sat there reading. There was a surge of gunfire and flying torches and the front rooms began to lace with flames. There were a few men working the press who scattered and ran.

Matthew managed to grab up his canvas satchel and notes and escape out the back, down the slope, and into that ravine of heaped trash.

From those rotting piles he watched through the smoke as hooded men dragged out the press and burned it. Beneath a clip of moon the metal blocks of letters melted in the flames. The steel rods of the press lathe bent and twisted under the heat. Others were torn from their struts and used to beat the managing editor, the one man they caught, till the bones in his back broke through the flesh.

• • •

The morning sun fell hard against the charred timbers. Some drifted through the crowd that had gathered there on the slope by that ruined clapboard frame. Those who worked for the *Flag* walked among the crowd shouting out their condemnations. They knew it was the Knights who had committed arson and murder, and they called out for help. The authorities questioned witnesses but to what end. One hooded man looked much like another, and the *Flag* had earned such enmity, one editorial at a time.

The next editor in line, one Randall Wilcox, stood on a chair and spoke. They had another press and a new location and would be writing about this, tonight, while continuing on with impunity in pointing out hypocrisy and lies and all efforts to undermine and corrupt the future.

Matthew stood among strangers. He looked at the place where the body had been beside the press. He was acutely aware of his own failings as a man. Last night pointed that out ever so clearly. A copy of his editorial lay in the dust. He bent down and retrieved it. He needed a shot of laudanum, and was reaching into the canvas satchel slung over his shoulder, when a voice called out, "Well, if it isn't Mr. Christman."

Turning, he saw Misters Latham, Holmes and Demerest. They were middle-aged men who had grown soft with success and harder because of it, and who shared the secret talk of bigots. Each had ruffled cuffs and a top hat of fine felt. They comported themselves with disdainful civility.

Mr. Demerest pointed at the editorial and remarked with a harsh flair, "Remember what happened to the snake in the garden, Mr. Christman."

Matthew answered, "Remember what happened to Adam, Mr. Demerest."

Matthew turned. It wasn't long before a hand got hold of that editorial. He looked up and was face to face with Mr. Demerest, who leaned in close and whispered, "That is precisely the kind of attitude the late editor at the *Flag* so prided himself on."

"The Great Knights of the Golden Circle," said Matthew. "What can you say about men when the courage of their commitment will only go as far as the sheet will stretch?" He then went to push past them.

Mr. Holmes got in his way. "There *is* one thing you can say. They are effective."

Then Mr. Latham added, "I don't think we have very much to worry about, not from someone with such woman's hands."

Matthew looked down at his hands. They were small, with soft, conical fingers. He stared back at the men. His mouth was dry. "They're not so weak they can't hold a pen," he said.

CHAPTER THREE

Through the small oblong framed second story hotel window Jason could see an endless forest of masts stretching out across Yerba Buena Cove and beyond that the small hump of earth known as Goat Island rose up out of the mist like the back of some mythic whale.

Jason sat on the edge of his cot in the corner of the room. As the long sleek fingers of his right hand floated the California Prayer Book across his palm, the middle finger cut the cards in half. He rolled the upper half of the deck away as the bottom half seemed to levitate from some unseen pressure. He repeated this motion an endless number of times, occasionally altering the direction of the break and the speed by which he continued the process. And each time he could call out the number and suit of the bottom card before it made its appearance thanks to the small gaper he had discriminately tucked into the ridge of flesh between his thumb and fingers.

The room wasn't much bigger than the cot, and the walls separating each cubicle were nothing more than canvas sheets stretched taut across the wooden struts and painted over.

The old man with the raspy voice in the room on the north side of his called out, "Jason, you there?"

He didn't answer.

"Jason? I know you're in there. I heard you come in."

With his free hand, he poured some water from a clay jug into a tin cup, took a drink, then answered flatly, "What do you want, Langston?"

There was a lingering pause. "I bumped into an old pard of mine last night. We panned the Cosumnes River outside Fiddletown in '54."

He shifted the cards to his left hand and began the endless process of manipulation.

"He's got a good claim on a stream up on Quail Hill. Been pulling in a clean fifty a day. Says he could do even better, but bein' as old as he is, and, well—"

Jason leaned back and rested his head against the window joist. The wind started to blow in from across the sandbars. Between the bilge water and the giant vats processing the sperm whales and spermaceti at the LONGHORN OIL AND CAMPHOR WORKS, the air was tainted with an acrid, bilious stink.

"You been out there eight times, old man," said Jason. "And eight times you went belly up. You've seen the elephant and it's just bone." Jason laid the cards and the gaper down by the clay jug then got up. He reached for his vest.

"I know, Jason." Langston cleared his throat. "But if you could see me to a hundred dollars for supplies."

After Jason finished buttoning up his vest, he leaned over and took the silver pocket watch that lay next to a stack of books on a candle box he'd been using for a side table. He wound the watch, then opened it, glancing at the small tintype that'd been cut and pressed into the casing.

The tintype showed a man and a woman. He was white; she was black. They sat side by side, hand in hand, against a flat dark drape. Their faces still the hope of youth.

"I know I owe you, Jason."

He looked into a section of broken mirror that was propped up against the wall above the wash basin. He had his father's long, thin face and the straight nose and high cheekbones that were his French heritage. But his eyes were the green of the tropics. His dark skin was not quite as dark as his Haitian mother, but dark enough. Stained enough so he had tried to cover it by letting his straight brown hair hang well below his shoulders, the sun bleaching it in the hope it would make the skin seem lighter. The streak of white along the temples softened the color even more. The moustache that hung over his lip, and the small imperial that grew on his chin beneath his mouth, these too, with flecks of early white, made his case. Defended his attempt to disguise the truth.

The old man didn't ask again. He could be heard mumbling as he dug around inside his head for a solution to his dilemma. Then a door opened and slammed shut.

Jason reached for his Bowie knife hanging from the same nail as his vest. A six-foot length of string leather had been run through the butt handle and tied off into a loop. He slipped the loop over his neck and hung the knife down off his back. It dangled waist high. Over that went his gray cotton coat.

His father used to say, there is a graveyard in our hearts of all the dead who lived there. Where was his father now, he wondered. He took the holster that was hanging over the back of the chair and checked his pistol. The late afternoon light drilled across the corner of the room where he kept his father's boots. They were tanned leather, knee high, polished until even the scars shined. These his father had worn when he commanded the 4 ème Regiment de Chasseurs à Cheval that marched for France across Europe, burning nation after nation toward history's reward. The boots were all that he had left of him, besides the watch.

At the door he hesitated, then moved the bed aside and lifted a cut section of floorboard where hidden was a blue metal candy box. Inside he kept his life, in cash. The currency was mixed: some foreign, some Secesh, a little gold, mostly Yankee green. He took out enough to make his play that night, a hundred he put inside an envelope. The rest was left inside the box, then hidden away.

The hallway was dark and stank of urine. In the harbor the hammering pile driver, staking out new wharf pylons, echoed down the corridor, a steady cadence of unceasing blows. He stopped by the old man's door. He took the envelope from his pocket and slipped it under the old man's door, silently wishing him good luck.

Outside the hotel Jason headed down the muddy street that ran past the moored and abandoned ships. Huddled there together in the dying light, the bleeding loss of detail gave birth to a mysterious sense of memory that always haunted him. As a boy, every Sunday, he rode piggyback behind his father on an old trace horse they'd borrow, through the village of New Harlem, past the Morning Star Church, all clapboard and whitewashed, with a sinking roof, and out into the Bronx hills across the river. As they rode along, his father would read to him in French from the epic *Chanson de Geste*—The Song of Roland.

Those great shadowed hulls banded together amidst the murky calm appeared to him that great stand of knights from the poem of his youth, there gathered up behind their saintly lord, Roland. The rear guard of Charlemagne, left behind to protect the pass, alone along the plains of Roncevalles, waiting for the final assault that would drive them into history.

• • •

Ahead the road bent around a rise that followed past the American Whale Company property. There, Jason passed acres of ground covered with cut sections of whale jawbone leaning up against wooden beams nailed to stakes driven into the ground. From a distance the stalks of bone looked like a forest of great palm fronds taller than a man. And when the wind blew up they shivered like wheat.

Farther on, a crew of blacks were carrying the shaved stalks of bone across their shoulders and dumping them in stacks along the road for the wagons to gather up. There was an endless monotony to their work. A drab, tiring gravity. Jason's life would be just like that except for the slight cheat in the color of his skin and the lie he lived with.

The shadow of a horse and rider cut across his path, kicked up dirt, then circled back. Jason looked up to see a young man, breathing hard, his fine horse lathered.

"Jason."

"Hello, Arlen."

"Didn't you hear me yelling to you?"

Jason shook his head no.

"I've been calling out to you all the way up from the docks."

"I guess I was drifting."

Arlen pulled his horse around and rode alongside Jason. "Drifting can be a dangerous preoccupation." Arlen took his hat off and wiped the sweat from his forehead, then slipped his hat back on. "I was heading over to Telegraph Hill. We got a transport wagon of ore from the mine that's two days late, so I'm going to see if we'd been notified."

As the work crew passed Jason listened to the men talk among themselves. The traces of their speech and cadence, their silent unities, returned him momentarily to the stoop outside the rooming house where his mother and he had shared a room.

"Jason, I can't stay and talk now." Arlen leaned down from the saddle and spoke so as not be overheard, "I think we've been robbed again at the mine. I may have a job for you."

"I gave up hunting," Arlen."

"To be a cheat at cards?" He mocked Jason with a laugh. "You may have given up hunting, but I'm not sure hunting has given up on you. We'll talk when I know more."

CHAPTER FOUR

Ocherous light. Dusk. Matthew trudged along the muddy road past the Parker house. Above the hillside's sandy emptiness was a hundred acres of ridgetop ringed with white and pink magnolias—the Whitehorse estate.

At the arbored gate he stopped and looked back over the city. The night was fast closing in. Lights from the campfires and cooking stoves gleamed like torches. Hidden from watchful eyes, Matthew got down a few more swallows of laudanum.

He took the path to where it opened up before the house. Three stories' worth of brick and mortar surrounded by a colonnade and capped by a cupola. A manmade crown trellised with thorny roses and four huge chimneys that reached up well beyond the roof.

Matthew turned as the front door opened.

Stepping out onto the veranda, framed in the hallway's candle-light, was Charles Julius Whitehorse. A tall man, he had no trouble filling out the doorway. He wore a fine silk shirt, but the sleeves were rolled up like any common day laborer.

"You must be Christman?"

"Yes."

Matthew came up the steps. They shook hands. Whitehorse had a thick fleshy fist and gnarled fingers. With his shaggy white hair, drooping white moustache, and wide weathered face he seemed more like a bucentaur than a man.

"Let's go into my den. We can get comfortable there and have something to eat if you like. Maybe a couple of drinks." Then he stopped in the doorway. "You drink, don't you, Christman?"

Matthew gave a little bite to his response, "What good American doesn't?"

"Oh, Mr. Christman, I'd heard you're a cynic. And you are. You're an honest to God cynic."

"Mr. Whitehorse, I can't quite tell from your tone if that remark is leaning toward a compliment, or an insult."

"It was leaning toward a compliment. You see, I hold cynics in the highest regard. They tend to be thinking men. Who don't bother trying to tell you what you want to hear. Oh, Christman, I was leaning toward compliment."

Whitehorse ushered Matthew into his den, which ran the length of the southeast wing of the house. Along one wall French doors opened out onto the veranda and beyond were the shadowed outlines of the barn, corrals and sheds. At the other end of the room was a fireplace made of quarry stone, large enough for a man to walk into. Whitehorse offered Matthew a seat at an octagonal gaming table.

Matthew noticed the inlaid rosewood crest that had once been the pride of some long since fallen clan of English nobility.

Matthew took out notepad and pencil. As Whitehorse pulled a bottle of blended whiskey and two glasses from a teak cabinet with beveled glass doors, Matthew jotted down a thought.

His vanity is furnished from the auction house of kings.

Whitehorse sat opposite Matthew, and said, "I hear you come from a good Philadelphia family. That your grandfather was on Washington's staff in the war."

"I guess my family's not as disreputable as some."

"And you went to Harvard, right?"

Silence. Then, "Yes, I studied law."

"But you never finished?"

More silence. Then Matthew shook his head no. "You know an awful lot about me, Mr. Whitehorse. I'm starting to get the impression that you're conducting this interview."

"When your editor told me it was you who would be coming to handle the interview I had everything you'd written that I could get a hold of brought over and read to me." As he pulled the cork from the whiskey bottle Whitehorse observed a momentary, halting expression on Matthew's face.

"I can't read, Christman. I can't read. I can't write. My son reads to me." He poured Matthew's glass. "I have no shame at being who I am. And how many men can say that about themselves?"

The wind scraped the branches of trees along the veranda roof. Matthew glanced past the shadows of the two men cast along the wall by the fire and into his own heart. He knew shame well.

Whitehorse went to pour his glass, but stopped to make a point. "I grew up in Baltimore, Maryland. Worked in a foundry down on Lime Street."

He now poured the whiskey, "Let's talk, Christman."

Matthew pulled out his spectacles, and wiped them clean with a faded white handkerchief. "Mr. Whitehorse, you come to our paper and want to do an interview. Why? We don't have a society column.

We don't do personal interest stories."

"Neither do I," said Whitehorse. "Now…as to the reason for this interview. As a businessman I make evaluations on everything I'm about to undertake, as to whether I proceed or not. We are in the midst of our nation's most critical undertaking. Evaluations are essential. And my evaluation as to Mister Lincoln's War…It might well prove to destroy this country's most precious resource. And you know what that resource is? It is our culture, Mister Christman."

He saw Matthew's eyes tighten and the lines around his mouth crease. Whitehorse put up a hand.

Whitehorse got up and went over to his desk. It was a heavy pine military campaign desk. He picked up a red brick and a small black silk pouch. He came back to the table, laid the brick down, then opened the black silk pouch. He poured six ounces of pure gold dust into a pile next to the brick.

"That's what built this country and the dreams that went before it." He pointed at the brick and gold dust. "Men like your grandfather fought for that dream."

"Men like my grandfather fought—"

Whitehorse cut him off. "One night my father wrapped me in a blanket and handed me to my mother. She was a big woman with a flat face. Just a flat, expressionless face. She took me across town to this old stone building. It was covered with ash from the smoke-stacks of the foundry behind it."

The sound of barking dogs from a den window, Whitehorse could see the outline of a man coming up from the corral with the animals circling around him and jumping. Whitehorse could tell from the man's walk it was Arlen.

"I went to work in that brick foundry as a day laborer when I was nine. But there's only so far an ignorant laborer can go." He threw his drink down, swallowing it fast, not for taste but result.

"I was ignorant. I was illiterate. That was on one side of the ledger. But I was angry and I was smart. And they were on the other side of the ledger."

He sat back against the pine campaign desk. "I was walking along the waterfront past Eleventh Street when something curious happened. There was no beach there, just broken stone facing the waterline. I noticed two crews of surveyors. One crew was running lines up from the shore tracing it maybe a couple of hundred yards inland. The other crew was checking the water depth along the rockface."

Matthew stopped taking notes to study Whitehorse as he relived those moments. A sense of anticipation seemed to overtake him. "I watched them all day drawing up their reports. I missed work. I was gambling I wouldn't lose my job. But I had to know more about this. I felt something in my gut. Well, I followed them after work. Can you guess where they reported to?"

Matthew rolled a cigarette, sat back and cocked his head, waiting for an answer.

"Mott Street, Office of the Department of the Navy."

He went to lick the paper closed, but stopped. Details were swimming out of his memory. "I've been in Baltimore a few times. There's a shipyard on the north side. It was put up in the late 'thirties."

Whitehorse's eyes glistened. "In '39. That was it. I sat up all night at the waterfront. Watched them the next day. Missed work again. I knew I'd lose my job now, but I had to come up with a plan. You couldn't fight the government getting the land coming up from the water. Not when they wanted something. No. But while the crew was having lunch, I stole one of their surveyor maps. Saw where they traced out the place. I saw where there was a couple of vacant lots just a block past the perimeter of the shipyard."

As Matthew watched Whitehorse stand to his full height he could see it all laying out. A shipyard needs buildings: sheds, tool and die casting, machine shop, repair shop, foundry.

"They'd need brick, and you knew how to make it." He lifted the brick off the table and held it up.

Whitehorse nodded. Matthew held the brick against the light, tracing out the history of a man built on the back of this fired stone. "How would a foundry worker get enough money to buy that land and set up those kilns?"

Whitehorse stared toward the fire.

"Mr. Whitehorse, where would a foundry worker get—?"

Arlen entered the room, letting the door hang open behind him. As Whitehorse introduced him, Matthew put out his hand. Arlen didn't bother with it.

"I need to talk to you privately," he said to his father.

"I'm finishing up an interview here. Can it wait?"

"No."

Whitehorse excused himself. He told Matthew to be comfortable, to have more to drink. Before leaving, he added, "I know you're familiar with the speeches given by men like Charles Demerest, as your editorials attacking him were read to me. This country was built by our culture. A culture that men like him and your grandfather helped create. You undermine *that* culture, you ultimately undo the nation. You will create an America that will forever be at war with itself. The country, in that way, is like a business. There must be singular unity for it to survive and thrive."

• • •

In parlored darkness, Whitehorse sat at the edge of the piano bench, his arms rested against his thighs, his head cradled in his hands.

"Didn't we hire enough men to guard those shipments?" He glared at Arlen. Empty breaths were his son's only answer. He spoke softly to himself. "It's Baltimore all over again."

"What?"

His father just shook his head.

"Let me hire a dozen men. Take enough supplies for the summer. I'll hire that hunter friend of mine. The gambler...To go into the hills and run him—"

Whitehorse cut him off. "You say one of the Till brothers is here?"

"Bayard. His cousin was one of the men at the relay station with the shipment. When I picked up the report at the telegraph office, they were already on their way in. He's got two gunneys with him."

"We'll deal with this after I get rid of Christman."

He got up to go, but Arlen grabbed hold of his father's arm. "I don't know why you're talking to him. I read to you everything he wrote. No good can come of it."

"I'm counting on that," said Whitehorse. "And now that you're here, there's something you can do to help insure it."

• • •

After Matthew left the room, Whitehorse threw open the French doors and waved Arlen and the others up to the house.

They walked along silently. The three men trailed behind Arlen. He was in a dour angry mood. He saw their manservant escort Matthew out the front door and close it behind him. He then told the others to head up to the house and let his father know he'd be there in a few minutes.

Matthew had taken out some tobacco and paper and started to roll a cigarette in thoughtful silence when he heard: "Christman. Hold on there. I want to talk to you a minute."

Matthew got a quick sense from the curt tone and aggressive way Arlen was walking toward him, there could be trouble.

"I want you to know something, Christman. I love my father very much. And I respect him. With all his faults and shortcomings. Don't insult him in your paper. You understand? Or there'll be trouble."

Matthew took a deep breath to keep the edge off and finished rolling the cigarette. He slipped it into his mouth. "Can I quote you on that in my article?"

Before the last word had died in the air, Arlen hit Matthew across the cheek and nose with an open hand. The cigarette flew out of his mouth. He tried to cover his face, but was not fast enough to keep from being hit again. He stepped back, but lost his footing and slipped. Arlen grabbed the satchel and pulled Matthew forward and hit him across the face again.

Matthew fought to pull free, his arms flailed at the panic inside him. Arlen hit him again, but this time so hard that with the satchel being caught up around his neck, he was spun about and fell flat on his knees. Arlen kept slapping him till his open hand was red and sore and streaked with blood. Then he shoved Matthew, who then fell over on his side.

He lay there till the front door opened and slammed shut, then struggled to get up. He stumbled down the gravel path toward the arbor gate. He stopped at the fountain and sat on the stone ledge. Matthew rummaged through his satchel. Trembling, he undid the cap on his bottle of laudanum. He drank to kill the shakes and he drank to calm himself and he drank to still the shame.

• • •

At the sound of voices, Matthew turned around quickly. He expected it to be Arlen coming back after him. Instead, beyond the low hanging branches, the three sets of French doors to Whitehorse's office framed an argument.

Through one set of doors Whitehorse paced like a caged animal. He was shouting. Framed by another set of doors at the far end of the room were three men. The best they could offer to his outburst were occasional short tentative responses. Two wore dusters and looked case hardened. The third, a boy about twenty years, wore a woolen serape. All three were covered with dirt and flecks of mud and gave the impression of having ridden a long way.

Matthew moved from shadow to shadow then sidled up behind a willow, peering out just enough to steal a view of all three sets of doors. He was still too far away to hear what was being said and the rest of the way to the house was open lawn.

Framed by the middle door, Arlen leaned back against his father's desk. Arms folded across his chest; every time Whitehorse made a remark Arlen nodded and glared at the men. The Prince of Arrogance, thought Matthew.

Whitehorse raised a half sheet of brown paper and waved it, then as if that wasn't enough to make his point, he slapped it with his hand.

One of the three men, the young one in the woolen serape, began to talk. He was angry and frustrated. He was unsure of himself and curled the brim of his hat in his hand then, unexpectedly, started to cry. He wiped at his eyes and fought to control himself, but couldn't. Whitehorse looked at the boy, then at the half sheet of brown paper. Disgusted, he tore it up and threw it on the floor.

That half sheet of brown paper—lying there in pieces, the draft stirring at its edges—played on Matthew's memory.

Had he drifted past it in the room? Or was it something else?

CHAPTER FIVE

"The Big Blue Heaven" was originally a livery barn of forty stalls for the Ellis Newcastle Hauling Company. In the spring of '61 during the first great storm of the season shards of burning light raked the bay. One levin bolt of Parabrahaman carved its mark in the roof of the livery killing five horses where they stood. Lying in the mud, their coats shimmering with smoke, bleeding from their nostrils and mouths, they were a pitiful sight.

The owner of the livery, Ellis Newcastle himself, lost not only his best pulling team, but his prized riding horse, Lulu. A short bald man with a quicksilver temperament and a superstitious nature that bordered on phobia, Newcastle sold the livery the next day and moved up the street. He had no faith in the adage that lightning doesn't strike in the same place twice.

As always, one man's misery is another man's fortune. Miguel Tejara Flores, a Spanish expatriate known for his peculiar lifestyle and flamboyant dress, saw the livery as a perfect location to open the gambling hall he had been dreaming about.

Lord Goose, as he was affectionately known—because of the

animal he loved so much and kept in a silver cage above the bar—supervised all the refinements of the livery himself from a bathtub in the middle of the dirt floor.

One aspect of the livery held particular offense in his eyes. The roof. He had no use for traditional roofs of any kind. At best he found their simple sharp angles desultory, if functional. He much preferred the great cathedrals of Spain where the hand painted arched coves were not only elegant but beautiful. So he ordered two great mainsails stitched together and hung from wall beam to wall beam. Then he had cables attached along its length and strung from the roof joists, and the great tarp was hauled up in what approximated a half-dome sky across the interior of the livery. This he had painted the shade of blue at midnight. Then, with speckled gold, he dabbed one horizon line to the other with the stars of the constellations.

As this was being seen to, he would lean his head back and look up at his personal heaven and converse with Jason, who sat in a large wooden armchair on his right. Here they shared the secrets of their lives over snifters of brandy. It was Jason who had added one last touch to the heavens—a lone shooting star, leaving a trail of faded gold across eternity.

Jason and the Lord had a special friendship. In many ways it was like a father and son as they were both expert mechanics with a California Prayer Book.

On this day, Jason ambled through the open double stable doors well into "hunting" time. Lines of men at the Monte tables along one wall were stacked five deep. Along the other wall men were hunkered down around the poker tables. Jason struggled to get around the wooden stand that was built in the middle of the livery where a fifteen piece orchestra played elegant classical compositions. And leaning up against the fine Italian walnut bar—the great silver cage,

home of his prize goose resting beside him as an eye-catching cen-
terpiece—was the Lord.

He spotted Jason, who couldn't help but smile at seeing the old
man dressed in a plum purple velvet waistcoat that had been cut
with squared tails. With his barrel belly and bony legs he looked like
some caricatured scrub jay.

"My dear Jason. I am so glad you are here." Then he whispered,
"This is a money night, my boy."

The Lord motioned for Jason to follow as he cleared a path
through the crowd. He pointed toward a table where four men were
wrapped up tight around a poker table.

"Table five. The four men playing draw. Now, the fellow with
the derby is utterly useless. He sets aside a weekly allowance from his
petty job. And it's pure spit. But the other three. They are dullards
with money, and that makes them particularly offensive and in dire
need of skinning."

Jason surveyed the table. A small man with a square head and
short hair had a pretty good stack of winnings. He was sitting next
to a lean young man with scraggly blond hair that hung to his neck.
He seemed a little slow for the game and his winnings reflected that.
He and the first man seemed to know each other from the way they
talked. The last man was older. He wore a pressed suit and tie, and
sat erect in his chair. He had that look of intent that usually comes
with mediocre play.

The Lord smiled through a new set of polished wooden teeth.
"I'll wait anxiously for my cut."

Jason began to circle the table where the four men were playing
poker. He occasionally stopped at a Monte or Chuck-A-Luck game
and laid off side bets. But his eyes scanned the play to pick up the
men's habits.

The lean young man with the blond hair was named Calvin. He was an average player and slow to anger. But the other man, Shawn, with the short hair and square head, was another story. He was a little more sure handed with the cards. He had an emotional streak and every time he got a good hand he leaned forward in his chair and butted his teeth together in a leer.

The third fellow was named Hotchkiss. He was conservative. But clean and steady. And if he had a good hand he pushed. But Jason had seen Shawn bluff him with a big tiger.

Shawn and Calvin knew each other pretty well. Maybe too well. After a dozen hands Jason picked up a move between the two men. Every time one had a good hand he let the other know by casually tapping his foot against the leg of the chair. The other man promptly folded.

It should be a simple blood letting.

The next time the Lord made his rounds, Jason had replaced the man in the brown derby and was floating a hand of straight draw across the table. The first half hour Jason let things run about even, setting up the fairbank. He took no major hands, lost none either. But he kept pushing up the size of the bet and not impressing anyone with his play.

Calvin looked over his cards and kicked up the bet. Jason knew he was holding a bullet and a pair of deuces. Shawn folded, as expected, since Calvin was running a hand. Hotchkiss met the run, but was taking a chance since all he was holding was a little dog.

Each man called for cards. Shawn was tapping his hand on the wing of his chair and staying with the play. Calvin looked his cards over, then bet up hard. He didn't pull anything and Jason knew it. He had him whipped with a pair of kings but let Calvin think he was unsure of himself and only cautiously met the bet.

Hotchkiss pulled a burn, and his little dog wasn't worth scratch so he folded. He excused himself, and walked to the bar to pull down a beer.

Shawn wouldn't take his eyes off Jason, as if somehow he could affect the outcome with a withering glance. Calvin sat back in his chair.

The orchestra had begun a melancholy rendition of "The Banks and Braes of Bonnie Doon," and the air was thick and rank with smoke. Shawn upped the bet, hoping to force the fold. But instead, Jason gracefully slid two double eagles across the plank table.

There is a moment in every game of chance, after the fairbank has been set and the hands are running in a steady groove, that an invisible force beyond the table begins to hold power over the cards and men. It is at that moment logic and reason, or at least common sense, are swept aside in the current of arrogance. Dust and coin are no longer dust and coin but significant stones of character each man is built upon.

Each bet is part of the age old conflict between who a man is, and who a man thinks he is. Each bet is pride. That is the foolishness of the game, which, not unlike life, shifts rapidly from the sublime to the ridiculous. Jason was always aware of this, and the mark always ignorant. But it could affect them equally the same, and that, sometimes even the best mechanic could not foresee. This was such a moment.

Jason lay down his cards.

It took a few seconds for the two black kings to leave their mark across Calvin's face and all he could muster through a sneer was, "Shit."

As Jason swept in his winnings, a fight broke out at the Chuck-A-Luck table just behind him. A miner had lost all his pickings and had grabbed hold of the chuck cage trying to rip it open and get at the dice he believed were either loaded or hexed.

Then a pair of thick shoulders plowed through the crowd that circled up around the miner. He was grabbed by a heavy chested Hawaiian doorman along the back of his shirt and flung to the ground.

Coco was a mute of low intelligence. But in this environment, where simplicity with strength, and dedication in service were true marks of success, Coco enjoyed a reputation as the finest bouncer on the waterfront. For this he had been christened the archangel of the Lord's staff.

• • •

Past midnight Shawn and Calvin had worked their way through most of a second bottle of whiskey. Hotchkiss had unloosened his tie and started to slump in his chair. Jason had culled Shawn's and Calvin's winnings by more than half. He had left Hotchkiss somewhere just under even to disguise his purpose. But the game had worn them all. The long hours had left the men sullen and in spite of themselves. Jason cut and dealt. Shawn leaned forward in his chair, letting it hang there on its two front legs. "Where you from, mister?"

Jason finished the deal, then lifted a cigarette that had been burning at the edge of the table. He drew in. "New York."

"New York?" Shawn let the chair rock easily. "I mean, what's your background?"

Jason put the cigarette down, took a breath, and reached for his snifter of brandy. "I'm French."

Shawn dug his boots in the caked dirt floor. "You're awfully dark for a Frenchman, aren't you?"

Jason smiled.

"You sure you ain't got no mixed blood in you? Indian, maybe? Something else, maybe?"

"Are we here to play poker or write the genealogy of my family?"

Shawn sat back. "I was just curious. We're all civilized here."

CHAPTER SIX

Coiled around a golden stem, a dragon lived. His skin was black, his teeth were bared, his eyes white dots with a fleck of red. He was breathing lifeless fire.

Matthew sat against the far wall of the opium parlor in solitude, looking at the dragon pipe. His back was bent. His hands unsteady. His legs were crossed. Faint orange glowed in rings around his head.

He lifted the golden stem with the coiled dragon and inhaled again. The smoke would burrow deep into his lungs and, just like smoke, would float along the rivered blood toward a poisoned soul. His eyes would falter in their course. So he would close them down like shades and stumble further on.

Matthew crawled along the floor. He tried to rally up his notes, spread around him like fallen leaves. He leaned his back against the wall, knees up, and tried to read:

I spent an evening in the den of a wealthy man, warmed by the fires of tragedy. Personal, historical, and fearfully, eternal.

My gracious host has carved himself, like any statue, out of the great stone facing of this nation's past. With that stone he has built a wall of ideas, a fortress to defend his needs. His name is Charles Julius Whitehorse.

His grand estate, which many of us who live in San Francisco are familiar with, drapes a sandy hill above the Parker house like a papal cloak; red as brick and trimmed with gold.

He is eminently successful, hard working, shrewd, tough, and I might add, charming. And like so many successful businessmen committed to public service—his own.

His past is our past. As an abandoned child, he was left to make his way under a soot stained sky, as dark as the muddy roads he walked along foundry row. His face bears the scars of contempt against his fight for survival. And survive he did.

He has built a life, brick by brick. From foundry worker to foundry owner. His story alone is worth its weight in gold and has bought as much.

I'm sure that in a certain light, any man would be proud to lay claim to the rich history that is Charles Julius Whitehorse.

He is a master of the self. Self sufficient—self reliant—and just plain selfish. And what frightens me most about this man is that all our dreams are his.

Matthew reached for the silver cup and took a drink. The water cooled his burning mouth.

Through a parchment wall was the shadow of a standing man being washed with lemon cloth by kneeling forms. One a woman, one a man. They ran their hands along his feet then up his legs, a slow rhythm drenched. They climbed like snakes along his length, and when they reached the hips, they rested. Then began a caress with scented oil.

The kneeling woman took the man and put him in her mouth. He reached down and stroked her hair. Her fingers slid up between his legs. And when she was done, the kneeling man took her place and began again. For Matthew the shadows were hypnotic forms in silhouette. Outlines to everything he'd ever felt. His heart was pounding against his shirt, running clean up to his head. In his dreams, as in his life, he had been either man. Because of this, every plan and every hope, every cherished thought his family had for him, was lost.

He sunk down and rested his head on the floor then curled his legs up like a child. The blood on his shirt had stained the color of wine. Looking sideways, just within his reach was the book, packed thick with notes and thoughts and letters from his youth. He reached out and ran his fingers along the leather cover.

In his mind Matthew could hear his father's voice. "You're a perverted disgrace to this family and your brother's memory. I am ashamed."

Matthew whispered into those smoky reaches, "Thank you, Father."

He tried to swallow but his throat was raw. Lying there, looking at the book, a distant note startled him—drifting there through his thoughts like the torn sheets of brown paper falling from White-horse's hand.

He sat up. His eyes fixed for clarity. He grabbed for his book. Thoughts and fingers scrambled past every page. Notes dropped out, sheaves of paper fell to the floor, letters tumbled into open air.

And then he found it. The envelope. Light blue and scarred with aging yellow. Inside, the letter his mother had sent to him long after he'd been driven out of his family. Just holding it brought back a lifetime of lost memories.

He slipped the letter out of the envelope. And within the folds, neatly creased, a half brown sheet of torn paper, just like the one in Whitehorse's den.

The edges of the brown paper had dried hard and cracked, so he carefully unfolded it. It was cut from the ledgers of the Telegraph Hill Relay Office. That's where he'd seen it before. That was what Whitehorse had been holding in his den. A message from the telegraph office.

• • •

Randall Wilcox, the new managing editor of the *American Flag*, was a slow, thoughtful man. Meticulous and prone to long reflections.

Matthew waited quietly, sitting across the desk in the tent that was Mr. Wilcox's office, while he read the editorial on Whitehorse, leaning close to the oil lamp for light.

Mr. Wilcox looked over the pages of the editorial. "This article troubles me, Matthew. Why he wanted it. His son's confrontation with you."

"Don't let it trouble you, Mr. Wilcox. And I won't be here after tomorrow."

All expression left Mr. Wilcox's face.

"I'm finished here," said Matthew. "I'm going down into the mining country around Tulare Lake."

"What in God's name for?"

Matthew pulled his chair closer to the desk. He opened his satchel and took half a dozen torn sheets of brown paper from the Telegraph Hill Relay Office and spread them out on the desk.

"I found out something tonight. These are copies of messages sent to Whitehorse from his mine out in Tulare County. They cover the last six months. See. He's been robbed seven times for over seventy thousand dollars."

Mr. Wilcox went from message to message. An arc of panic and urgency rising in the torn half sheaves.

"How'd you get these copies?"

"Bribery...I had a long, quiet conversation with one William McCall. He's head man on the graveyard shift at the relay office. I just left there."

Wilcox sat back, surprised.

"Whitehorse *appears* philosophically linked with the likes of Demerest. The mine is in Tulare...That's the heart of redneck country. And a stronghold of the Golden Circle. Whitehorse wants to be interviewed... by the *Flag*. Might he be trying to curry political favor to protect his business interests there?"

Mr. Wilcox considered all this thoughtfully, then asked, "Are you running away, Matthew?"

CHAPTER SEVEN

Inside the Big Blue Heaven, beneath the section of roof that was hit by lightning, was a door that led to the tack room which had been transformed into the Lord's private office. Coco stood by that door, his legs astraddle, as they were for years on the quarter decks of whalers, maintaining a steady vigilance.

Jason pushed through the crowd and brushed up beside him. "I see you got a little exercise tonight."

Coco nodded.

Jason motioned toward the door. "Could I steal a minute of his time?"

As he opened the door, Jason saw the Lord sitting in a klismos chair of European origin behind an oak table that he used as a desk. The oil lamp cast a churched glow on four businessmen in high backed chairs spread around the room smoking cigars and drinking Madeira. When the Lord saw Jason, he nodded. As he walked out and closed the door behind him, the wooden smile he'd offered to the men disappeared.

He and Jason stepped off by themselves. "Jason, I've gone from pariah to patronage. These bourgeoisie have offered to partner with me in setting up another gambling hall. Of course it will be a silent partnership as propriety demands."

"Of course."

"It's a wonderful country, isn't it?" A twinkling thought crossed the Lord's mind. "Maybe I could run for mayor eventually. I've always felt I had a flair for politics."

"What would be your campaign slogan, Miguel? A hand in every pocket."

The Lord's delicately plucked eyebrow rifled upward. "I suppose you've had a successful evening."

Jason reached for the Lord's hand and opened it palm up and laid out his take in green and gold. The Lord savored the moment by weight and feel. He reached for a belly pouch made of wolf skin and corniced with the creature's head. He poured his earnings in, full now as a bloated belly. He gave a shake and the furred skull snapped and bared its teeth.

• • •

Outside, a drifting night was growing cold. Jason pulled his collar up and smoked. Up past a row of rooming houses, the view opened out below where the roofs fell away like steps. A fog had begun to crest along the reefs. There were just a few lights flickering here from the rooms above.

He heard muddy steps and the hammer's cock too late. Before he could turn to fight or run he was shoved against a wall and hit. He tried to grab his gun, but an army Colt pushed hard against his chest.

"Try your luck, carriage man."

Their faces were black outlines. All sense of emotion and meaning lay now in their actions. Calvin grabbed the gun from Jason's holster and threw it into the street. They forced him up the sloping hill toward two small warehouse sheds that sat like headstones against the moon. Then through a short causeway between the sheds. Halfway, they stopped and backed him against the clapboard siding. Calvin edged the Colt up under Jason's jawbone and into his neck hard enough to make him choke.

"Well, carriage man. Let's see our money." Shawn worked fast, emptying Jason's pant pockets and lipping them. Hotchkiss watched the causeway, first one end then the other.

Calvin stayed fixed on Jason and he could feel the blood pumping up through his neck. "Half looks to be gone."

"You spend fast, carriage man. Maybe you're carryin' something else we could get a little interest on for our money."

As the hands began their search, Jason stole a glance up the causeway. The fog had started to drift in across the hill. There was no help in that.

Shawn found a loose deck of cards in one coat pocket. He held them up and threw them across Jason's face. They floated to the ground. He tried the other coat pocket and felt something caught up in the corner. Its sharp edge cut him as he pulled it out.

"Well, look at this." He held the mirrored chip up close enough to Jason for his breath to fog the glass. "What do you see in that gaper, carriage man?"

Jason drew all expression out of his face.

"See what else he's got tucked away," said Calvin.

Shawn started through the rest of the coat pockets but found nothing. He tried the inside coat pocket. The shirt pockets. Nothing. Then he started with the vest pockets.

Jason stole a glance down the causeway. The hillside was giving way to black. He eased his hands back and let them go flat against the wall and slipped one boot forward, feeling for a good spot of balance.

There was nothing in the upper vest pocket. Nothing in one lower vest pocket. Then Shawn tried the other vest pocket. Jason could feel the fingers find the watch.

Shawn pulled it out and looked it over. "Very nice. Real silver." He held it up for the others. "Where'd you get this, carriage man? Was it willed to you in a rigged game?"

There was no expression on Jason's face. No fear. No sign of weakness or panic. He hoped Shawn would just take the watch and slip it into his pocket or throw it on the ground and crush it with his boot.

Shawn rolled his thumb across the lock catch then pressed down. The casing popped open. The faces in the watch were reprised in the face of the man before him. Shawn looked up and shook his head.

Jason felt the clapboard siding behind him and tried to ease forward just enough to make space between himself and the wall.

"It seems the carriage man had a rascal in the family. Take a look." He dangled the watch for Hotchkiss to see.

"Calvin our boy ain't no full French, if he is at all. His mama's black as a Sunday button." He bit at his lower lip. "This won't pass."

"What do we do with him?" said Hotchkiss.

"I say we put this dog down," said Calvin.

"We're playing on velvet now, carriage man."

"We can't shoot him. Not that."

Shawn looked at Hotchkiss. "Why not? We ain't short of bullets."

"It's one thing to strip him down and whip him, but—"

Jason let one hand slip along the border of his coat till it passed behind his hip. He stayed fixed on Calvin and that tarnished metal barrel staring at him. Jason drew in a deep slow breath.

"I've never been involved in shootin' a fella," said Hotchkiss.

"You ain't gonna shoot him."

Hotchkiss went to walk away. "You do what you want. I'm leaving. Keep my money."

"God damn. He cheated you too."

In the moment it took Calvin to look away, then back, Jason grabbed the knife that hung from the leather loop down inside his coat. He came up fast and slit Calvin's throat.

• • •

Jason stared down at his father's boots. That's all he could manage as he walked the length of Kearny Street. He was lost to those moments that he knew would cut his life here as swiftly and irrevocably as he'd cut that throat. His hands were in his pockets, balled up into tight fists. In his left hand was the watch.

He'd have to leave. That night. He'd get back to his room and take the money out of the blue metal candy box. He made his way back home along the shore road. Through the mist he spotted a platoon of Union troops stationed up around his boarding house. Four enlisted men with rifles walked the perimeter. Another dozen or so had broken into groups of two and searched the sheds and service buildings along the docks.

Why were they here? He stepped back and let the fog close him in. He found a spot behind a shed wall where he had a full view of the front of the rooming house.

The kerosene lamp in his room gave full measure to a Sergeant and two enlisted men who were going through his belongings. They opened his books and reached into the pockets of his clothes. They tossed each item aside. One of the enlisted men gutted his mattress with a bayonet and tore out the stuffings.

In the next room an Army officer questioned the old man, Langston. He stood there solemnly, and after each question just shook his head in calculated ignorance.

Could either of the three men have been in the army? Certainly not Hotchkiss. Unless he was a supplier and had friends who were officers of high rank. But what about the other two? They weren't in uniform. And in their conversation never even hinted at it.

In his room the two enlisted men bent down out of view. Sections of ripped up floorboard were handed to the Sergeant who threw them in the corner. It didn't take long before one of the men stood up, holding the blue metal candy box with all his money.

• • •

One of Coco's jobs around the Big Blue Heaven was to clean up the Lord's office after a business meeting or liaison, and make sure nothing of a "delicate nature" was left behind.

As he loaded wine glasses onto a silver tray there was a tap at the window. He turned. Jason waved to him through the grimy panes.

Coco went over and unlocked the back door and let him in. Jason looked tired and the creases around his eyes warned of desperation.

"Where's Miguel?"

Coco motioned with the wave of a hand.

"I'm in trouble. I need to see him. Now."

Coco looked away. And in that moment, in those placid mooned eyes that couldn't look into his, Jason spotted the truth.

"The soldiers were here, weren't they?"

Coco took the last wine glass and placed it neatly next to the others on the tray. Then he nodded.

Jason could barely manage a breath. He leaned back against the table. "Was one of those plowboys in the army?"

Coco glanced back at him and raised two fingers.

Jason slapped his hands against the oak tabletop. "Talk about coppering the odds."

Coco watched as all chance of hope drained out of Jason's face.

"Coco, I've got to get some money and be out of here. There's Union troops all over my place. They found my stash. I'm bust. Dead bust. I've got to talk with the Lord."

Coco rubbed his hands across his face. His arms were tattooed with the pagan symbols of the islands and the crass motifs of his years at sea. He offered the wave of his hand, but little more.

Jason came up to him. "Remember back, my friend, when your mates left you stranded here to hike it for gold?" There was anger in his voice and bitterness. "And you were living in that pigeon hutch."

Coco tried to turn away, but Jason grabbed him by the arm.

"There's no place for that right now, is that it?" He grabbed the cloth pouch that hung from Coco's belt and held his magic. "When you had the fevers and were carving those pagan dolls of your soul so you could try and fleece your way into heaven, who got the god-damned quinine. I need some of that magic you're carrying there... friend."

There was shame in Coco's face, but he would not break faith with the Lord.

Jason was lost to all possibilities now, save one. He went around the table and sat in the Lord's chair. He found some letter paper, and tore a sheet in half. He took a quill pen and ink and wrote out a note.

"I need to get this to Arlen Whitehorse. Will you do that for me?"

• • •

A walkway squared the shantied boathouse anchored to pylons in Yerba Buena Cove. According to Jason's watch there was only an hour left to dawn. Still no sign of Arlen. He leaned against the railing by the door and smoked. There would be inevitabilities with daylight.

Moments later he heard a set of oars cut the water in slow measured beats. He stood back in the doorway as the bow of a Columbia River boat, the Solitudo, eased through the mist.

Jason could see Arlen standing in the bow as Coco rolled out the oars. He was carrying a gunnysack and a Navy cape. As Coco tied off the boat, Jason pulled Arlen up the ladder to the landing.

"You're down to one on the layout and three in the hand," said Arlen.

"You think I could even cover that?"

Arlen passed Jason the gunnysack and the Navy cape. "I brought some gear for you. There's a blanket in there and a Colt in the blanket. It isn't much, just what I could pull quick."

"Thanks, Arlen."

Coco climbed the ladder and both men reached out and pulled him up the last step.

"Let's go inside and talk."

Arlen hesitated a moment, and glanced at Coco. "He and I will talk alone?"

Coco looked toward Jason. Jason nodded.

The room was dark till Jason bellied a kerosene lamp. The walls were lined with crates. The room smelled of mildew and rotting wood.

Arlen sat on a crate. "You made quite a name for yourself tonight."

Jason grew solemn. "What did you hear?"

Arlen took cigarette paper and tobacco out of his coat pocket. "The word is those three fellas called you out for cheating. And when they were heading up Vallejo Street, you jumped them. Knifed one and belly shot the other. You tried to fire down on the third fella but he got away."

Over by the window Jason leaned against the wall. "They'll hang you for a lie as easily as the truth. What difference."

"Yeah, well. The fella who got his throat cut is a Corporal in the Third Dragoons. And the fella that was belly shot and is lying up there now in the Marine Hospital is a Master Sergeant in the same company. It's bad enough they're Army, but that Master Sergeant was a hero in the Mexican War. Jason, every jackdick First Lieutenant is hoping to slip the California collar around your neck."

Jason came over, sat in a chair and leaned forward. He would live or die with things as they were. He looked up at Arlen. "Can you see your way clear to spottin' me?"

Arlen lit the cigarette and let it hang from the corner of his mouth. He pulled a money pouch from his inside coat pocket and tossed it to Jason. "I can help you, if you can help me."

Jason looked through the pouch, at the short stack of bills that ran a few hundred dollars deep. He looked up at Arlen.

"What could I do for you?"

Arlen took a minute, and thumbed at some tobacco caught on

his lip. "Our mine out in Tulare. Over the last year some bastard has robbed us about a half a dozen times. He's seventy thousand on the long side, and we're nine men to the short. It's bad all the way around. We've hired gunneys to guard the shipments. But they've been shit. No one even knows what this fella looks like.

"We're sending an expedition out into the hills. A dozen men. Equipped for the summer. There are these brothers, the Till brothers. They're magistrates out in Tulare County. One of them will lead the expedition.

"Jason, the men I hired are gunneys." He tapped his finger against the side of his head. "But none of them are topsiders. I need someone who knows the hunt. Who can get himself inside the head of this fella. Shooting him will be one thing but…we can't shoot him unless we find him."

Jason began to think through this, weighing the probabilities of what was behind him against the plausibility of what lay ahead. He glanced at the pouch of money on the crate.

"That is just to get you downriver and meet up with the expedition. You track for them, you'll be taken care of."

"This isn't really my line of work."

Arlen stared at him caustically. "Tell that to the Union Army."

Jason looked away, "Yeah."

What was left, really? He could hear the creaking hulls of the dying ships somewhere on the bay. His breath escaped all cold and smoky. The windowpane was starting to sparkle around the edges with the coming light.

"You're asking me to hunt this fella down and kill him. Not just track him out. You want me to gore the ox."

• • •

Jason sat in the bow of the Solitudo looking back toward the city. Coco rowed, searching for a place to beach along the Marin County shoreline.

The boat rose on a crested wave then bottomed out along the sand. Coco pulled in the oars, and both men jumped out of the boat and hauled it up through the surf.

The sun was past the ridgeline, and the haze had begun burning off. A hard wind was blowing in across the peninsula and they had to cover their eyes to protect them against the sand.

"Well, this is goodbye."

He put out his hand. They shook. Then Coco ran his hand in a line across his mouth and pointed at himself.

"No. I'm not angry with you. I understand how things are."

Before Jason turned to head up the beach road, Coco untied the pouch that held his magic to his belt. He slipped it into Jason's pocket, and raised his hand to the sky.

"I guess I could use a little magic."

Both men pushed the Solitudo back out into the surf. Coco jumped in the boat as it rose through the breakers. He pulled in the oars, and with one hand raised the huge oar like a spear. Jason waved as Coco began to row back toward the mainland.

Jason slipped on the old Navy cape. He took the Colt from the gunnysack and slid it into his belt.

The army would be sending out telegraphs by now that he was wanted for murder. The word would bleed its way slowly downstate. He decided it best to hoof it inland to Sacramento, hopefully beat the spring rains, which could be treacherous this year, with all the snow that had fallen in the Sierras. From Sacramento he'd work his way south to Stockton, then fare it by boat down through the sloughs to the mine. He foresaw weeks of hard going just to get there.

The day was giving shape to the outlines of buildings along the mainland. Smoke from the boilers of the steamers and ferries rose in plumes along the harbor. The Solitudo grew smaller and smaller till it disappeared with the rolling tide. Jason knew the hacks and drays would be lining up along the wharves as the day's cargo was unloaded. The vendors would be setting up their stalls along the street to sell their goods. The bar hands at the Big Blue Heaven would be preparing for the next night of rounds. And the Lord, who he thought a friend, would sleep late and well.

BOOK TWO

CHAPTER EIGHT

It was the night of the dying moon. It was the day when the sun found itself reflected a hundred different ways against the cracking surface of Sleeping Water Lake. It was the time, along the rim of the Western Sierra Nevadas, when the spring rain and melting frost ran a course in ribbons down through crevasse and rivulet, and great solemn drifts of snow lying draped along the granite walls dissipated and joined the steady stream in its rush through ravine and hollow.

Above the fall line each small running crease met and mated with a large crease, then hurtled on to meet and mate with a still larger crease till the gullied narrows thundered down sloping roads of lavaed rock and converged in chasms.

It was here the slate and shale had cracked, leaving deep grooved scars in the brown clay of the tablelands and the torrent found another path down through the arroyo secos. The remains of placer mines — the paltry miner's shack, the long toms, the riffle bars and sluice boxes, the rotting signs of a world gone bust — these were all swept aside. Just so much driftwood now, pocked from mites.

This torrent turned a dark, dirty, ugly brown as it swept up the rock and sand, mud and gravel, of those spoiled hills of poisoned sludge left like great primitive burial mounds to the miner's failed dreams and expectations.

The watered avalanche made its way out of the foothills through long spurs, carving new channels, gouging great holes through the topsoil and leaving eroded blisters, cutting at root and branch along the swill line. Here, the great chasm spread out its branches through the grasslands to the sea.

The onward crush rode a crested arc that flooded its terraced banks and left mounds of slate and shale and stratified gravel that buried roads and river crossings. Mud, laced with quicksilver and iron chromate, hemorrhaged out into the marshlands, tainting the sloughs, killing off all life there, and depositing a malignant silt that would take the wind a lifetime to blow away. On the plains outside the city of Sacramento, a brown white slime twenty feet deep buried wheat farm and orchard leaving desecrated husks to rot in summer.

Then the rising tide rammed itself against the levee built in a ring along the eastern rim of the town, a sodden wall to defend Sacramento from becoming a barren floodplain. With this onslaught, the spring of '62 was ushered in.

There was little the captains of the city of Sacramento could do. They just watched and waited and pledged mounds of earth to their cause. For days the water rose. So they prayed. And then, the flood peaked, cusping at the rim of the levee. God had answered their prayers.

But dawn brought great thunderheads from the west. Dark streaks of mercury bled through the orange mist. The air stayed damp and chilly, and the copper weathervane on the second story roof of the Rettin Rooming House spun on a rusted spire. Then the rains came in slow distant drops.

By the first night, running trails streaked the road. By the second night, the railroad tracks, which ran flat out along the waterfront, were sunk in a quagmire, leaving only a thin band of iron rail headers visible. By the third night, hundreds of flatbed wagons filled with dirt ringed the waterfront. Crews of men in slickers filled sandbags. Lines of men carried them up the battered mastaba walls trying to shore up broken seams of earth.

Hetty North watched all this from the sewing room window of her cousin's rooming house on Second Street. Streaming lines of rain half obscured her view, but she could make out a roadway of men with torches on top of the levee wall lighting the way for the men carrying the sandbags. Beyond that, the great mastheads of the river schooners listed hard to shore as the flashing tide lifted their hulls and hammered them against the wharves.

The sewing room was dark. Hetty stood there quietly. In the parlor she could hear her cousin Sarah and the other women talking. Out in the mining country, alone at night, the rain had always been a comfort. No matter how lonely she felt. No matter how unhappy. But tonight was different.

Where are they, she worried. They should have been here the day before. What if the bridges were washed out like she'd heard? No one could get through. But what if something happened to them? What would she do then?

She leaned her head against the wall, and her dark hair, which hung loose, fell across her cheek. She brushed it back with her hand. She began to agonize and it angered her. With every trip, with every mile of trouble, with every chance she'd taken and every mistake she'd had to survive, she felt she would have found peace with it all. But it eluded her still. Growing up she'd learned to be steadfast through her loneliness, through lost expectations, through tragedies. But it gave her no peace.

There was a sudden surge of rain on the second story roof. She looked back across the room. There in the dark, by the wall, she could just make out the leather steamer trunk which she brought with her out of the mining country. The metal bands underneath the leather had long since worn through. The brass lock was badly scarred. One whole side of the coffered frame was singed from a fire.

Her thoughts drifted toward Sarah's two small sons in the bedroom at the end of the first floor hallway. They'd been restless when Sarah had put them to bed so Hetty stayed behind and read to them from *"Mr. Midshipman Easy"*.

Through the arched doorway the light from the parlor fell at a harsh angle along the hall. Sarah and the other women sat at an oblong table near the fire. From the sewing room, Hetty could make out the profiled form of Geordie Frohmann. She was a squarely built woman with gray hair pulled back in a bun and braided.

"I tell every girl in my class, every one, mind you, come to life as you come to class…prepared. Not just intellectually, but socially. Be conscientious in your thoughts as well as in your person. And be knowledgeable of the laws passed by our legislature because many of them have gone a long way to undermining your security."

Hetty quietly approached the hallway and watched from the shadows. Sarah, who was embroidering new curtains, commented without even looking up. "Geordie, you're not going to start again with the divorce laws, are you?"

The other woman at the table, Annabelle Mulford, whose short red hair and blue eyes stood in marked contrast to Geordie's gray demeanor, looked up from her writing. "What about our divorce laws? It seems California's are the most progressive in the country."

Hetty entered the room. She walked with a severe hitch, and her left boot, which had been specially cut with an extra two inches of leather sole to compensate for being born lame, left a harsh clump on the wooden floor with each step. She passed around the table and stopped behind Sarah's chair.

Geordie continued, "Do you know they're calling California 'The Principality of Legalized Immorality.' That's what judges are saying."

Hetty looked over at Geordie, who was wiping at her mouth with a napkin. "This permissive law you're railing against says that a woman who works side by side with her husband is an equal partner and as such earns half the profits and can sue if she doesn't get them. It also says that a woman who opens a business with her own capital is fully protected. If that's legalized immorality, we need a lot more of it."

"Amen," responded Annabelle.

A rush of wind drove the rain hard against the rooming house and the glass rattled. The room suddenly quieted, as if the rain owned them all.

"Hetty," said Annabelle, "your cousin tells me you have a business downstate."

"That's right. In Tulare County. At a mine called The White-horse. I come up here every few months to see Sarah and order more goods."

"That must be quite an adventure for a single woman," said Annabelle.

"It's many things."

"A fair amount of men down there have money?"

"For as long as they can keep hold of it."

"I'm working on an advertisement. Would you mind if I read it to you?"

"What could *you* possibly be advertising for," asked Geordie.

Annabelle was a bit self-conscious, but answered, "A husband."

The improbability of the statement caught the others off guard.

"You can't be serious," said Geordie.

"Most of the men out in the mining country are single," said Annabelle. "And a good number have done very well for themselves. I see articles in the paper discussing the shortage of women in the state."

"We live in a preposterous age," said Geordie.

"I wasn't asking you."

"The women in this state used to stand for something," said Geordie. "They were the ones who built the churches, the schools and the hospitals. Not the men. Women were the ones who began the benevolent societies. They were the ones who brought—"

Hetty cut her off, "I'll remind you of something else many of the women brought to this state. They brought allegiance to the same rancid ideas of their fathers, brothers and husbands."

"Is that remark aimed at me?" said Geordie.

"And they allowed a world to be built on those ideas."

Geordie raised a hand in anger. "Name me one of those 'rancid' ideas."

Hetty stood up straight, finding her balance. She walked out of the room.

"Those remarks were directed at me," said Geordie.

"That's not true," said Sarah.

"They were directed at me. But I understand why." Geordie could hear the slow heavy clop of a boot falling away along the hallway toward the stairs so she spoke loud enough for Hetty to hear. "It's her physical infirmity and the scars on her face. She is angry and disillusioned."

Hetty stopped at the bottom of the stairs. The hallway was dark and empty. She rested her hand on the balustrade as Sarah came to her defense.

The parlor went silent, leaving only the sound of the rain overrunning the gutters and the gears turning the hands of the clock. Hetty walked to a sideboard at the end of the hall. She viewed herself in the mirror above it. Her cheeks were drawn in sharp angles down to her mouth, and the smallpox she'd suffered as a child had left her face sloughed, like so much broken ground. She had often thought she was nothing more than a cutter's stone, scarred by the sculptor's chisel then cast aside.

She ran her hands along her face, so unkind to the touch, and let them come to rest beneath her cheeks, leaving only the upper half exposed. Her forehead was high and proud. And her hairline formed a black oblique crest at the peak like the delicate turn in a tiara. Her eyes too were black, stark black, and centered with a canary yellow iris.

If only God had fulfilled the promise started there. If only he could be called upon to reshape the battered frame that haunted her there through the dark. If only...

In that moment the edges of the mirror started to shudder. Because of the dark, unsure of what she saw, Hetty came forward and rested her fingers on the glass. Against her hand the surface spasmed. Then stopped. Hetty drew her hand back from the glass. She could hear her cousin ask, "Did any of you feel that?"

"What?"

"Stop. Both of you. Sit still, Geordie."

The shaking started again. Cups in the sideboard behind Hetty began to rattle. One of the cups tipped over and rolled to the edge of the sideboard. Hetty reached to grab the cup when a jolt rocked the house. Hetty fell hard against the stairway railing. And the ground beneath the house felt like a thunderbolt was ripping through its belly from one end of the hall to the other. The mirror dropped and shattered against the floor.

Hetty covered her face and turned away as she lay raked by breaking glass. Annabelle screamed out. The house began to quake. Hetty pulled herself up and made her way back to the parlor. At the door, she ran into Sarah. Her face was white. And she was trembling.

"The levee can't have given way. It just can't."

Geordie looked out the window beside the front door. The levee had given, and a great gray demon of water was coughing up ground. The shattering tumult leapt the front yard fence.

Annabelle put her hands up against the side of her head. "I can't swim. I can't swim. What will I do?"

"Get upstairs," shouted Geordie.

Sarah grabbed Hetty by the arm. "Help me get the children."

Hetty tried to keep up with Sarah as she raced down the hall. A foaming wave engulfed the yard, charged up the veranda, raking the lanterns from their hooks, then hurled itself against the house. The windows shattered. The front door was blown open and torn from a hinge. It hit Geordie in the face, leaving a deep cut above her eye.

The mad rush of water began. The search for every corner, for every open chasm, every hidden pocket. The tide grabbed at every-thing it passed, splattering up its dirty brown bile on the walls and ceilings, knocking over tables, drenching candles and flooding the hearth. The rooms went black.

Annabelle tried to follow Hetty but the water tossed her aside. And the next wave sent her and a chair tumbling into the sewing room.

The churning tide rushed down the hall, eating at the open space. Sarah had made it around a corner at the end of the hallway that led to the back bedrooms, but the rolling black wave hit Hetty in the back and washed her along the floor where she was rammed up against the wall. The sideboard was lifted and slapped against the ceiling, then thrown like a piece of clapboard where it wedged between the stairwell and the wall, blocking the turn in the hallway that led to the back bedrooms. For a moment the sideboard acted like a barrier and slowed the flood, forcing it to turn back on itself. The rush spiraled around Hetty as she who was reaching up for something to grab onto so she could stand, and swamped her. She went under. Her fingers clawed at the wall. Her head bobbed up. She was spitting out water and gagging. She got hold of the back of the sideboard.

Sarah had made it to the bedroom and forced open the door. The water was up to her knees and a rushing stream poured over the sills. It was pitch black and she couldn't see her children. Frantically, she called out, "Danny, Charles!!"

Charles tried to stand. "Mama, we're here, behind the bed." The water slapped him down. Sarah searched through the dark. The bed had been tossed all the way across the room. Her boys were crying and panicked. She lifted herself over a bureau lying on its back and saw them both, huddled in the corner, drenched and shaking. "Hetty! For God's sake, where are you…"

Hetty took hold of a thick ornately carved dowel that supported the upper half of the sideboard. She tried to get leverage and pull it down. But the sheer weight, and the rushing water against its back, kept it jammed in place. If she couldn't move it, she couldn't get through, and more harrowing yet, Sarah and the boys couldn't get back. Hetty yelled up the hallway to Geordie. "You've got to get the door closed long enough to slow the water down."

Desperate, Hetty took hold of the dowel, but this time lifted herself up, got a boot anchored on the lower shelf and wedged her body between the wall and the back of the sideboard. She leaned hard against the wall and started to kick. Once. Then again. And again. The heavy leather thud echoed in the alcove.

Annabelle struggled against the current, got hold of the back of Geordie's dress. Geordie hauled her to her feet. Side by side they lifted the door and, like a huge ancient shield, pressed it against the current. Hetty saw the water rise and spiral and the frothing run turned, and rushed toward the parlor.

Sarah made it down the hall, carrying a child in each arm, and collapsed near the sideboard. "Hetty, please."

Hetty pulled her leg back and kicked again. Still it didn't move. Her muscles were cramping and her shoulders, rammed hard against the ceiling. Her strength was failing. She pulled her leg all the way back, and kicked again.

"It's moving, Hetty!"

Geordie lost her balance, and slipped. The weight of the door fell on Annabelle and her grip failed. The door dropped and the rushing tide drove over the top, swamped the women, and flooded down the hallway.

Hetty could hear the water charging her, the children crying, Sarah's faltering voice. She forced her hands against the ceiling, bent herself back farther, grabbed all the strength and breath she could steel, and drove herself at the sideboard.

The stairwell railing that the sideboard was jammed against snapped. Hetty was thrown into the water as a two foot circle of black burst between the wall and sideboard.

Hetty struggled back to her feet, using the railing to stand. "Pass me the boys."

The water was rushing up waist high. Sarah lifted Danny and slid him through the gap. Geordie and Annabelle slogged through the freezing, black tide. Hetty carried Danny over to the stairs and put him down.

"Get upstairs!" He was too afraid to move. "Do as I tell you," she screamed.

Charles was already squirreling through the gap when Hetty turned around. Geordie made it to the stairs and took Charles. As Sarah squirmed through, Hetty and Annabelle got hold of her arms and pulled.

The women were exhausted black silhouettes making their way along the upstairs hall. Below, the beams creaked as the water pressed against the walls. Sarah held Charles' hand and led the others to her suite of rooms.

"We'll get out on the roof where they can see us."

"Who'll see us?" asked Annabelle.

Hetty, carrying Danny, walked behind Annabelle. "There'll be boats out to pick up the stranded."

Geordie stopped at her room. "I've got a lantern. We could use it as a signal."

They entered Sarah's bedroom. Hetty put Danny down on the bed, went over to the window that led to a flat roof above the front parlor and looked out.

Annabelle sat next to Danny. She turned to the others. Her voice shook. "I can't swim. So you're all gonna have to watch out for me."

Through the rain Hetty stared up toward Second Street. The road was rolling black and window high. Some of the ramshackle, one story houses had collapsed. Beyond Third Street, two wide hulled fishing boats rode the crest alongside a row of warehouse sheds and were hauling the stranded off a roof.

Hetty turned and looked over at Sarah who was going through her armoire and pulling out a couple of old woolen coats. "I see boats up past Third Street."

"You hear," Sarah told the boys, "there's boats. We'll be all right."

As Sarah got the coats on her boys Hetty remembered. The trunk. The trunk in the sewing room. By the door. It couldn't be left behind.

Geordie came back carrying the lantern. Annabelle, watching on the roof, leaned her head back in. She wiped the rain from her face. "Hurry with the lantern. One of the boats is coming along Second Street."

Geordie put match to taper. A yellow flaring light filled the room from wall to ceiling. Each face stood out against the black, each face was a stark memory of the hours before the flood. Sarah noticed her cousin wasn't in the room.

"Where's Hetty?"

"Isn't she out on the roof?" asked Geordie.

CHAPTER NINE

Fingers guided Hetty's path along the wall, the water ice against her breasts, lilacs from a vase lifted with a wave like a funeral wreath, and from somewhere, her cousin called her name.

When her boots stumbled on the trunk, her hands stretched beneath the inky black. With a breath, she followed. A trail of bubbles left a mark. No response begat a desperate call again from Sarah, as bubbles burst upon the air and disappeared in silence, broken only by footsteps racing on shaky timbers.

A shattered chair shaped buoy followed by a chafing dish, a cloth woven tapestry, a cooking pot, a rooster with a broken neck swirled by degrees through a maze to circle in the alcove like a dumping trough, when a gasping shadow on the wall appeared. Hetty grasped the trunk's slick leather sash and held. From broken step to broken step a slow wave folded out upon itself as Hetty pulled the trunk toward the stairs. More movement from above, the echo of a voice as a boat was pulling up.

With each slow exhausted foot upon those stairs came a thud, then a cut and rake, another thud and another cut and rake. The trunk lifted up the terraced woodwork, water streamed down its side. The trunk twisted and the leather handle snapped. It fell. The locker's brass clip sheared along the railing and out onto the steps spilled bags of gold. A coffer full.

Hetty squatted down and stuffed the small, dirty wet canvas bags back into the trunk scrambling for time as men climbed through the window to help evacuate the women and children. Reaching the stairwell, her cousin called to her.

"Hetty. There's a boat here and—"

Hetty looked up quickly. Her cousin on the landing stared at her in disbelief.

"Go back and wait on the roof."

Sarah refused to move.

"Sarah. Go back and wait on the roof."

Instead, she came down the steps slowly.

"Hetty. What is that you have there?"

Sarah knelt beside her cousin. Each face lost to shadows. Sarah looked down at the stairs and there beside a torn canvas bag, nuggets shined against the dark stained wood.

"Where did you get all that?"

"Just go and wait on the roof."

The men were calling out.

"Answer me."

Again the men called out.

"We're here by the stairs," shouted Hetty. Then, with her hand, swept the remaining nuggets from the stairs. They pocked the water, then were gone. She slammed the trunk lid closed.

"Where did you get all that?"

"It's not your business."

Sarah leaned against the railing.

Two outlines filled the upstairs hallway entrance. "Hey…we've got to get out of here."

Hetty looked past her cousin and up toward the men come to help. "I've got to bring my trunk. It has everything I own in it."

Sarah stepped back up the stairs, silent to the lie.

One of the men, tall and rail thin, with sideburns cutting a line down to the lip, pushed past Sarah. "We got no time to be draggin' her. The levee's caving like a sandhill."

"Well, go on then," yelled Hetty, trying to drag the trunk. "I'll get it up to the roof myself."

"We won't wait for you," shouted the man.

"Don't then. There'll be other boats."

"This whole damn building could go!"

She paid him no mind. She kept laboring up each step. Sarah disappeared down the second floor hallway.

Whether it was out of pity, or because Hetty seemed like some kind of madwoman, the other man, the one who hadn't spoken came past and pushed her aside. He bent down curling his hand around the broken leather sash. His long dark hair hung across his face in wet threads to the collar of his worn Navy cape. There were streams of water trailing down through his moustache. Jason looked up into the black stairwell to the man who'd been talking.

"Can you help us here?"

· · ·

Hetty followed behind her cousin across the roof. The rain had turned fine, a hard drizzle driven by the wind coming up from the river against the falling pitch of the upper roof in haphazard furrows.

At the edge of the roof, a boy no more than fourteen, wearing a slicker torn then patched with canvas, held a guideline attached at one end to the bow of a deep hulled shrimper while the other hand curled around his back and ran through his hands like a pulley winch. He was bent against the roofline. The shrimper was rising and falling with the heaving tide, and an old Russian was anchored to the rudder stick forcing the boat to heel just feet from the roof beams. A black crested wave drove the shrimper against the support beams shearing them like pitiful dry reeds. The boat was filled with the stranded, helpless except to bail the watery slime flooding around their feet.

The boy cried out to the women in broken English. "Go…to end…roof…I pull…You jump…Jump!"

Hetty glanced over at her cousin who only looked away.

The prow of the shrimper rose on a running wave, and as the boy pulleyed the guideline the shrimper edged up along the roof. Geordie and a Mexican in overalls who worked the livery at the end of Second Street stood up in the boat and stretched their arms and Sarah stepped out along the edge of the roof and the two feet separating her from the hull of the shrimper might as well have been two miles. But with her boys wailing, and the others calling, and the old man screaming in Russian, she took a breath and jumped. Outstretched arms caught her, and all fell backward into the bow of the shrimper.

Hetty waited, and the boat jerked from port to starboard. She leaned against her thick boot fighting for balance. When she saw the boat lurch in toward the roof she jumped and landed hard against the others. The shrimper lurched again and she was thrown over a seat.

Out along the roof Jason and the other man hauled the trunk along the grated shingles. The shrimper fell again as the tide was sucked back down then driven back up by the wave behind it. The old Russian was pressing the rudder stick hard to port, but having trouble holding, and a businessman stripped down to a vest and shirt front climbed over his seat past Annabelle, and anchored up beside the Russian against the rudder.

On the roof the other man faced the same span of two feet and made it clean. Jason pushed the trunk over the edge, and the boy, his hands white as bone from lack of blood and his palms raw red from the hemp line scouring at the flesh as it wound through them, pulleyed in the line and the steamer trunk fell, landing against the side of the hull. Hetty grabbed hold of it and as it hit against her shoulder it drove her down under her seat scoring the inside hull casing.

Another wave drove the boat back up against the roof supports and an oarlock was sheared off as if guillotined. The water washed over the roof, swamping Jason and the boy, sending them tumbling across the wood shingling like pebbles.

Jason got a hand on the guideline. The boy, all tangled and turned round the thick hemp cord, kicked his boots against the gutter. Snapping, it gave way, but his heels gouged the cedared squares and slowed his fall. Jason got his footing and pulled the guideline hard, lifting the boy.

He called out. "Get up! And we'll pull the line in hard. Get her bow in close against the roof. Her bow."

He understood. "Yes. Okay. Yes."

"Then we jump."

"Yes. Yes. You jump."

"No. Goddamn it. We jump together. Together. One of us can't hold the line in here alone."

The boy looked at the boat rising on a wave then wiped the rain from his face as if seeing better would help him think better.

"Yes. Okay. Yes."

They coiled the guidelines round their arms and leaned. The shrimper rose on a slow black arc, the bow rolled toward the roof and Jason yelled to the boy.

"Let's jump. Now. Now!"

They made for the edge with heavy clodding steps, grabbing at the air for balance, and then the shingles were gone beneath them.

From the boat the two seemed printed against a sheet black backdrop and the hull of the shrimper lunged up to meet them and hit them square. The boy's ankle was caught up under a seat joist and his weight carried him backward and then pinned the ankle like a pry bar, shattering it.

In broken English, the old Russian, his voice a harsh groan, kicked at the oars and ordered the others to row. Each scurried for a seat. Jason in the bow, the boy in pain slid over to the oar opposite, his leg dragging and bloody.

Hetty sat in front of her cousin who stared at the trunk then pulled her boys near as if Hetty's actions might in some way be suspect. The Mexican sat opposite her, winding a rag around a gnawed oar handle. The tall man with the sideburns behind him and opposite Geordie and Annabelle tried to wedge an oar into the remains of the sheared lock, but its broken clasp forced them to anchor their grip together.

At first the boat moved in short palsied spurts, so the old Russian kicked his whaleboot against the hull like it was the top of a drum and soon the oars found their rhythm and formed a sleek line. They made their way out into Second Street, now a black lake, its only markings the remains of rooftops. As Hetty pulled, she could see ahead the current hemorrhaging out across the rain dark floodplain, the surface of which shimmered and was speckled with detritus as if some great, lost world had coughed up the relics of its life.

The shrimper was pulling slowly under the weight of its cargo and the water it had taken in. The businessman in the vest and shirt front had a clay jug in one hand and a storage tin in the other, and on his knees was bailing water as fast as it accumulated.

Annabelle began to weep seeing bloodless white corpses on the oily surface scum, their lifeless arms rising as if to wave them in.

Sarah whispered to her friend. "Look away. Just look away and row." She covered her own children's eyes, each with a palm, and bowed their heads against her breast.

The old Russian knew that soon he'd have to turn hard to port and guide the shrimper toward the hills west of the city where the evacuated were being taken. He called to his boy to watch for any floating debris they might come upon beyond the broken face of the warehouse that could swamp the boat.

The boy dragged himself along the seat, and hanging over the edge, leaned out and scanned the running surface ahead for any signs of danger that could be cutting a breaker line against the current. He waved to his father. "Okay, Dada, okay."

His father geared against the rudder stick. The shrimper rolled to starboard past a warehouse and into a sweeping eddy. Pulling flush past the warehouse, the current widened out, spiraling, and they had to bear down on the oars.

The boat rose on a breaker curling out from the great mortared escarpment of warehouses; then past that silent passage echoed a queer, violent scarring that swelled beyond and above them.

Pulling at the oars slackened then slowed, and all looked through the black ahead. The darkness here was inviolate except for the shrill atavistic grating, like a rusted axle slowly rotating and in so doing began a thousand more rusted pivots turning.

The boat slowed on a rise, then flattened out. The old Russian wiped his face and called to his son in confusion. The boy, his leg numb and swollen, could not help to guide him now and pleaded to Jason. Jason stood in the bow searching and saw in outline, blacker than blackness, clipped, twisted, broken gnarled arms, cutting along brick walls, clawing at window casings and an illusory form shaped out itself. Two levantine juniper trees torn up by the root, like two great warriors fallen in combat and died together had become entwined, and rolled, drifted, surged with the current. And caught there, impaled through the casing, a wagon, its canvas hood torn free, floated back and above from one arced branch like a guidon and fanning out behind the roots, snared by the tracer lines, were four mutilated pull horses.

Jason turned to the boy, and by the look of terror on his face he knew he had seen this monolithic train of debris. Jason swept his arms across his chest in desperation.

"We've got to clear those buildings. Drive her starboard. Drive her starboard or it'll roll us. Do you understand?"

The boy screamed out. His father hooded his eyes against the rain and got his first view, as the tumbling barked columns raked walls and tore out brick, then caught in the charging current, swept out into the eddy toward the shrimper.

The old Russian canted the rudder stick and the others were thrown against their oars. Sarah grabbed her boys and forced them down under her seat.

So the current drove this lifeless demon, which, in turn, drove the current before it. And rising, the shrimper bellied on a living wave. And the water rushed over the hull as in a baptism. And the dark horned snake rammed the prow. And the screams could not be heard above the shattering branch. And the roots sabred the hull casing. And a woman cried out to God. And a bark lance drove through the shoulder bone of the old Russian, then was torn away. And the children huddled beneath the seat well choking on bilge. And the rain washed away nothing.

Hetty anchored herself against the leather trunk filled with gold for ballast. And the bloated corpse of a beast was thrown across the deck. And the man with the sideburns was buried beneath its weight and died in silence. And the great junipers rolled, and the tracer lines jerked and dragged along the deck the bloated corpse, and the boy fell and was pinned beneath.

The great junipers rolled back and shattered the oars to port. And Annabelle was thrown to the flood. And Sarah hid her face and covered her children with her life. And Jason lifted an oar and wedged it beneath the blood soaked hide of a dead pull horse to free the boy. And Annabelle sank only to rise again. And the old Russian, fallen, stared in shock as the rudder stick went mad. And the boy clawed at the horse's head. And Geordie grabbed Annabelle by the hair and pulled her back on board.

There were more screams. And there were only helpless souls everywhere. And Jason tried to lift the dead animal's thick roaned chest. And the Mexican and businessman tried to help lift the beast. And Hetty dragged herself across the seat and tried to move the beast's head. And the boy was gasping for breath.

The wagon's canvas hood unfurled above the deck. And clawing root tore away at the underbelly of the hull. And Jason still could not move the bloated corpse. And the boy was dying. And Jason cried out as he lifted. And the boy grasped hold of Hetty's hand. And the oar snapped and Jason's hands were pierced with shards of wood. And the boy's head rolled back under the sagging chest. And blood spurted out from his mouth as his heart was crushed. And the rain washed away nothing.

Caught in the maelstrom, man and lifeless demon were spinning. And the surging junipers dragged the tracers, and the horse carcass was pulled across the deck while the corpse of another rose up on the starboard bow. And the tracer lines tore like ruptured veins. And the dragging harness metal struck and stung like a whip. And the harness metal dug out the flesh on Annabelle's face. And the harness metal coiled around Geordie's throat and pulled her into the flood. And the oarless boat was left spinning.

Geordie tore at the tracer line strangling her and was lost. And Hetty fell back against the trunk, holding the dead child's hand. And the living were covered with slicken and blood. And the living were helpless and huddled there together. And Jason could not stop staring at the fallen child. And Hetty would not let the child's hand go. And the rain washed away nothing.

CHAPTER TEN

Before me the earth goes from black to gold. The light slowly eats away at the ground like a creeping mist as it climbs the hills west of the city where the evacuated have been taken. Along the hillside, a parcel of humankind faces the time of desperation in the storied looks of those across the flames of each campfire. When the darkness evaporates around them, each personal tragedy becomes part of a larger, more devastating tragedy. For with the changing tide of color comes the harsh, tearful truth. Sacramento, our Gateway to the West, has been ravaged.

At the cusp of the river that circles the center of town are two tears in the levee wall where hemorrhaged through an ocean of slumgullion. Lying against the muddied escarpment are the schooners, from topsail to scow, like fallen giants along the edge of some great ditch, their mainsails broken and covered with mud, floating in the gray morass. Near them, floundered on a sandbar by the J Street Dock, is the steamer ACROPOLIS. The admiral of the river, all shining brass and shimmering white, where legions of patrons passed their Sundays of memory in the sun of her upper decks.

From my vantage point, where I write in safety, I can see beyond that sodden wall, the city...

Matthew was sitting on a crate. He stopped writing and leaned back against the rusting wheel of a dray left alongside a guttered section of road. He closed his notebook and reached for the cigarette resting on the metal axle rim. I have run from one disaster, he thought, only to meet another.

He walked down to the river and looked out upon Sacramento. It was now a shimmering flood plain reflecting the light of a thousand suns, and dotted with roofs and boats channeling up the lined rows of treetops, that were guide marks to where the streets once were laid out. What troubled Matthew most was that he had been lucky. For seven days he'd pushed it hard from San Francisco to be in the city when the rains came, and what happened. The bridges had been washed out when he reached Sacramento, and so he was left to the safety of the hills.

On this side of the river the tide had crested well beyond the pylon docks where the river packets were moored. And along the newly running shoreline, smaller craft used in the evacuation had been tendered for a mile down the coast.

Standing by the shoreline, Matthew saw before him, floating on the surface of the brown tide, a town's worth of letters. Most drifted loosely to the shore, then were plucked back by the shrinking tide. The paper was wilted and the print indecipherable. They were probably from one of the river packets that had sunk at its moorings.

Squatting there in the mud, he pulled his book from the canvas satchel and noted what he saw, then added:

A life lost on the shores of the West. Am I like those letters?
I do wish I had been across the river when the flood came. Will

I die somewhere down country? And would I be better for it?

· · ·

The old Russian shrimper beached just past a grove of willows about a half mile south of the Front Street Wharf. The shoreline there had risen enough so the willows were bob sawyered. Jason sat on the husk of a fallen bay laurel by a fire they'd built near the boat. Sarah cut strips of cloth and bandaged his wounded hands after he'd washed them clean.

The river road which wound past them down the peninsula was packed with people and wagons in a state of evacuation. From the rains there were deep gouges in the clay roadbed causing the wagons to list and totter.

Jason noticed Sarah stop cutting rag strips and stare at Hetty as she talked with three men who had pulled off the road in a carreta. After a short conversation, they followed her to the shrimper, and two of them climbed into the hull and lifted out the trunk. Sarah's eyes became grave as the men carried the trunk to the carreta and loaded it into the back.

Hetty followed along, talking with the third man. He was not much older than her, but his beard was already matted to the gray. They talked a little while longer, then shook hands, and he climbed into the box seat and guided the horses back into the roadway.

· · ·

"I want to talk to you, cousin."

Hetty followed Sarah to the shoreline where the tops of the willows brushed against the surface of the water in the wind.

"Where did you get all that gold? And who were those men that took the trunk?"

Hetty remained firm in her silence.

Sarah crossed her arms. "So what are you? Tell me that having a small business in the mining country made you that wealthy."

"I should not have brought the trunk into your home, but I did."

She went to walk away, but Sarah grabbed her by the arm. "Take notice of all that was suffered here. Take notice. Because much of it was your fault."

"Am I responsible for a flood?"

"No, cousin. But you are responsible for that trunk. That trunk you would not leave without. That trunk you made those men carry, then drag, then lower into that boat. Had it not been for that trunk, we would have escaped sooner. And having escaped sooner, we may have well avoided the disaster that befell us."

• • •

When Jason stood and reached for a tin of heated coffee, he spotted a cavalry guidon making its way above the heads of that trammeling mass along the road. A slow snake of uniformed Dragoons picked their way past the wagons and stragglers. From the red and gold tassel on their kepis to the red braided baldric, he knew they'd be the 1st Dragoons of California, who'd just arrived from San Francisco to begin a sweep toward the border.

In slow double file they filtered off the main road onto a short sandy spur, halted, then dismounted and began to water their horses. Trailing up with the last platoon were prisoners taken along the way. They, too, were on horseback, but their hands were chained through a carved hole in the cantle that was run under the horse's belly to a set of leg irons. Across each of their backs had been stitched a large piece of rag or tarp with the painted nature of their individual crime. HORSE THIEF. — EMBEZZLER. — ROBBER. — SESECH. — MURDERER. Martial law was the order of the day.

Jason put the coffee tin down and reached for his gunny and the Navy cape drying by the fire and, without either word or gesture to the others, silently fell in with the stragglers along the road.

Making his way south he came upon the confluence of the Sacramento River and Steamboat Slough. Along the road women from the benevolent societies struggled with crates and barrels, loading them into carts and flatbed wagons and towing sleighs. Another temporary hospital had been set up in a connecting row of tents.

On the downriver side of the road, traders and hawkers had set up stands, or spread out their frayed woolen blankets on the soggy hillside. They hung wooden signs they carried itemizing goods for sale or trade.

Jason glanced back over his shoulder and scanned the trace of road he'd come over. About a half mile back, a single line of dust caterpillared in his direction. From the steady cadence of the dust rising to the front and disappearing to the rear, he knew it'd be the Dragoons. Taking care, he made his way off the road to lose himself among the scheming goods-sellers.

Waiting for them to pass, he pulled a tobacco pouch from his shirt pocket. He felt around for rolling paper only to find it missing, when he heard a Frenchman crawling through a conversation in broken English.

He turned and there at a hawker's stand, made from the remains of a rotting kitchen door propped on rocks stacked table high, was an old Frenchman with a beard all black and greasy, sweeping his hand across two dozen rifles and pistols laid out in what was meant to approximate neat order.

"Of all these…my feelings, Monsieur Purloin." He pointed at the pistol hanging in the hand of the young man standing before him.

"Christman," said Matthew. "My name is Matthew Christman… not Purloin."

Matthew swung the canvas satchel over his shoulder and shifted the pepperbox to his right hand to get a better feel.

Jason watched the sallow faced young man draw on his cigarette and try to maneuver that clumsy mess of a thing, insultingly called a weapon.

Jason went over to this Matthew Christman and excused himself. He held up his tobacco pouch. "I'm square for tobacco. But lost for paper. Could you spare me enough to roll one?"

"Sure." Matthew rummaged through his satchel, the pepperbox dangling from his right hand, nose down like an albatross with a broken neck.

"I got some matches, too, if you're short."

The Frenchman kept busy talking, some to himself, some to the sky above him.

"You say this gun's accurate?"

The Frenchman nodded with enthusiasm. Then he glanced at Jason, his dark eyes squirreling around in their leathery sockets. Jason knew the Frenchman was trying to figure if he'd mule with the sale. But he turned away as he finished rolling the cigarette and watched along the road for the Dragoons. Their flags cleared a short rise less than a quarter mile back.

"Can I help you?"

Jason looked back and answered in French. "No, I just needed some rolling paper. So you can relax."

The hawker eased a bit before a countryman.

"There's some rust on the barrel," said Matthew.

The Frenchman turned to Matthew and mumbled, "Monsieur Purloin." Then he gave him a dressing down with his eyes and waved the rust away. He pointed at the gun, his finger doing a bony imitation of a dagger. "Inside is firing…inside…Blanc-bec. Inside… clean!"

Matthew nodded as if being suddenly educated to an understanding. The Frenchman stole a look at Jason, who said nothing. Jason interrupted Matthew long enough to bum a match. He lit his cigarette and looked back along the road.

The Frenchman started to dismantle a British Brown Bess, replacing the hammer fittings. He spoke to Jason, rumbling through his thoughts in French. "I hate the people here. I hate this country. It is a pigsty. No, wait. Let me not insult a pig that way. It is a nation of stillborn."

Matthew looked at both men in a pitiful state of uncertainty. "I'm not really knowledgeable about weapons. I can't shoot very well." He was hoping for support somewhere in a look, a word. But was offered nothing. "Like I said, I'm heading out into the mining country. I've never been down to Tulare County. So I thought it might be best to, well…"

Matthew took off his glasses and rubbed his eyes. He looked at the pepperbox.

Jason stared through a row of tents and trading stalls toward the road. The Dragoons were making their way single file through the lines of carts.

"How much?" asked Matthew.

"One hundred dollars."

"A hundred?"

The Frenchman nodded gravely.

As Matthew tried to weigh the deal, he took notice of the Walker pistol wedged into Jason's belt next to the pouch of magic Coco had given him.

"Excuse me, but, would you mind if I ask you something?"

Jason looked back at Matthew.

"About the gun." He pointed at the pepperbox. "The gentleman is asking a hundred dollars for it. And I wanted to know if…"

Jason hesitated, then picked up the pepperbox in his bandaged hands. It was a clumsy excuse for a cutter. With its six rotating cylinders running full barrel length along a core. It looked more like a piece of pipe fitting than a pistol, and less serviceable. He checked the action. The rotation on the center axis was erratic and slipped. The spur trigger was loose, and the release retarded. The weapon wasn't built front heavy for recoil, so it snapped up like a river snake after it fired. If it fired. Jason put the gun down. Even when the damn things worked, they didn't.

Jason glanced at Matthew and in that moment observed something relict there. A vestige of decency, maybe. Worn with sadness, but nonetheless…

"It's a gun that will match the man, I'll say that."

Matthew wiped his glasses clean. "How much do you think I should pay for it?"

If there ever was a sheep, this boy was it. Jason called over to the hawker in French. "This pistol isn't worth dirt. And the goddamn thing will probably blow up in his hand the first time he fires it."

There was a black sense of pleasure in the Frenchman's face. "Listen," he said to Jason in French, "if you can help me sell the gun to that sheep there, I'll give you twenty dollars."

"I'll help you fleece him, but a hundred dollars? You might as well kill him and rob him. He's a blanc-bec. Fifty dollars…I get twenty."

The Frenchman had no pettied vision of himself and bobbed his head from side to side. "Look at Monsieur Purloin there. He looks like the type that shits in his tent."

"What is this discussion here?" asked Matthew.

Jason ran his hands along his moustache. "He says you're quite an unusual fellow, so he's thinking about the price."

The Frenchman stared at Jason, scaling the possibilities of a sale on his terms versus being stuck with such a prized piece of craftsmanship. He snapped his fingers, then followed with an open palm.

"You just bought yourself a pistol for fifty dollars," said Jason.

"I appreciate this."

Jason offered silent thanks by looking away. "Don't forget cap and cartridge."

Matthew poked through his satchel and came up with two double eagles and paper. While Matthew was intent on finding a length of belt suitable for holstering the pepperbox the Frenchman quickly tossed Jason a double eagle.

Matthew turned to Jason. "I want to thank…" But Jason was already making his way along the path running between the trading stands.

Matthew scooped up cap and cartridge and hurried off, following after him. He strode up alongside Jason. "I wanted to—"

"I was thanked," he said.

They moved across the hillside running parallel to the road, with Jason taking occasional bearings of the whereabouts of the troops below.

"Which direction are you walking?"

Jason pointed to the south.

"Me, too. I'm heading for Stockton Landing to—"

"Tulare County."

Matthew bore a surprised look.

"You mentioned it back there to the Frenchman."

He nodded, recalling. "How far are you going?"

"Stockton Landing," said Jason. "Then on south to the southern mines. Tulare County, I believe."

CHAPTER ELEVEN

I am sure, like so many others, you believe in "Hallowed be Thy name." But we both know that's so much fool's gold, don't we? Be careful, Mr. Whitehorse, in time you may end up like that brick you so proudly exhibit in your den, just so much dead stone.

Demerest tossed the paper down on the table after going through Christman's final editorial in the Flag. "The self-serving little bastard. It's a disgusting assault on your good name."

Whitehorse sat opposite him. He held the chewed down stub of a cigar between two fingers. He was sullen and hadn't touched his scotch. They shared Whitehorse's private table at the rear of the "Mule Deer Club" on Halleck Street, just across from the American Theatre.

Mr. Demerest adjusted the ruffled cuff on his shirt. "I'll tell you how I would handle this. I'd use the treatment my old daddy used on his farm. One day 'one of them' talked back. Just came out with a 'So you say' response. Well, my old daddy had the bite of a snake but he kept closed council. Now what he did was this. He took 'So you say' and tied him down. Bound him head to foot and tossed him in the barn for two days."

Demerest took a sip of scotch and pulled his chair in closer to the table and flourished on the memory. "For those same two days, my old daddy starved the hogs." He winked. "Starved 'em good. After two days, they get to rooting and squealing. And they were about ready to turn on themselves when my old daddy took 'So you say' and had a couple of his own carry him out from the barn and toss him into the pen with those starving hogs. They hunkered down on him fast…I will tell you this. You could hear 'So you say' screaming all the way down to the road."

Demerest punctuated the next thought with a quick finish to his scotch. He sat back. "'So you say' lost a leg. And most of his lower arm. A part of his ear and the end of his nose got all carved up."

He slipped his fingers into the pocket of his green felt vest, rummaging for a spack of tobacco.

"He was useless after that. His mind, too. Gone. My old daddy kept him as a warning to the others. I'll tell you, Charles, that old nigger would have to just see a pig."

Whitehorse sat back. The smoker was quiet. He looked out the window to the veranda where the empty tables were little more than catchbins for runoff.

"Charles," Demerest said softly, "that boy deserves what the editor at the *Flag* got."

Whitehorse bit down on the stub.

"The lathe rod is a great equalizer."

"Amen," said Whitehorse.

Demerest looked around the room to make sure they had the privacy he needed to continue. "Charles, we always have room in our 'castle' for another native son…"

• • •

A buggy made its way down the coast road toward the landing at San Leandro. The mist had crept up from the beach. There were no fires anywhere, only the steady drizzle. More felt than seen. With its leather top and tassels at the wings, the buggy emerged out of the enameled wall like some hearse trolling a bleak netherworld.

The landing had been deserted now six months. The Szyamanski Supply Warehouse on the wharf shut down. Just an amorphoric shape floating above the shoreline in the stench of low tide. A retching spillage.

Two figures walked the parapet of the wharf in long blue coats. Deft eyes turned to the road when they heard the chugging breaths of two mares. The buggy cleared the fog and sifted its way across the sand, coming to a stop at the wharf.

Whitehorse stepped down from the buggy seat and was ushered into the shed by the two officers. There was little light in the shed. Bare outlines formed and reformed around two kerosene lamps beside each other on the floor. A Union colonel named Madsen came forward from the shadows. He was a young man to hold such rank. He was unshaven and dogmatic.

"Well, Mr. Whitehorse, were you successful?"

The shed door closed behind Whitehorse. He slapped his hands into his overcoat pockets. "Demerest will initiate me into the Knights sometime next week."

The colonel knelt behind the kerosene lamps and looked over to his captain. He was older, and the hand of his left arm was withered from birth.

"You were right about the editorial," remarked the Captain.

Whitehorse nodded. "The Christman boy is a zealot."

The colonel glanced up at Whitehorse. "A patriot, Mr. White-horse. The boy is a patriot."

Whitehorse looked down on the colonel and his youth. "Zealot, Colonel."

The captain rested his shriveled hand across the good one. "We need names. As many as you can get. And the quicker the better before there are outright hostilities here in the state."

"I'll get names, captain."

"And Demerest?" asked the colonel. "Where is he in all this?! What rank in the Knights?"

"Of some rank, I assume. He is monied, after all."

The colonel ran his fingers through the dust on the floor. "Well, what are your conditions for this?"

Whitehorse squatted down before the boy colonel. "Contracts. My business is iron, my business is brick. And one last detail. I keep using the Knights to protect my mine. That was my entré to Deme-rest. And they're all that's out there in redneck country to try and keep it from being robbed."

CHAPTER TWELVE

There was a bare skin of dust left across the brown surface of the whiskey in the cuptin.

Jason and Matthew sat together in the sunshine of the road along the river, two hours south of Rio Vista. They balanced themselves on handcarved stools barely fit for sitting, in the shadow of a wagon, where imprinted on its canvas hooding with a meager legibility was written: AUGUSTUS ROADSIDE—EVERYTHING FROM PICKLED ANCHOVE TO QUININE—MOSQUITO REPELENT A SPECILTE.

"Were you in Sacramento during the flood?" said Matthew.

"Yes," said Jason, staring into his cuptin. "I got there during the rains and holed up in a livery on A Street. The place was owned by this boatbuilder and…his son."

He finished the wash left in his cuptin and blinked lifelessly.

"Is that how you got out? In a boat of his?"

Jason nodded and blinked again. "We made it to one of his boats. Even managed to pick up some stragglers." He blinked again. "Then things went bad."

Matthew watched him as thin lines creased above Jason's eyes. "Is that how you hurt your hands? In the flood?"

Jason turned his hands over. The dust had coagulated in clumps where the sweat had seeped through the bandage. "Yes. What takes you down country?" asked Jason.

Matthew leaned forward. Jason saw in the boy's soft fingers a tremor. He noted a blemish of bloodless color beneath the eyes. The silent trademarks of addiction.

"I worked in San Francisco. I was a reporter for a newspaper." He hesitated. "Circumstances dictated I leave my job. So I thought…" He took a drink. "I thought I'd go into the mining country. Write about what I see there."

"Unlike most on the road," said Jason, "you don't appear strapped for money."

"I come from a well-to-do Philadelphia family," said Matthew, and then, rather uncomfortably added, "I live…on a remittance."

"I see."

Matthew emptied his cuptin, tapping the bottom for the last remaining drops. "What takes you down country?"

"A friend," said Jason, "asked if I could try and help him close a business deal."

• • •

They tramped over most of the afternoon. They were tired and talked little. Each silent to the conspiracy of their separate journeys. Farther along a crass row of one and two story buildings began to form out of the dust along the horizon.

Jason pointed. "Look there."

Matthew put on his glasses.

Through a wavering haze, Stockton Landing did not seem so much a small port city on the San Joaquin River, but rather some vast singular entity where the gray spired mastheads of the brigantines and sloops beyond the rooftops reached up and dissected a flat blue sky.

The road switchbacked through the landing, and they had to press among a crowd knitted about a flatbed wagon where the relic of a man in a black suit of frayed cotton stood with arms outstretched like some storefront Jesus recently crucified. A scrapheap scarecrow of a being. He spoke, no shouted, with a preacher's fever and stamped his foot at the dilapidated flock in passage.

"Pilgrims. Yea, Pilgrims. Listen to me now! Listen to all! Listen to the passings of things replete. Look around children, look around. You stand at the great cathedral to the West."

Matthew stopped to listen to his rantings, while Jason pressed out a narrow space in the crowd by the river path.

"Hear me now. One and all. Yea. The Catholics have preached this country with their curdled blasphemy and curried the native out of land and stock. And to the Spanish they've done the same. False prophets of the Royal Highway.

"It is time, Protestants. Both men and women, equally made. Sons and daughters of Adam. To go forth and take this land back from the Catholic butcher and give it to God. Yea." He stomped his foot again.

Jason slapped Matthew on the back. "Come along."

They pushed past a plank table stacked with Bibles where some of the preacher's acolytes handed out the sacred text freely, pressing them into the hands of all who went there.

A tired but shiny faced woman squeezed a Bible into Matthew's hand. "Remember, when you're downriver, you're a soldier for Christ."

Jason suffered the same indiscretion as a man grabbed hold of his bandaged hand and laid there a copy of the St. James, then wrestled his hand closed. "You too, brother."

Just so much extra weight, Jason tossed the book into the bleached grass beside the muddied pathway.

"Don't dump it, boy, don't dump it," came a voice all cranky and cracking.

Jason and Matthew stopped, then turned, and there hoisting up the book and wiping the mud from its sleeve, was a thickly carcassed old man with a drooping shoulder and wide flat hands and a wire gray beard that'd grown wild over the collar of his tattered benjamin.

"Not yet, anyway, boy. Not yet." He forced the Bible back in Jason's hand. "Downriver at the landings you can get yourself twenty-five cents to a drink for one of those. Yeah, brother, yeah. Ain't no Christian been better served." He winked. "Are you two spindlies making your way downriver? Or are you just here for the sermon?"

"We're heading downriver," said Jason.

"Tulare County," added Matthew.

The old man nodded. "Tulare County. Another of our illustrious shitholes. Gentlemen. My name is Hoole." He put out his hand. "I've a boat waiting, if you're wanting."

He pointed to the western side of the levee.

There, poled along a mudded embarcado was *JOB'S DESCENT*, a belligerent scow sloop, flat bottomed and square backed, with a Chinese style junk sail but made of cloth instead of matting and held together with an unsightly gambit of colored patches, raw and ill-stitched sections of flags and table silk and shirt fronts and women's dress fabric and sheeting. The deck was loaded down with barrel and crate and hay bales and a goat was tied at the main mast.

"I think we can do better," Matthew whispered.

"Better, but not sooner, spindlies. So what will it be?"

• • •

They ran south till dusk died away. They passed other sloops journeying up from the southern mines and barges drawing more slowly in midchannel. The steersmen shouted to each other, trading news of the river and the tides.

After dark Matthew sat on the gunwale abaft. Torches were mantled larboard by the bowsprit. Flaming banners that searchlighted the river. To the west, the Mount Diablo Range was a spectral of ragged crepe.

Matthew looked up toward the pulpit where Hoole steered, and tossed him a question, "I heard some people in Sacramento talking about a fella robbing the southern mines for over a year now. You know of this?"

"Yeah. I heard some."

Jason had been sitting quietly against the sheerstrakes, head bowed to his chest. Now his eyes opened and his head came up slowly.

"Like what?" asked Matthew.

Hoole pulled an azimuth compass from his pocket and bore down on Polaris.

"What have you heard?"

"Not now, boy…not now."

Matthew noticed Jason stand. His attention was drawn past where the river arced to the east, and a candle shaped flame jumped above the treeline. As they watched the fire, a short burst of rifle shot was caught on the wind, then gone.

• • •

Where the river bent back against a buttress of lavaed stone, a small inlet formed. The inlet was an incendiaried wall of yellow and gold reeds. The junipers, firesticks rooted to the shoreline. Their stenciled outlines burned then cracked, the limbs blackened then exploded against a luminescent night sky. And there before the pyred earth a sloop lay half sunk in the shallows. Its deck too, awash in flames. A smoldering wooden reef.

The three men jumped from the scow where they'd anchored in water knee deep. Hoole carried a shotgun against his chest and called to the helmsman of the other boat. Jason and Matthew walked his flanks. They made their way through the reeds along the embankment to look for survivors.

The wind picked up and carouseled the flames, a thousand demon spires skinning the surface of the water, where from the blackness floated a body.

Matthew called out to the others then pointed. The three moved forward, struggling past the reeds. Matthew got hold of a cold arm. The body rolled. Jason pushed back the hair that hid the face and below the eye where once was bone was now nothing but an open bloody hole.

"I recognize this fella," said Hoole, turning away from the wound. "Travels with a gent named Claron. Owns a sloop. That must be his boat." Distraught, he cupped his hand to his mouth and shouted, "Claron! Can you hear me, man!?"

Hoole's dying voice drifting above the treetops.

Silence.

The keelson burned through. The hull gave way, choking them with smoke. A flock of birds, dabs of black, swift against the sky, were there then gone.

Jason spotted the mark from where they'd flown. A stand of trees beyond a ragged field of buckgrass. He slid the Walker from his belt, checked the load, cocked the hammer, "You two follow along the shallows. If you find something, holler. I'll make my way up that field there."

"If somebody fired down on these boys..."

Jason nodded, but he was already digging at the embankment with his boots for footing.

"Be careful, boy," called Hoole. "The fire'll eat that grass faster than you can turn if the wind kicks."

The ground was a patchwork of shadow and smoke that left bewildering signs. Jason trailed up through the high reeds, moving forward, crouched, a figure black and ferret-like. He espied a tuft of heeled ledgegrass. He squatted down and fingered the edge of broken tips to judge which direction the boot followed. His throat burned, his eyes watered.

Farther on, the running boots met and mated with a double set of boots in a clumsy stumbling march over a set of flat heeled shoes. Here the ground was carved and chewed, and after a few more paces a furrow of broken weeds widened out where a body had fallen and was dragged to its feet and fell again. But before being dragged on, it left there a factory shoe with a torn heel, and a toe ripped, then patched, and ripped through again.

He lifted the shoe and looked it over, then cast it aside.

Matthew shouted and Jason turned and saw him standing in a circle of chest high tules waving his arms as he tried to clear a body from the spreading reeds.

Jason and Hoole rushed into the water. Hoole pulled at the buoyed head. His voice trailed off. "It's Claron."

The dead man's hands were bound behind him, and taut around his neck was a shorn section of Union flag used to strangle him with.

Hoole's voice cracked. "Well, God has seen his share tonight."

Jason reached over and pulled at a leg only to see it booted.

They had to shout now to hear each other over the burning timber. "Was it the Secesh?" yelled Matthew.

"Claron was a Union boy who talked Union. We all said he talked too much for this section of the country."

"Whoever it was tracked through that stand of trees."

Hoole wiped the sweat off his face. "Stupid boy. There'd been threats against him from those jacktraders and gunmen that come hooded out of the hills. The 'Golden Circle.'"

• • •

Exhausted, Matthew sat with his back and head resting against the scuttle butt. The bodies, which they had pulled from the river, lay in state before him, amidst baled hay and barrels of salted pork. Matthew's head tipped back to drink and there Jason stood looking down at him. The honey colored bottle made a tentative approach to his lips. He drank, then tried to set the bottle down.

"It's just like San Francisco. When they beat the editor of the *Flag* to death." He glanced back upriver. "Why is there always fire?" He looked up at Jason. "Why?"

Jason sat on a crate opposite Matthew. Next to him there, boot to boot, were the corpses.

Matthew's head leaned against the cask, and he looked up through the rigging, "My brother would be at home here. He loved to sail." Above, thin banners of mist made their way across the heavens. "He's gone. Mexican War." His tone was sharp, bitter. "Another reasonable cause. He was on a scouting mission for his troop. Running the advance. Got caught."

He took another drink. "The Mexicans put him before the firing squad. In the desert. Somewhere near Churubusco."

Matthew stopped. He looked down at his notebook lying open in his lap. Matthew began to drift. He whispered, "My brother was a brave boy. I am older now than he was when he died. And I am nothing."

Jason sat there quietly. Matthew's breathing slowed as he fell into a drugged sleep. Jason got up, leaned over and reached for the bottle. He lipped his tongue along the edge of the rim and tasted.

Alone there, looking into the satchel, the restless nature of the truth began to eat away at him. Why was this boy, this broken thing, so ill-equipped, traveling to Tulare County? Why was he asking those questions of the helmsman?

Sure that he was out of Hoole's view, Jason started to pick through the satchel. From glass case to cotton shirt with buttons missing. To the barest toiletries. Past the packed notebook. To the bottom of the canvas bag where, bundled, he discovered half a dozen torn brown sheets of paper from the Telegraph Hill Relay Office.

He undid the binding and read through each, one by one. And, one by one, bit by bit, the disquieting truth became clear.

Later, by the pulpit Jason came upon Hoole tying off the rigging.

"The boy has seen the Chinaman, hasn't he?"

"I believe he's gettin' a good look at him right now."

Jason sat along the gunwale and anchored his foot against the deck timber. Hoole watched Jason pull tobacco and paper from his shirt pocket.

"Roll me one of those, would you, boy? Back there at the inlet. I saw how you picked up sign. You've done your share and more I'll bet."

"I've done some," Jason answered.

"I assume you know of The Golden Circle."

"I know of them."

"I'll speak honestly to you if I can," said Hoole.

Jason lipped the paper and his fingers smoothed it over.

"You ain't no picker. That's obvious. But you look like you hustled a few. Now, I can see a fella of your type, young and smart, and with your talents, get it into his head to take the trip downriver. Spot himself a place. Tulare County for instance. Try to jackrabbit some bounty. That fella that's been raking the mines, carries a good price."

Jason stood and handed him the cigarette. Hoole slipped it into his mouth, then cupped his hands against the wind and waited for an offer from Jason to strike some light.

"I don't know anything about that," said Jason.

"Your friend was asking a lot of questions about that fella."

Jason struck the match along the pulpit posts. The light grew rosy yellow, a handheld moment in a cupped black universe.

"Tulare County is a pestilence. Between that Whitehorse Mine and the hardscrabble boys in the hills. And those Till brothers, magistrate and tax collector. Stand away. Stand away."

Along the headway streams of gray mist stalked the shoreline. Hoole watched a moment, the smoke curling from his mouth, the wind across his beard, the studied eyes—a chapeled painting of a man. He glanced at Jason, taking in what he saw there.

"Be careful, boy. This country has a black heart."

Jason mocked a smile. "Not that black." He turned and walked away.

CHAPTER THIRTEEN

Daylight across Greyson Landing. River packs unloaded onto a rickety wharf. Jason and Matthew jumped from the pier to the sand.

Hoole leaned across the railing and called to them from the pulpit. "Hey, spindlies."

They turned.

"Don't forget to give my greetings down country when you piss. And keep clear eyes now. Remember, in a lick comes grass and summer. And I hope you've still got your lives by then." He stumped a couple of fingers against the side of his head. "And your minds."

• • •

Hetty washed her face with water from a bucket on the steps of the stagecoach shanty just up from the landing. As she dried her hands on her canvas leggings, she saw Jason among the small clusters of men filing past. He was with another man.

Jason and Matthew reached the porch. Jason took notice of Hetty and he nodded and she nodded back and then, without words, he continued inside with Matthew to purchase tickets for the coach.

As a couple of grissel heels trudged over to the mud wagon and labored it into the roadway, Hetty gathered up her carry bag. Jason walked over to her, followed by Matthew, who was peppering some tobacco onto his rolling paper. Introductions were made all the way around.

"What brings you down country?" asked Jason.

"I'm a merchant. I have a business and warehouse at a mine in Tulare. The Whitehorse."

"There sure aren't many of you ladies down river, working it alone."

"There's few to begin with, that's true. And they got weeded out pretty quick. You need to have a temperament for it."

"And a fair amount of sand, I bet."

"A fair amount. I was in Sacramento ordering more goods… when the flood hit."

They walked out into the roadway.

She looked at Jason. "It was a difficult time. In Sacramento."

"Yes," he answered.

They continued on quietly.

The depotman rushed out onto the porch and kicked at a brown skinned boy who was lazing on a broom along the steps, ordering him in Spanish. "Goddamn your ass." The boy jumped back and the depotman kicked at him again. "Get over to Mr. St. Lowe's tent and tell him and the others to gather up, that the coach is being rigged."

Jason heard the name, and his attention was drawn away from the others who conversed among themselves. He watched the boy run to the tent and call politely to those inside. Jason waited as the mules were eased back into the traces and the popper climbed aboard and filled the jockey box with stones. The tent flap opened and stepping out into the sunlight was St. Lowe, in a black suit with a Hawkin rifle slung across his back and a stovepipe hat in one hand and his head shaved to skin because of the scalping he'd suffered years back. His face a violent angled "V" to the chin. Right away Jason recognized this ruddy faced bountyman from spotting him a number of times at the Big Blue Heaven.

Following behind St. Lowe was his son Leon, who was just as tall as his father, with the same violently angled face. Walking between them was a woman with pense eyes and a long, thin nose who could be as easily with the father as with the son.

They trooped past the corral and stopped at a root cellar where St. Lowe pulled back the bolt on the cellar door and Leon disappeared below. He came back up, leading on a leather leash about the neck, a black, no more than twenty. His face was swollen with fluid from a beating, and right away Jason saw he was one shoed, and that one shoe partner to the one Jason had found back at the inlet. Now the three together, dragging the black behind them like a dog, had their place in Jason's mind from the tracks near the burning scow.

St. Lowe pointed at the back of the mud wagon. "Leon, bind this murderer to the booting." He swung his Hawkin down from his shoulder and tossed it to Leon. "And place yourself atop there on the dickey."

St. Lowe turned and glanced at Matthew and Hetty. He floated his stovepipe hat in salute. "Brothers and sisters. Hallo. And excuse us bringing this thing aboard. But my son, Tess and me are journeying to the magistrate in Tulare County for a little justice."

Matthew looked the beaten manchild over and walked past St. Lowe without even a glance at him. "And the booty collected, I'll bet."

St. Lowe smiled. "Yes, sir. That is correct. It's a privilege to travel with such an observant and outspoken fellow."

• • •

Their coach followed the hogback through slow defaults as it trimmed the landing. The day passed on the western side of the river, the black struggling and tied to the booting.

"You've been doing your share of note taking there, Mr. Christman. I'll say that for you."

Matthew looked up and across the aisle to St. Lowe. He closed his notebook, with a finger in place. "I keep a journal."

"Keepin' a journal. Aye." St. Lowe nodded, resting a thoughtful elbow on the sill of the coach window. "It will suit you well in a country like this. Yes, it will. A great wall of paper is a proper defense against the dangers that ail you."

St. Lowe took to watching Jason, who remained occupied with himself and the passing country.

"Do I know you, sir?"

Jason looked from the window toward St. Lowe. "I haven't any idea."

St. Lowe sat back. His fingers flicked at the brim of his stovepipe. "Maybe it's just I've a sense of you." Then St. Lowe's fingers danced through an imaginary deal with a California Prayer Book.

• • •

The coach trailed over broken country. The air was still for hours. The mud wagon halted at an Indian well, rimmed it was with faded stone paintings of snakes and birds and spinning moons and shaded by a grotto of cypress.

The popper watered his charges first and then the others took their turn from a canvas pouch. All except the prisoner, squatting in the sun like a heeled beast by the wheel well; alone, he slunk toward the boxed shadow of the booting.

Tess saw him crawling from the sun and shouted to Leon who leaned down from the dickey where he was covered by a parasol. He tapped the Hawkin against the casement rim and shifted his head from side to side.

Tess walked over to the prisoner. She grabbed him by his neck leash and kicked him hard in the back.

"You have no right to do that," remarked Hetty.

"Thank you, miss," said Tess, as she passed.

"The man needs water."

"Thank you, miss."

"Are you going to give that man water, or am I?"

Jason, who had been at the far end of the grotto skimming the hills because of disturbing sign, made his way back through the trees.

Hetty reached up and pulled a water bag from the jockey box.

"Don't do that, ma'am," called St. Lowe.

Hetty uncorked the bag and squatted before the prisoner. His hands begged the water pouch when a shot drove through the air above them.

The prisoner fell prostrate on the ground. Hetty lost her footing and stumbled back.

St. Lowe walked to them and grabbed the pouch. "I told you, ma'am, I'll not have it."

• • •

In a grotto at the edge of spring all things are known. Even those done in His name. I was raised to believe. I was raised on the seed of Pilgrim's Progress. On Christian's fabled walk from Doubtful City to Enchanted Hill. The walls of my thoughts are lined with each pillared soul who gave him strength or fell away. Those were the cherished memories of my mother, framed by the bedroom window in summer, the candle lit beside her as she read to me. And to my brother, Charlie. I was taught then the world was built in two great arcs. One black...one good. But that truth does not exist. And I was a pauper for ever having believed it did.

• • •

Jason walked alone, well behind the coach. He did not allow himself to feel any kinship for the shackled man before him. Instead, he attended himself to any detail he might glean from the face of stone abutments to the west.

Matthew climbed down the back of the coach and fell in line next to Jason. He motioned toward the prisoner. "Did you read the wanted sheet they tagged to his shirt?"

"No point."

"Says one 'Josiah' killed his Mormon owner at a community of theirs down in San Bernardino. Says this 'Josiah' is about thirty and nearly six feet tall." Matthew pointed. "He's not thirty. And he's not as big as me and I couldn't find six feet standing on a box."

"No matter, you know that."

"Yeah, maybe. But I intend to make something of this when we get to the county."

Jason warned, "You better watch yourself."

Matthew looked his way.

"Back at the inlet. Those tracks I came upon, dragging a body. Well, the factory shoe I found was a perfect mate to the one 'Josiah's' missing."

Matthew stared at 'Josiah', his mismatched steps laboring forward.

"You think those fellas on the boat were contrabanding 'Josiah' upstate?"

"Maybe." Jason slipped his bandaged hand into his belt. "I know this man St. Lowe from a gambling house in San Francisco. Execute caution, or we could all be up to it, gratis."

Jason and Matthew walked on for a bit, their steps sweeping aside the stalked weeds.

"St. Lowe said he thought he knew you, or had a sense of you. What did he mean?"

Jason glanced at St. Lowe, walking on the far flank of the wagon, his stovepipe sitting tilted on his head in a haughty arrogance. "You are the questionest asking man, Monsieur Purloin."

Matthew's face fell askew at the remark. "Now that is what the trader kept calling me back in Stockton, and I was sure it was a heartfelt insult."

Jason smiled and ran his hand through his moustache. "Monsieur Purloin...Purloin means...Baby wool...Virgin wool. You're a *blanc-bec*...A white face...A raw ass."

"That bastard." Matthew jammed his hands into his pockets.

Jason came over and slapped him on the back. "Don't take it to heart, Monsieur Purloin. It's a natural state of affairs most all have come through...Anyway, that's not our most serious problem at the moment."

Matthew glanced at Jason.

"We're being followed."

"What are you talking about?"

"Been so since the well."

"How do you know?"

"There were signs there. A rider. Left with our approach. Moved up into the hills and has been following our flank since."

Matthew looked back as if somehow he might see something even though he knew better.

"St. Lowe," added Jason, "he's seen it too. Been scaling the hills, that's why he's walking that side of the wagon."

Matthew glanced at St. Lowe, who saw him staring and gave a flick at his stovepipe.

"Do you think there'll be trouble?"

"Don't know. Maybe it's just that fella you've come to write about. Or is it to *find?*"

Matthew stopped. Jason eyed him but kept walking. "You know, the one who's been robbing all the mines down in Tulare. The one you asked the helmsman about."

CHAPTER FOURTEEN

The prisoner huddled against the coach wheel where he was chained, shivering in the black light of evening. He was given neither food nor drink. The others were spread about the ruin, an old boar's nest built by trappers well before the Rush, on a promontory above Yellow Sulphur Road.

The stockade itself was little more than a hut made of flat cedar logs and a pine bough roof matted with sod. The palisade was a ravaged battle line of brittle spruce spotted with gaps. In the failing moonlight it appeared as teeth in a bone dry skull.

St. Lowe sat alone against the hut wall on a stump shell, his Hawkin within reach, intent on any sound or smell that might warn him of the rider who had been following. But the only sound so far was that of Leon and Tess behind the hut, who contented themselves in the darkness. For a moment he listened and shared in the bounty.

A plank table was placed near the fire, and this was where Hetty sat alone. Her food was yet untouched on a tin plate before her. She occupied herself by tearing neat strips of cloth from an old muslin sack she'd begged from the station attendant. She washed the strips clean and then placed them on stones within reach of the warming touch of the fire. When dry, she took them and a bowl of water to where Jason and Matthew sat on a pair of fallen timber posts.

They stood as she approached.

"Sit, please." She looked at Jason. "Would you mind if I spoke to you privately?"

A bit surprised, he answered, "If you want," then looked at Matthew.

Matthew reached for his satchel and stood.

"Thank you," said Hetty.

Matthew made his way back across the compound and passed St. Lowe as if he were just a part of the stump itself. Hetty turned to Jason.

"Those bandages are filthy. I brought some changings."

Jason lay his plate down and looked at his hands. She sat before him on the fallen post. She loosed up the bindings. She took a strip of cloth and wadded it, then dampened it with water. She lay his hand on hers, flattening the palm and spreading the fingers. She began to clean away the dried blood and dirt.

Her movements were precise and gentle. As she leaned toward him, her eyes lifted only once to look across the darkness into his. Her hair fell across her face and she looked away and her fingers hesitated beside the laceration.

"We don't know each other but for that night in the boat," said Hetty. "Yet the experience renders a feeling I know you…and can speak."

"We were lucky that night," he whispered.

She did not answer. Or could not. The rising and falling beneath her coat deepened.

"Were we?" she finally whispered back. She looked up at him.

"May I ask you something?" she said.

"If you want."

"That night. Had we escaped off the roof sooner. Had I not held us up so long. Had I…Do you think all that happened could have been avoided?"

He saw before him the same face she'd worn in front of her cousin there on the flooded sandplain.

"I haven't slept since," she confessed. "I find myself…I can feel the boy's hand, as truly as I can feel yours now."

He hushed her with an answer. "We did our best."

"You all did."

He leaned in closer to her, the wind brushed her hair across his face. "We all did. All of us."

"Can you say that honestly?" She pulled the collar of her coat up around her neck. "If I hadn't made you men bring that trunk—"

He cut her short. "Yes. We would have gotten off the roof sooner. And we might have avoided those trees tumbling out of the hell of it all. We might have. What difference?" He paused, then, "Suppose we made mid-channel a few minutes sooner? Suppose we did? If we'd come upon that rolling monster in mid-channel when it was moving with the full force of the current, what then? We'd have been sheared. Cut in two. We might all have gone to the black."

• • •

The mud wagon made its way south, following a pony trail that paralleled the vast slough of tule grass which braced to a man's height or more down through the gut of the state. Jason watched for the rider who had been following but none appeared. He looked at Matthew, who walked alone, sipping laudanum.

"You better stick to choc, paper man," shouted St. Lowe.

Tess called out to St. Lowe and she pointed and he followed her line, and there to the west a small cluster of riders sized up out of the savannah in a slow procession.

Jason made his way around the back of the coach for protection in case of trouble. He checked the load in his pistol and looked up into the black face before him tethered to the coach. He then shifted his gaze to the gaunt figures forming out of the bleached dust.

The prisoner whispered again. "You're one of us. I know."

Jason turned away as if he heard nothing.

Leon climbed atop the coach. The horsemen disappeared into the tailings of a depression but appeared again shortly in the slanting light. Leon called out to his father, "Five spics..."

They were mesteneros with a string of wild ponies tethered to their riatas. They were swarthy and dust covered and they sat forward in their saddles and man and beast seemed all a part of one being. The reguardas across the horses' chests were mottled and scarred from many weeks in the brush and they were as shiny as Gallic shields from the sun.

They passed the coach with a cautious distance, and St. Lowe remarked quietly to his son, "You can smell the stink of them from here."

The wind took their serapes and Jason could make out the brace of pistols that hung from their weathered britches and the worn stocks of rifles tilting up out of the tazas.

Moments in passing. The tapping metal of a bridle ring. A muzzle peaked at an alien scent. A still coach, rattled through with wind. All was otherwise silent.

Jason took notice of each man. One in particular. Older than the others. He wore an oilskin tarp, cut like a poncho, over a frock coat. His horse was black. And it, too, was old. From its size and the width of its chest, Jason knew it was born of mixed blood. Native stock mated with the French Percheron. This was no brush horse. It wore no reguarda across its chest, and its chest was unscarred. Then, the rider. He was no mestanero. He wore no armitas to protect his legs. And his pistols were of a heavy caliber, and they were worn from use, but clean.

Hetty came forward and offered greetings to them in Spanish. They looked among themselves in silence, and then one returned the greeting and raised his hat. Soon the others followed. All except the old one. Hetty spoke to the men in Spanish.

"Good hunting, I see," she said.

"Good hunting," one said back.

"If you mean to trade those ponies for goods, I own that warehouse at the mine and would trade."

The riders took note of this among themselves and continued on.

Hetty's eyes drifted over to the old man and his eyes to hers, and there Jason detected between them something more than the informal passing of strangers.

"Is all well with you?" the old man said.

"As well as might be expected with things as they are," answered Hetty.

His hand issued across the saddle and Jason saw he was missing an index finger. He followed off behind the others.

All waited by the coach till the riders were nothing more than impassive shadows diffracted by the haze.

Jason walked the ground their horses had passed over and found a shod mark to match the one at the well. He turned and there was St. Lowe.

"What line of odds would you give me, Mr. Clay, that one of them greasers is the trash that's been following us?"

• • •

The coach led a slow procession through the loamy vega that was bordered on the east by a great slough and on the west by an open trace of marsh. Here a hailstorm of gnats infested the air. All were forced to cover their hands and faces with gloves and bandannas.

The driver guided his charges up a thin mistake of a trail that slanted one way then switchbacked another in its slow confused ascent to a plateau where the gray stone shimmered like the inside walls of a kiln.

They fell among the rocks and stripped away their bandannas and bindings and gulped at the cooler air. Then the driver shouted out, his voice resonant against the rocks.

They rose and clattered as they weaved their way about the stone outcroppings and assembled up around the driver on a slate ledge that viewed the valley of their approach.

To the southeast, the great slough opened into Lake Tulare which painted a blue clean halo in the earth. Running west from the lake was the Tortoise River. It cut a line toward the foothills that climbed to the summit of Peneche Pass.

But there for them to see was the burned remains of a rail bridge across the Tortoise River. And trapped along both banks an assemblage. Man and wagon. On the northern bank, which defined the border into the county, were four wooden rails, driven into the earth as stakes almost ten feet high. Small groupings of men gathered under each stake. Most stood. Some sat. But all stared at the four wretched whites crucified and left to rot.

CHAPTER FIFTEEN

They came upon the dead espaliered on those railroad ties. The living talked among themselves that these were the four ore wagon drivers and guards taken at the relay station in the midst of Peneche Pass one week since.

With a blade, the skin had been excoriated in long strips. Leather thongs were spread through the open tidings and wrapped tight to cinch each carcass to the mastings. Where needed nails were driven with an iron hammer into bone as anchors. Bones had been shorn of flesh, flesh shorn of bone, as if lightning had had its way. Eyes were picked clean as the pockets of vagabonds, leaving dark wells to eavesdrop on the living. Their privates had been stripped. The cullions left to rot on the earth as a sign. Red ants climbed the worn rails up to festering holes.

About their necks hung small bags of gold. Hammered into the tops of the two center posts were strips of batten. On each, scratched out in bone black, was a warning. Upon one was written "JUSTIC-ERIO RA." Upon the other "EL TIEMPO."

This is no petty thief on the outskirts of a few trinkets. Not from where I sit beneath the trussed corporeals of the last confrontation, the grisly details of which I described to you earlier.

Here at the river, stranded on both sides, while they try and repair the bridge are upwards of a hundred. They are miners and merchants. They are Mexican sharecroppers, their wagons loaded with dry fodder and caged chickens. They are tillers of small acred plots around fresh wells in the hills. They are families of distant nationalities in passage. There is even one group of Chinese. English is lost on them, and they travel to some stream near the mine where they, too, search for gold. Those who have lived here for a while, each have a different story to tell, but to tell it at all, there is a war going on in Tulare. On one side is the "Caesar" of the county, Charles Julius Whitehorse, and his legions bastioned at the great Whitehorse Mine. And on the other side there are no legions, only a lone buscadero who has robbed and murdered and issued a warning on wood...*the wicked will be chastised by a virulent justice.*

I've finally reached the goddamn promised land.

• • •

"Hey, paper man."

Matthew looked up from the boot step of the coach where he'd been sitting. St. Lowe was yards away squatting beside the capped banks of the Tortoise. His shirt was off, and Tess was cleaning the sweat and dust from the white skin of his chest.

"You gettin' it all down there, paper man? All the misery?" St. Lowe pretended he was overtaken by a rush of passion and his fingers scratched urgent ideas out in some imaginary notebook.

"You better save some room in that book of yours. There might be more misery to come. At least an obituary's worth is my guess."

• • •

The old man moved among the rocks. He no longer wore the oil-skin poncho over his white frock coat of African wool. He carried a canteen and a Sharps slung over his shoulder. His collar was pulled in against the rising wind of a failing day. He had perched amidst gray stones well within view of the river and the dead he'd left there hanging to draw them to him. A careful rifle shot away when the light and wind were set.

• • •

Jason stood as he saw the approach of riders out of the blood red of the sun. Singular plumes of smoky earth kicked up by the hooves fanned across the rim of the flat vega.

Those gathered along the river stopped what they were doing. Those carrying a rail beam laid it down. Those hammering up side-posts, quit and stood. Women washing clothes on the banks cupped their hands above their eyes and their children, naked, circled around them. The silent Chinese, alone by their wagon, whispered among themselves of what they didn't understand, and waited.

Jason walked over to Hetty who stood near the rocks, where gathered the women. Matthew was there next to her.

She turned as Jason sided her. "They've been expecting the Till brothers."

Quickening their approach, the riders began to loom up out of their own makings, a dozen in number.

"There's an awful lot of them working for the county in one family."

"St. Lowe will make a lot of friends with that bunch," said Hetty.

The riders drew up past the burned husk of a great oak. Orders were given and four came forward while the rest spread out back from the river.

Hetty pointed. "The four coming to the river are the Tills. The rest I've never seen before."

Matthew put on his glasses and swung his satchel over his other shoulder. "One of the merchants by the fire told me they're putting together an expedition of professionals to go out into the hills all summer and hunt the fella who's been robbing the mine and left that stringed quartet."

"The expedition will fail and leave a mark for what it is," said Hetty.

Jason moved off quietly a few steps to get a bearing on the men he'd come to serve. With their ruddy faces and flat noses and ruddy brown hair and beards, all except the youngest who was clean faced. Four abreast, with pistols hung from shoulder holsters and shotguns strung across their backs, they trotted toward the river. A chanced line that conjured up visions of Varingian horsemen hired to defend the steppes of Constantinople before the Golden Gate of its princes.

Jason could hear Hetty point out each vermined brother for Matthew.

"The one with the broad brimmed felt hat and the feathers poking up from the brim, that's Emmit. He's sheriff. The one in the derby and blue woolie, that's Serranus. He's tax collector, but profiteer is nearer the word for it. The one on Emmit's right in the muleskin coat, that's Bayard. He only comes out of the hills when they mean to exact their will. And the youngest there is Daniel, and all that can be said of him is that he is shiftless and a drunk and bears no resemblance to the heritage of the name he was baptized with."

Matthew recognized Daniel as the boy in the serape, crying in Whitehorse's den the night of his departure.

Reaching the river the horses' heads flared up and they skittered in the mud at the smell of death. Daniel rose in his saddle. Seeing the bloated malignancy that was his cousin hanging there, he screamed out, "Christian!" He drew his horse from the banks into the stream.

Emmit called out to him but the boy kept swimming and then Emmit ordered his other brothers forward, and with crops they drove their horses from the mud into the black current where they sank and then pulled up and swam. The riders straddled their backs till they reached the other side, all floundering legs and knobbing hooves and shaking muzzles.

Those about the shore scattered. Emmit harnessed in the mecate, and stared at those trimmed there in death. His eyes raged. His head cocked around with bared teeth. He noticed the Chinese by their wagon. He wielded the hat from his head and pointed a feathered brim in their direction. "Serranus, get those goddamn pigtails away from here. Drive them upriver. Drive them into the river! I don't care. But be done with them."

Serranus peeled a coiled whip hanging from his rifle scabbard and unfurled it with a fast extension of his arm. It beat a mark in the dust as he kicked his horse forward.

Emmit leaned back on the cantle. "Bayard, get that bridge fixed. Get every man here who can lift his arms working. And Daniel, get Christian down from there. Get him down, boy."

St. Lowe squatted on a stump by Tess and Leon. He fanned himself with his stovepipe as Serranus rode down upon the Chinese. In a massacre of tumbling footfalls, they scrambled under wagons or along the embankment or laid down flat on the ground by their crying children.

"The meek will inherit the earth," St. Lowe propheted from his stump, "but it will be a sore patch and only big enough to be packed in."

Daniel dragged over an old wooden chair and leaned it up against the cross post and ascended slowly. He stood rickety beneath the living mask of lost manhood. He reached for his knife. He slipped the knife under the leather bindings at the ribs. The skin was falling away like wet cake, when a powdered concussion of fulminate exploded out of the hills and rattled across the glassed surface of the lake. A stringy thread of blood spit from Daniel's neck onto the yellow grass a foot away. He tottered there a moment then fell backward, arms out.

• • •

We scattered like vermin. I bellied up under the coach and was almost run down by one of the Tills rushing to his fallen brother. I could hear screaming and shouting and orders given, but it all ran together in a black chorus of panic. I was choking on dust and it burned my eyes and I curled up behind the wheel of the mud wagon and prayed I was out of anyone's line of fire. From where I huddled I could see Hetty grabbing up the children and herding them into the rocks along the embankment. I could see across the river the small puffs of gray poison from the rifles of the men picketed through the brush. It was a faint popping, more remote than real. But I'll be damned if they knew where to fire since there'd been but one shot. The men still on horseback rallied up and fanned out in a long line and charged the hills. They were in open country and ripe for a clean shot. But they had numbers. And they had been paid. And I guess they believed well enough in their luck. Then another discharge of thunder from somewhere along the blue stone ridgetop brought the truth home.

• • •

The Tills' men walked the hills at sunset with their rifles. They bled the ground for sign. St. Lowe squatted at the spot where the shot had come from. His eyes and fingers worked the ground. Emmit waited there near him.

A spot of crimped grass edged around a stone outcropping left a mark where a horse had been staked. There Jason stood. Alone and well away from the others.

The shod mark again. The same one that had followed them since the well. Jason's father's boots sifted at the soft earth about the mark. He knew now who it was that fired down from the hills. The old man riding with the mesteneros. Jason could see the man's chiseled fingers resting there on the saddle horn. And the sober pull of his Percheron. He could still hear the low guttural words of the rider talking to Hetty as Emmit descended the crooked stone pathway toward him. At that moment Jason might know more about the Mexican than any other, save Hetty North.

And if there were truth to that, what was there between her and the old man that he could use to hunt him out?

• • •

My eyes looked upon the stakes now barren of bodies and saw the battens posted there with their warnings and I thought about the man who had written them and where he'd come from to reach that point.

The buscadero could have killed anyone at the river, but he chose his marks as clearly as one would choose words to form an idea. Mr. Wilcox, this "ain't" no knight carrying the children of Christ across the river in a poem from our youth to a House Called Beautiful. Nothing like that. He comes of something more ferocious and more dangerous, and bounded to a truth that foresaw a willing conspiracy against what we are. And he will leave the ground raw. And he will leave souls raw. And there will be more blood. But he's a knight nonetheless, and he has no name. At least none that's spoken of. So I will anoint him with one. I will steal it from John Bunyan, and when I see him, if I see him, thank him for it. For I will call this buscadero...Greatheart.

CHAPTER SIXTEEN

Jason lay sleeping. But his sleep was haunted. Haunted by memories and the thoughts that memories arouse.

Later, he walked through the dark, past the bridge. Downstream, he could see the Tills and the riders they'd brought along saddling up and heading back to the mine. He considered his private conversation with Emmit when Hetty and Matthew were by the river. And the trap he'd planned to draw the Mexican out.

• • •

The iron wheels shimmied across the wet rock, and the coach descended the grated embankment and pulled up at the edge of the river.

Hetty waited with the others on the shore. The driver asked St. Lowe to offer up his prisoner in a treacherous maneuver to help guide the mud wagon across the bloated channel. The prisoner was untied from the rear of the coach. The bindings on his hands were loosened, and under the warning eye of the Hawkin, he was shoved to the front of the wagon to take hold of the lead harness and pace out before the trembling beasts and keep to a steady line. Those attending to the bridge or waiting on opposite shores gathered up to watch. The popper stood in his seat and wailed out his whip. The mules' ears went back and they rushed forward into the brown muddy.

The water rose to their chests and the mules balked. The prisoner loosed his grip on the harness rope and he grabbed hold of the lead mule's bit. The mule's head kicked back as they bolted forward under the whip. The prisoner stumbled and his legs were almost trampled by the mules.

On shore an old man pulled out a drum and tuned up a cadence, rolling out a mock tempo of war, both encouragement and disdain.

The coach spasmed and shot forward. Spasmed and shot forward. A listing, fragile wooden box against the black rush of the river. The channel beneath the mules' hooves was a silty marl and the mules' legs buckled. The coach slipped off a stone lip on the river bottom and jammed against the trace hitch, sending the back wheels into the air and out of the water. The driver lost his balance and grasped onto the brake stick but it snapped and he was thrown into the river.

The driver was taken downstream as his arms grasped at the air like a drunken picker. The coach was mired in the middle of the river as foamy riffs swirled up around the wheels. The prisoner held firm to the leads. He was the last anchor before destruction, as the mules had frozen where they stood, splay legged against the mud, trembling.

The men along the opposing shores argued amongst themselves in confusion. St. Lowe held up his rifle and the rumble of his voice commanded the black to abandon that mud wagon and swim back to shore and be quick.

Hetty watched that poor exhausted soul rest his head against a mule. Swim back and stay alive so you can be strung up to fill another man's pockets…or be shot where you stand. A grand choice.

There came the rattling echo of the drum. A pitch of voices followed with stark epithets. Dirty this…useless that…mongrel thing…mindless beast. She'd heard it all before, as had he—every voice from the river back to the first insult colored against them. It was the mud wagon they wanted, not the man. He was just another mule. But none came forward to help. None.

The wagon may as well be his coffin as any, so in that black moment, he reached up and gripped his hands around the harness bit and rooted his feet. He began to pull. It might be futile to pull, but pulling all the same. For if he was no better than a mule, he was no less. She saw he would exact his will upon one moment in time and make it stand for all the moments lost to him.

He screamed out a haw. The mules' ears kicked back. Their legs gathered up the courage in his voice, and the coach humped forward foot by foot. Then stalled again.

History will not record what passed here this morning. It will find no documentation in the "honorable" lore of the bleeding wound known as America. Unless what I say stands. And what luck would that have to be.

But in a moment of profanity, out of the hateful fragments of men's lives, something profound transpired when Hetty stepped down into the water.

Each step slow and hobbled. She went forward. She battled the current. She got hold of the boot rack as the coach spurt forward another foot, and she was almost cast away. But she held. And foot by foot she clung her way along the coach, along the trace lines while the mules kicked and bucked, and she came to stand beside the prisoner. She said something to him, took hold on the leads and they began to pull together.

For a moment there was silence. Stiff and clumsy. There was shame to that silence. Then, across the river came an insult against her. And then another. A man grabbed up a stone and hurled it at the coach. A man on this side of the river followed suit. Some gamey young bummer ran to his wagon and pulled a Confederate flag from his trunk and rushed back to a cairn of silted stone and stood atop it waving the colors like some great killer of bulls.

The drummer beat out a miened cadence more fierce for the madness it inspired. They jeered this woman and man with hatred smoking up dust in their rush for stones.

There were some voices in our favor calling out. But none came forward against the arc of stones that rushed the sky. A hail of hate, the reward for this insurrection. The stones were no longer being flung just at the coach. The mules were struck and they retreated back against themselves crying. The coach floundered like some ark in the shoals of a great storm, and a shiny mule lost its footing and went under in a panic then rose again spurning water from its muzzle as its teeth flared in agony. I heard Jason, who stood near behind me, speak to himself out loud, "Not again. Not again."

He pushed past me into the swell. He tore the bandages from his hands and shouldered himself up against the rear of that mud wagon and braced to push. He shouted to Hetty, and she nodded, and they went to task.

St. Lowe raised his rifle and I believed he would shoot them dead but he fired a round into the sky and Leon pulled his pistol and followed his father with a secession of rounds. Others joined up behind them. The air was filled with rabbled fireworks. Small powder clouds spotted up against the sky, a flickering carnage, but that tottering wooden box with its doors hanging open jostled forward a few more feet.

A grievance of stone and gunshot cried out. And that drum. The goddamn drum in the hands of that toothless old man grinning like the idiot son of idiot sons. A barefoot penitent of some asylum.

And those three there alone together, scrabbling it out. Iron hoof and iron wheel, bit by bit, before churning shoots of black tide.

And here I stood. Stark and still. Where my heart would take me my legs faltered. I remembered what I wrote. And what I felt. And what I knew. And they meant nothing weighed against my fear. But today...today...I began my fall from the good grace of cowardice as I felt the teeth of white foam snapping up around my legs. I heard the whoosh of stones around me and saw them pluck up the bits of tide. I saw Hetty shout to Jason, and she pointed to me. Jason turned and reached out a hand and grabbed hold of the satchel across my shoulder and hauled me up beside him against the boot rack.

"Well, Monsieur Purloin, I see you brought your satchel."

I went to speak, when a hand-size piece of granite careened off the boot rack and squared me in the chest. I dropped to the water. Jason pulled me back up. I felt sick, and he shook me hard.

"You think you could get up on that seat and guide those mules?"

I told him I couldn't do much worse than that damned driver, so he shoved me around the coach and warned me there was no brake and I stumbled, one hand on the door and the next on the wheel spokes, slipping on the slick stone bottom till I got hold of the jockey box. Next I knew I sat shivering in view of it all. A witness to a drama as I pulled back up on the leads. Across the river I caught sight of the flag I had written for rise up on a branch staff. But the man who waved it shouted down on us and spat. And there were those who followed that flag, and they shouted down on us, too.

A stone hit Hetty in the back and she fell against the mules. I hollered to Jason and he and the prisoner rushed to clear her of the whelming flume that tumbled and trapped her under the harness trace.

Before I could twine the leads around my hand the mules reared hard and sent me toppling down into the jockey box. The coach hitched around, grating on the river bottom. It shook and wavered with each hump and cleave. The spokes ground against the iron rim of the wheels just before splintering. At that moment I thought we were going to come apart. That we would be swept into a silent eternity, where a century from now, our bones would be panned up in the silt with the other dregs of forgotten rubble from our times.

They stood Hetty up, and she hung there straight and pale as straw, resting her arms against Jason's shoulders. He spoke to her, and her head bobbed up and down at dizzy angles but she pushed away both men to get them back to the mules. She got hold of the harness bit and sagged against a mule's chest for support then she looked up at me and I heard her yell to drive those mules on.

Stones punched into the river everywhere around us. The ting of gunshots passed overhead from a confusion of directions.

I slung my head down so I could only see the mules and the shaly cut of the riverbank beyond, and I put the leads to the backs of the mules, and we went to task.

Before them all. Embattled against that assemblage with those three pulling, and me on the box seat. We must have carried enough weight in that configured union of castoffs to carriage out of the foul mud that held us, for I felt the coach wheel back up straight and we kicked forward a foot. And then we bought another. I saw the mules lean against their straps. Their heads went back and up. They heaved and snorted and flutes of dun graveled water brattled up through the spinning mandala of the wheels.

We were moving now. The brown flood gave way. And gave way again. We were almost running. I saw Hetty rise up out of the water onto the cut bank. I saw Jason follow. The prisoner a step behind. The mules rose up with ears pricked and I felt myself lean back as the coach rose from the tide.

CHAPTER SEVENTEEN

The coach followed a cart path along the lake, through trampled rushes and mud, which would come to an end at the mine.

The driver lay inside the coach stretched out across the seat, his shoulder and arm broken and supported by a rolled blanket across Tess's lap. Hetty sat up front behind Jason and Matthew, who took turns guiding the mules home. By late afternoon the mules hauled the coach over a crest of rocky hillface and they entered the valley of the Whitehorse Mine.

Jason and Matthew, side by side, viewed a blight of two dozen buildings that prefigured a town this side of the river. Hewn from pit sawn plank and split timber. Roofs of tarpaper and corrugated tin. A threadbare and haphazard streetless alliance. A flat rail tie bridge offered a single crossing to Gull Hill where the rag bungalows and tumbledown huts lined a mud broken path filled with muckmen coursing down the hillside from their shift of chaffee work.

The coach pulled up to a corn crib impostering as a Relay Station and began to disembark. Hetty pointed out her cabin to Matthew and Jason. It and the ramshackle warehouse were by a shallow creek which broke from the river and ran into the hills at the far end of the valley.

She offered to let them bunk there and if they came by at dusk they could share dinner.

After she was gone, Matthew took his satchel and walked to the edge of the river and squatted down. He smoked. He looked down into the water where the iron piping spewed out its talused waste in a roil of rusty gravel and tailings. His eyes followed the gilded veins up the hill, each section bracketed in place with bark puncheons. They trailed cliffside, a shimmering line upward past spotty pines, their boughs the grim color of smokeblack. Up past the housing for the chemical tanks. Up past the housing for the ball mill. Up past the housing for the heavy crushers. Past the founders' shaft and sheds where blackdamp rose in thin tiers, and windless, hung there then circled. Then on to the battlement penthouse of pylons grappled against the granite overhang.

Matthew stood as Jason approached, stretching uneasily, carrying his Navy cape and sack. Matthew took a shot of laudanum. Jason looked past Matthew across the river for a cabin with a corral and a sign posted for the magistrate's office. He spotted the place about halfway up the hill, just as Emmit had described it.

"What's your plan, Jason?"

Jason turned to Matthew. "Buy me a horse if I can find one that isn't a rocker. Then I'll… take care of my business." Jason put out his hand. "Good luck, Monsieur Purloin."

Matthew looked at his hand, hesitating to take it.

"Get back on that mud wagon, Monsieur Purloin. Go back. Or go on. But leave."

"Thank you. But, as you can see," Matthew said, waving a hand toward the sludge poisoned banks, "there's another river to cross."

• • •

Here they separated, and Jason wound his way through a jumble of patchy brush and the scrap huts of the merchandisers till he came upon a mud corral with a dozen horses sided up to a hovel of a smith shop. On the porch of a raggedy falsefront a trader of arms sat with his back against the wall. A couple of muckmen conversed around a table at the near end of the porch over a half bottle of skinny. They watched Jason squat there looking over a reliquary of arms and knives spread out on the porch. Some faulted, some worn.

Jason began to piece together a rifle out of the odds and ends of failings. The men at the table studied Jason as he framed up a crescent shaped butt stock with the body of a Jennings, then bolted it into place.

• • •

Hetty could see Matthew through the doorway of her cabin, sitting on the front step and penciling in his notebook. She set a table for both men and herself. There was a sense of uneasiness in her movements.

Matthew closed the notebook and reached for his bottle resting against the sill. Hetty came and stood behind him in the doorway.

"He rode out into the hills," said Matthew.

"What?"

"If you're wondering about Jason. I saw him more than an hour ago. He got a horse from that smith shop and rode out into the hills."

She rested quietly against the doorjamb, feeling the coolness of a breeze against her muslin blouse, when a wagon approached across the clearing. It pulled to a stop and three Chinese miners stumped out of the rear. Solitary and quiet spoken. Their English a rubbished heap of half words and raw sounds. Overworked men in overalls and pigtails stained with dirt.

On the opposite side of the wagon Hetty talked with the driver who climbed down out of the box seat. He and Hetty came around the wagon and made their way toward the light of the coallamp resting within the open face of the shed doors.

Matthew watched from the breezeway as the driver handed Hetty a list of supplies. The faces were not more than a bare outline in pencil sketch. The driver was a good sized man with a thistle patch of a beard.

Yet there was something in that caverned voice and peculiar slouch to the broad shoulders, and the arms too long and dangling out of sorts with the carriage of the body, that threatened to awaken in Matthew some sort of recognition. As if something lost and forgotten in the attic of his past were suddenly thought of, as it reappeared, a varied image of itself, long hidden in the recess of some dusty opened bandbox, amidst the other treasures of childhood.

"Neville?"

The man half turned.

Matthew took another step closer. "Neville Faire?"

A strip of features formed out of the silhouette and reformed in the fire opal light of the coallamp. The man's face hung there uncomfortably on stooped shoulders.

"It's me, Matthew Christman."

"I don't know any Matthew Christman, I'm afraid."

"Charlie's kid brother. Charlie Christman? You both served together in the war with Mexi—"

"I don't know any Charlie Christman. And whatever you called me a minute ago...my name is Ed. Ed Candles."

• • •

Between forkfuls of Brunswick stew, Matthew recounted for Hetty details of his and Charlie's life. He told how he had followed Charlie and Neville when they rode downtown on a rainswept night and stood among a crowd on the steps of the First Church of Christ by Independence Hall and heard speeches from Congressmen and pastors, and a legion of honored veterans and officers who praised service to this nation, born of a pride in our Manifest Destiny. Who condemned the Mexican daemons to the south and the danger they posed to the wholly American empire. There had been shouts and cries, and Matthew recalled how frightened he was. There was a call for volunteers, and Neville and Charlie, flush with dreams of youthful arrogance, joined a generation of God's children as they coursed around the square behind a platoon of drum rattlers to Independence Hall, where the wind blew tired wet flags, and their fate was signed to company after company.

Matthew leaned forward. Beads of sweat hung from the fragile bones of his cheeks from too much ale and laudanum. He then told her of his troubles in San Francisco. Of his humiliation under the boot of Arlen Whitehorse. He whispered in a shaky voice of his plan to write about the outlaw he now called Greatheart.

• • •

Later, as Matthew wandered the shabby village looking for Ed Candles, he heard:

"Hey, paper man."

Tess stepped forward from a dark patch of shanty porch. That smiling shill of a face looked him up, then down, then up again.

"You got skin like parfleche, you know that, paper man?"

Her nose cut a crooked middle to her face, like a ship carp'er's adze and there was something to her eyes that was feverish and languid in the same breath.

"I can't wait to see what you're made of, once we're out there in the hills."

"What does that mean?"

"It means we ain't takin' no mud wagon with us on the expedition for the paper man to hide under."

Standing there he was a statement of bewilderment.

"Wait a minute," she said, "maybe your partner don't want the paper man with him on the expedition."

Matthew began to understand. "Jason?"

• • •

When Hetty heard her dog begin to yawp, she sat back and leaned around looking through the open doorway. The frame of a horse and rider poured up out of the darkness and into the moonlight. Her dog backed into the light cast through the doorway from an approaching footfall of boots, until Jason stopped at the door.

"Am I too late to come by and talk?"

She stood. "No, come in, please."

He stepped through the doorway lowering his head.

She motioned for him to sit. "Have you eaten? There's still some…"

"No, thanks."

"Coffee?"

"That would do."

Jason took off his Navy cape and laid it across a frail chair by the table. Alone, he took account of the room. A plank framed bed with feather and straw matting. Roughhewn pine shelving for plates and cups and books. A simple oak writing desk with ambrotypes of Sarah and her two small boys.

She came back with a steaming earthenware cup.

"What took you out into the hills?"

He took a sip of coffee. "At the Trader's where I bought a horse, I overheard some of what the Tills are planning for the expedition. You know an expedition goes out into the hills tomorrow?" He took a cigarette, already rolled, from his shirt pocket.

"Yes."

"Emmit has gotten information of a place somewhere close to one of the passes where the old man camps."

"What old man?"

He took another sip of coffee, but his eyes stayed vigilant. "The old Mexican. The one who's robbed the mine."

Sitting in that light left her bare to any change of expression, "What makes them say he's an old Mexican?"

"Those battens back at the river for one thing. They don't know he's an old man. They don't know he rides that black Percheron." Jason struck a match and let it hang from the tip of his fingers. "I do, though. We both do...don't we?"

He lit the cigarette and drew in slowly. Her bearing altered, if only at first.

"I think you're mistaken," she said.

Jason stood and shouldered his Navy cape. "They've got a cross waiting for that old man, and they won't kill him before they splay him. They've got blood invested now."

He walked to the door. "Is it all right if I bedroll here?"

She looked up at him. "Of course. You can bunk with Matthew

in the other common room."

He nodded. "Warn him while you can, Hetty. By morning it may be too late."

• • •

In the common room black with silence, Jason watched from the window to see if Hetty would go to warn the Mexican and make his job of goring the ox all that much easier. He tried not to feel anything about the way he was using her, when the door flooded open, and in the breech stood Matthew.

"Why are you sitting in the dark, Jason?"

"I prefer it."

"I need to throw up some light."

"There's a wick on the table there by the door."

Jason observed Hetty walk from the house up through the breezeway. A swath of light bled up around Matthew sitting along the edge of the plank table.

"The sins of men are interesting predicaments, aren't they, Jason?"

"If you say so, Matthew."

Jason watched the cadaverous old man that worked for Hetty lead a saddled plowhorse up from the shed.

"Where do you think lies would stack up in the sins of men, Jason?"

Jason did not answer. He got up and slipped on his Navy cape. Matthew grabbed him by the arm.

"So you're leaving with that stinkin' expedition of bloodmen?"

Jason took hold of the hand that held his and peeled it away.

"Mind yourself now, Matthew."

Jason could hear Hetty's boots along the gravelly bits of pathway.

He started for the door but Matthew pushed himself in front of Jason again.

"You're an insult to who you are," said Matthew.

"What does that mean?"

"I saw your watch. The night you woke and walked to the river. It was on the ground by your bedroll."

Jason's teeth flared. "Goddamn you."

He hawked through the breezeway. He could make Hetty out in the muddy light trotting that plowhorse up a stitch of trail through scrub oaks. He headed around the back of the cabin where his horse was tied and saddled. Matthew followed him.

"How did they buy you? What trouble are you running away from that they could buy you? Or are you just a different shade of St. Lowe? You left from San Francisco. Do you know the White-horses? You one of Arlen's drinkin' buddies? One of the old man's field hands?"

Jason did not answer.

Matthew rushed Jason as he stepped up to his mount, and found the clean square of his back. Both men slammed into the withers of that horse.

Jason near stumbled and turned on Matthew with a claw of fingers rooted up under his chin, forcing the skull to bend down to the neck, then drove a muddy bootprint into the heart of his coat. Matthew fell backward, a huff came rushing out of his windpipe.

Jason turned to catch sight of Hetty but the soot black hillside had hidden her. Then the night air behind him filled with the ratchet click of a hammer. Jason's head cocked around to face that foolish looking pepperbox.

"So you've finally found your will, heh, Monsieur Purloin?"

Matthew breathed heavily behind the barrel of that percussion monstrosity.

Jason felt with his stomach the butt of the pistol snug in his belt. The river, glassy beyond Matthew, shaped him out there in the night. Jason could see how afraid the boy was having to confront such punic treachery, with his fingers a clumsy mass about the trigger.

He let the boy have no time to consider the gravity of what stood. He jumped back jerking that grulla's head around. It shied and kicked and there was a weaving and blending of half images in the open space between the two men.

Matthew fired.

But that pepperbox failed him in a false discharge of rusty hammer on loose cap. There was just a pilfering of gray smoke.

Then came a second shot sweeping across the void that ended with a frail cry.

CHAPTER EIGHTEEN

Across the bay from San Francisco, a phaeton climbed the hills toward Point San Quentin. Upon reaching the hilltop the phaeton turned west at a carrefour and soon passed the quarried walls of the prison where a regiment of Union troops were bivouacked across a fielded palisade.

Whitehorse carriaged Mr. Demerest up through South Beach, past where hulls of steamers and brigantines were being outfitted. The great shelving of their skeletal frames were rift with moonlight, and so appeared as the baleen of some colossal creatures of myth sleeping at the gateway to the underworld.

They passed beyond the last remnant of lights from the prison and descended a dry wash flanked by a sand facing of gully wall. The only light now, frail as it was, came from the headlamps of the phaeton. Wobbly patches of illumination about the two draw horses.

Toward the crest of the next rise Whitehorse was sure he spotted a man with a rifle by a set of trees. They continued on. Whitehorse was uneasy. About half a mile ahead the road passed around a huge sandstone rock where two men sized up out of the pitch with rifles raised and ready there in the roadway. Whitehorse pulled in the leads and the horses slowed and a grisly looking apparition came up to his side of the carriage.

"If you're traveling through, the creek ahead is washed out and you can't make a go of it. So you best turn back."

The man took another step closer. Deep set eyes in a thin wooden face. Whitehorse slowly reached for a pistol lying there on the seat between himself and Demerest. He felt Demerest's hand come to rest on his.

"Sorry to hear the creek is out," said Demerest. He lifted his hand from the gun and rested it palm open across his heart. "We've come a long way to walk inside the burning circle."

"And why would that be?" said the wooden face.

"There's no safety outside the circle now, is there?"

"Not so they say."

Whitehorse noticed Demerest's hand come forward and rest on his knee. Dangling from a leather cord in his hand was a medallion of hammered gold about the size of a silver dollar. It appeared to be stamped with an eight pointed star embossed upon a Templar cross and encircled by a wheel. There was writing on the medallion that Whitehorse could not make out.

"What about your friend here?" said the man.

"He's come to be initiated."

The creek was nothing more than a boy could jump, and the road meandered down through a soft ribbon of sandy hills that formed the edges of the peninsula. Ahead, fires seemed to alter in position and direction through a climb of trees. In a clearing cut between a half moon of hillside, a dozen bonfires marked the circumference of a vast circle before the fallen hull of a barn.

Over two hundred men talked among themselves and drank as

Whitehorse and Demerest walked among them. Whitehorse recognized men of some repute and men he'd done business with, and others recognized him and came forward with a hand.

In time all stood within the circle of fire sequestered in that half moon agora. Speakers went to task on the propagation of a new state. Poor men with rough vernacular and men of education, their way provocative and image ridden. When the speakers were done, the new members were asked to come forward and introduce themselves and bespeak of their feelings and ideas. One by one they came. One by one they went. But all watched and waited for Whitehorse, who was the last.

When it was his time, he walked forward and looked about this insurgent army of citizens. Whether from Carolina or California, the faces of a ruffianed nation never change. Eager and angry to impart their will. Heeled by laws they have no respect for. By ideas they have no respect in. By a concourse of embittered events. A disenchanted generation of men. Waiting like vassels at the edge of a dawn camp.

"Like many of you, I am an uneducated man," said Whitehorse. "Shanty poor and shanty worked. I can't read. I can't write." He opened his coat and slipped his thumbs up under his suspenders. "I once stood before Rome. Before the greatness of Rome. Before a civilization so proud, and so strong, that it was over one thousand years before any nation could approach the glory that was Rome. I learned many things in Rome. For it is best to learn from those who have learned well."

He took a step forward. "The Romans had a vision of life. And you can see it in the cities they built. For when they built these cities, they were planned for a certain spot and a certain size. And if those cities grew too large, they did not expand them. They planned a new, larger city. And it was built. Order and organization. That was Rome when Rome was great."

He went from face to face and began to move about this circle of men, and they bent back to accept him and reform around him like some living cell.

"But in time, those planned cities were flooded with foreigners of a different color. And freed slaves. And primitive labor from the colonies to the north. They began to eat away at the grand tapestry that was Rome. The cities were now polluted. The cities grew beyond their will. Soon the plan that had built Rome was forgotten. Order and organization, these became nothing more than words. And in time Rome fell.

"The State of California is like Rome. Strong like Rome. Proud like Rome. Rich like Rome. Truly a nation in its own divine right at the far end of the world. And if we are to be part of the future, we must build as the Romans built when Rome was great. Where no nigger black...no Indian red...no pigtail yellow...no greaser brown, will find a home. They must be run out or run down before they can steal our cities and our way of life. For in the new Rome, the Holy Trinity we will worship will be God...good...and white."

• • •

The old Mexican sat on a stump in front of the stone shelter he'd built into an overhang of rock well back up in the hills. He ate the cold white meat of a rattler in his fireless camp. Along the arroyo that led up to his shelter the wind carried the scent of an approaching horse.

He gathered in his rifle noiselessly and waited till he recognized the clodding hooves of Hetty's plowhorse.

She reined in her mount and struggled down from its back. She was tired and breathing hard and filthy from the ride.

She took his hand in hers and he placed his other arm about her shoulders and pulled her against his chest as one would their child.

"How are you?" she said.

"Older, hija, older."

They made their way back up to the camp, he leading her mount.

"Why have you come like this?"

The ride into the mountains was a difficult passing and she sat wearily, her leg and foot in pain.

"Did things go bad in Sacramento?"

"Ah…I got one trunk through. Union soldiers picked it up in Sacramento."

"The rest?"

"In my storehouse. I'll go back in a few weeks." She took a breath. "I came tonight to warn you."

"Of what?"

"The expedition leaves tomorrow."

"Yes. I saw today as they made ready. I was not fifty paces from the oficina of the Tills. I sat with the other peon beggars near the river and I watched."

"They have a plan."

"There are many plans, hija."

"They mean to trap you." She leaned closer to him. "They know about one of your camps."

His eyes lowered and he looked into the heart of a black scheme.

"Which one?"

"That I don't know."

"How did you come by this?"

"A man who traveled with us on the coach. He overheard them

and warned me."

"The one with the dark skin and long hair?"

"How did you know?"

"When I rode past with the mestaneros to see you were safe. The one with the dark skin can read sign." He paused. "He knows who I am?"

"Yes."

"He served you well at the river when you helped the black man take the coach across."

"You came back, Joaquim?"

"I saw."

He walked over to his cojinillo sitting next to a rusted skip bucket used for carrying water. He opened the leather flap and found his punche and dried hoja.

"The one who helped you, is he a friend?"

She took an awkward turn. "He could be, but...he seems to be a decent man."

"Ah." Joaquim spread the punche across the dried husk but remained thoughtful. He struck a match against the shelter stones and the dried husk burned harsh and quick, and he drew in the gruel smoke deeply.

"The time is now, hija, to find others here you can trust."

There was a feel to his voice that was disquieting to her.

"There was another man on the coach I could trust. He came downriver to write about what is going on here. To write about you."

He laughed to himself and looked up at the moon. "The frail boy with the sandskin?"

"Yes."

"Even if willing, he is not enough. He is still blue meat."

He looked up at the moon. There were no saints, he thought.

"There will be no need to come here and meet," he said. "I will be abandoning this camp tonight and moving deeper into the hills. I will make them pay hard to find me."

She walked over and stood beside the old man, "What's wrong, Joaquim?"

"An old shaman once told me the best that heaven has to offer is there are no pockets. So no place for money, no need for guns."

"What are you saying?"

"I am no longer good enough for my own rifle," he said.

"But at the river?"

"At the river I baited the trap and the fool Tills come. I was close enough to bleed them. But I was too close." He shook his head. "One of their number will read that sign," he said. "Men like the one with the dark skin and long hair. And they will see my weakness." He looked at Hetty. "We need others. You see, hija, I am becoming sandblind."

• • •

A lantern jugged from the old man's arm as he moved up through the breezeway. He spotted Hetty leading her plowhorse back to the shed.

"Hetty."

She turned.

"The boy's been shot."

She dropped the leads. "What boy? Matthew?"

"The boy staying here. He's been shot."

• • •

Jason wandered through most of the night trying to find the tracks left by Hetty's plowhorse. Luck had eluded him. Tomorrow he would have to leave with the expedition. Now one of many.

Just north of the mine were the frame ghostly remains of the original founders' shaft and sheds Whitehorse had built. They fell to fire, and now keeled weakly against the hillside. A transom ran from that founders' shaft to the valley floor, and overhead, ore buckets dangled like rusted planets from a wire cable in the night wind. Iron creakings above a mud graveyard of miners. Grated mournings that fell away in the hidden whisper of the trees.

Jason leaned against the massive plating of a fallen ore bucket. The metal jaws torn away from its casement head. A corroded beast lying in death on the gouged shale. He looked past the board head-stones toward the river and Hetty's cabin. Past those clapboard thumb outlines thrown up haphazardly across the ground as if the earth shook and defied the clean order of their remains. And for what he'd done, lying to the girl, shooting the boy, he felt unquestioned shame.

CHAPTER NINETEEN

In the blue light of beginnings, twenty men odd and one woman roosted about the rotting portico of the magistrate's office while the Tills laid out their directives for the expedition.

There were men whose English was spotted with their wretched antecedents. Others there remained silent, looking neither at others nor themselves. They were blighted gunneys wearing California pants and shod stitched jaquetas or stout benjamins and calzoneras and floppy hats. Each carried weapons of choice from rifles with bores the circumference of a double eagle or sabers and machetes slung from leather baldrics. There was a Scotsman named McLime with a fiddle looped by a horsehair rope around his back. There was a bullate faced bog of a man named Hennet with cracked yellow teeth who wore a brace of Volcanic pistols that hung to his knees. A walleyed boy named Perty with a hawhole for a mouth and a cheek crushed from the fastening loop of a bent rod.

Bayard called out to this coarse peerage, "My brother Emmit and I have asked St. Lowe to take charge of the day-to-day operation of the column, and here's how things will be. Clean and fast, boys.

Clean and fast."

Jason watched as Bayard waved his hand for St. Lowe, who stood and centered himself on the porch step to have his mind with the men. He scanned the portico and then looked down at Jason sitting there by his boots.

"You have heard what Brother Bayard has said. Now as for me. I'm a Christian and a redneck with a temper. So stand warned."

St. Lowe slipped his hands into his pockets. "It is our job to run this bastard into a hole. To accomplish this it is necessary to find the meaning of the man. That is so in a hunt." St. Lowe took off his stovepipe and dangled it from two fingers. "He's already told us plenty. Aye. He ain't just some rat thief beggar. Not with the sinful thing he done back there at the river. No. He means to leave his mark against this mine and so, against us all. Everyone. And we know he carries a big bore rifle but ain't a cherry shot, not from the telling sign he left where he rifled down on us.

"Now I hear most of you are fair hands. We'll see." He looked down again, studying Jason. His remark now was directed at him. "It seems we have at least one man who can read sign besides me—"

Before St. Lowe got any further, he was interrupted by shouting, and the men turned. Serranus was down near the river waving that hat of his frantically. The men rabbited through a dozen patchways in the brush hauling up their pistols and cocking the hammers. Except for Jason, who followed along at a disinterested stride.

Serranus stood over an open latch door to a stone root cellar. The last remains of a hut lost to fire. As the men rushed up around him Serranus called out to St. Lowe, "That nigger prisoner of yours is gone."

St. Lowe shoved his way through the pack. Leon jumped down the cricked steps and disappeared into the hole. St. Lowe bent down and ran his hands over the iron clip latch bolted into the stone and then looked over the hewed log cellar door. They were as virgin as when he bolted down the door the night before.

Leon gophered up into the light. "He's gone, Pop."

A rush of epithets spilled out of St. Lowe's mouth and he took his stovepipe and flung it against a stone face of rock. He stared across the river to Hetty's cabin. "He didn't break out. Aye. He's had a pair of hands to help him."

"Woman's hands," said Tess. "Or that bugger's."

St. Lowe ran his fingers across a flash of teeth and looked over at Bayard. "You give me a day to get the nigger, and I'll join you in the hills."

"You go with us, or you leave now."

St. Lowe noticed Jason rearing the pack, his arms tucked casually into his belt.

"Leon…Get yourself an extra horse. No. Get two. Go after that nigger. You run those ponies to death, but you bring him back. You bring him back alive. Then you find us in the mountains. I'll get the truth out of him. Aye. If I have to shave him like a sausage."

• • •

Matthew lay in his own damp, all twitch and tic. His thigh swollen and scored by a Walker pistol. He could hear the muckmen somewhere across the river cheering the expedition as it filed out of camp.

He struggled to sit and reach the light pealing in across the window sash. He was halfway up and shouting, "I want to see him," when Hetty got him back down, then ran a wet rag across the burning slick of his face.

Along the road, they were coming across the bridge and up

through the village. A winding strop, twenty men odd and one woman, and a string of pack mules clickety clacking with supplies. And somewhere in that vile cadre, a fiddler kicked up a Celtic march to their stirring enterprise, and there was a rousing of hats and rifles.

• • •

The column made its way south along the old toll road passing a flurry of wagons heading for a settlement in Tehatachipi. By late afternoon the sky had turned the color of gunmetal as they began their ascent of San Lorenzo Pass. By dusk they rode against an oblique drizzle. They came upon the camp abandoned by the Mexican. Sign led away toward the gray shadowland of the mountains.

St. Lowe strode his horse alongside Jason's and they marched together with Bayard, the column being two hundred yards back.

"I hear you travel with some pretty rich company," said St. Lowe.

Jason looked over his shoulder at the grisly company of ordinaries.

"I was speaking of the Whitehorses."

"Oh," said Jason.

The second day out, thunderheads. The company moved through the drenched uplands, when a crack and roll rumbled up through that funneled trace from somewhere at the rear of the column. The mules began to scatter. There was a second crack and roll rumbling onward and the column turned back on itself in a mad rush. There was a fusillade of pops and a heave of thunder burned the sky white. Jason drove his grulla across the stream in a convergence of men to where lay one mule shot and one of their number pinned beneath a dead horse, fallen himself by riflefire.

• • •

Hetty sat leaning against the jamb of her cabin door. Matthew lay sleeping in her bed, his leg ravaged with poison. The night was black around her. She drank coffee laced with mescal, waving the clay mug toward the silent void before her. Pleadings for Matthew and the old Mexican. Somewhere in the darkness a saddlepack clanged like tannic. She watched. Across the stone slurry that framed the woods, three mules approached and came to a halt ten feet before her.

Ed Candles dismounted, but the two Chinese he'd brought with him remained on the mules. "I heard the boy stayin' here got himself shot."

"I got the bullet out," she said, "but…his leg…"

Ed looked back at the two men and waved them on. A young boy of eighteen jumped down from one mule and crossed over and helped the old man down from the other.

"That tired looking old pigtail there is part of the clan that works the river with me. He's some kind of priest medicine jockey back in his homeland. Maybe he could take a look."

Hetty stood, and waved the tiny figurine of a man toward the common room. The bed glowed from the stoked fire and candles. The priest sat beside Matthew, who lay there unconscious.

That old priest fingered about the infested bullethole. Then the priest rolled his thumbs forward peeling back Matthew's eyelids. He leaned in close and slipped two fingers into the hollow of Matthew's mouth, gathering up tailings of spittle on the edge of his fingers.

Hetty watched from the foot of the bed. She looked to Ed, who was sitting at the table and handling the rusty pepperbox that bore a part in Matthew's troubles.

The priest started gibbering in his native dialect with the young cleric squatting by the bed, who nodded and opened a blanket rucksack. He began to remove implements necessary for this undertaking. He took a silver pan and filled it with water and balanced it on two cindery cords in the hearth. He sprinkled a handful of moxa across the fire and it burned up a harsh gray pungence. He laid out a bamboo cloth, placing on it spine edged dagger blades and obsidian knappings and other rare stones sharpened for cutting. He took a pipe and filled it with dried roots and bract. He lit the pipe and inhaled, then leaned over and opened Matthew's mouth and began to blow the ghostly smoke into his lungs.

"You sure this...priest...knows what he's doing?"

"At least as good as you, Miss North."

• • •

For two days the column drove in hard pursuit deeper into the mountains. The rains came in abrupt violent storms that barely cleared before they began again. Jason guided them on their ascent toward the peaks. The trail here was a quarried etching of the remorseless will of nature. They followed hunches and the spartan leavings of a horse, and once or twice the distilled mintings of a rider black before a moment's sun.

At night they camped along a vantaged crest spread out for half a mile in groups of two where they huddled like silent mounds before an unfailing wind.

Jason was partnered with Hennet at the point of the ridge. Jason watched for sign while the other cleaned his prized Volcanics.

"That stupid Mex makes no sense. But you know how they are. Now if it was me, I'd leave this county for a few months. Wait till things settle down."

Jason wondered himself why the Mexican didn't run. Maybe he had others in the hills, and a trap was being set. Maybe he meant to run all summer till exhaustion and discontent wore the expedition out. Or maybe he would just try to cut them down one by one out of sheer contempt.

Hennet held out the pistol. "She's a beaut, ain't she?"

He slipped the weapon into Jason's hand proudly.

The sheer weight of the archine barrel was enough to bow even Jason's hand. As he raised the big bore octangle .38 against the moon, he ran his thumb across the scroll engraving. He slipped two fingers into the brass lemniscape lever cocking it down and back in smooth rapid burst. Then Jason stretched out his hand and swung the pistol down, letting it balance for a breath on the distalled lever then swung it back again.

"That repeating pistol is hell in a crowd, boy. Makes two men out of one. And I'll tell you what else. She is a clean shot. I even got a butt stock mount for that model. I got it in my saddlepack there."

Jason handed him back the gun, and Hennet went to oil ragging the blue barrel.

"I was at a gun trade auction in San Francisco about four months ago, and I heard that Wesson and Smith, the fellas what invented that gun, went belly up and a new company called Winchester bought the patent and is planning to make a rifle out of those repeatin' pistols."

Jason had turned away and was scanning the distant hills, where he noted a slithery lathe of smoke.

• • •

Hetty sat in the dark alone wondering why Ed Candles had made her swear he had not been to see Matthew, when she heard:

"What day is it?"

Startled, she looked across the room and saw Matthew's feeble shadow trying to sit. She got up and crossed the room and knelt beside the bed.

"Oh, Matthew."

"What day is it?"

"What day...Sunday."

"Sunday?" His eyes blinked and he tried to place himself back in his own life. His mind seemed to ruffle through the dark and he could see Jason again firing down on him and he looked to where his leg should be. "Did I lose my leg?"

"No, Matthew. No."

• • •

It was still dark when the men grouped in a circle and Bayard set his orders for the day. St. Lowe squatted beside Jason.

"You sight anything at your end of the ridge last night, Frenchman?"

Jason smoked and glanced at St. Lowe. "I spotted nothing."

The column made its way up a series of connected meadows and scrap rock beds crossing creeks and streams flooded from the spring rains. The sky had cleared but a ground mist climbed to the cannon of the horses' legs.

St. Lowe rode beside Bayard. "That pork eater was lying, for he had to see that smoke as clear as me."

Bayard eyed Jason, who covered the left flank of the column. "He's a friend of Whitehorse's, and I have to catch him in an open act. Then we slit his throat."

"Aye, Brother Bayard. The politics of it must be done right. And there are many ways to slit a man's throat, but it is always best to get him to hold the knife."

Ahead, the grooved walls of a canyon and four adobe huts with thatched leaning roofs. Bayard ordered the men to fan out in a line. They drew up their weapons, and the horses snorted and tugged at their leads.

There was a rush of dogs that swirled before the horsemen. The padron squatted by the fire eating his morning meal. His wife sat beside him on a wormeaten, high-backed chair. They watched the dusty row of horsemen as they came on. The padron, counting their number, waved his sons away from their rifles.

He stood and paced forward to meet these foreigners who halted up before him, and offered greetings in his half-caste English.

Bayard leaned on his wood saddle horn. "We're with the magistrate's office back in Tulare, and we're huntin' a greaser who's robbed the mine and murdered a dozen men in their employ. Now, we've tracked him through these canyons, so if you know of him, I expect your help."

Jason watched as the padron maintained a stoic conviviality. "We know nothing of any robberies. Or of this man. There is just here my family. We would, of course, help the alcalde if we could."

McLime strung up cords of acrimony on his fiddle. "An ya go teh chirch on Soonday an nevar beat yur wife."

The men hooted and jawed, and the padron eyed McLime with caution.

Bayard brushed his horse forward, and the padron was forced to step back. "We'll see, old man. Hennet, take a couple of the men and search those hovels. Perty, you take a couple more and check for hoof markings on those mestenos."

Jason watched the men begin to ransack the huts, dragging out women and children who were hiding there. They kicked over cooking pans and water buckets. They grabbed up food and serapes and any trinkets that suited their fancy. Perty opened the corral gate and fired his rifle into the air, and the horses shot forward rushing through the camp, angling left and right and spilling past the chickens and the dogs.

Perty yelled to Bayard. "All of them horses was unshod."

Hennet came lumbering out of a hovel talking through a mouthful of cornbread and grease. "I found something interesting here!"

He was holding up a small canvas bag, and he walked up to the padron and shook it in his face and it rattled. Then he threw the bag on the ground at the old man's feet and tumbling out came the gravelly yellow metal.

Bayard looked from that bag of gold lying there to the padron. "Where'd you come by that, greaser?"

"We sold our ponies to the woman trader at the mine. She pays us in gold."

"Or maybe one of your greaser clan robbed an ore wagon."

"If you ask the woman, she will tell you."

Bayard sat a moment, when Tess called out, "I don't know why you bother with all this talk." She swung down from her saddle and pushed past the men and knelt before the pardon. She grabbed up the bag of gold in one hand and in the other she curled her fingers around a stone as big as an ax blade. She stood and tossed the bag to Bayard and walked over to the old woman who had been sitting there without saying a word, her hands folded on her lap. Tess stared at the padron.

"Now listen to me, you spic bastard. You don't tell us where that greaser is, I'll stove in your bitch's head with this rock."

The old woman looked up at Tess and the rock in stark disbelief.

"Answer me, greaser! Or I swear…"

"Put the goddamn stone down."

The men turned to face Jason. St. Lowe craned his head around.

Jason kicked the grulla forward. "You kill that old woman we'll have everyone in their clan climbing through these hills sniping at us."

St. Lowe shouted Jason down and stared at Bayard. "If they don't give us what we want, kill 'em all!"

Tess shouted again, "Answer me!"

"Have her put the damn stone down, Bayard."

Bayard hung on a moment, confronted by that which flew in the face of common sense. Before he could make his judgment, judgment was carried home. Tess stove in the old woman's skull.

"Stupid bitch," shouted Jason.

The old woman tumbled out of her chair sideways and landed with a dull thud. Blood spilled from her nose and mouth. The padron let out a coarse wail and rushed Bayard. Hennet swung out his hulking Volcanic and hammered a fusillade into the padron's back, dispatching the old man where he fell among the startled shying horses.

Bayard then ordered all those in the village to be killed and their homes burned, save for one boy. He was put afoot to warn every greaser villaged in the hills the Mexican must be handed over, lest they suffer the same fate.

CHAPTER TWENTY

One boot and an alder staff left their mark up through the breezeway. Matthew was still weak and stopped at the edge of the cabin. He rested against the wall and looked across the river where the burning vats processed ore. He glanced at the storehouse. The shed door was closed, but crooked lines of light from a candle beaconed through creases in the slats.

Alone, Hetty loaded bags of gold from small crates lettered with different dry good labels into a trunk no less weathered than the last one she'd carried to Sacramento. The shed door creaked open. She closed the trunk lid and latched it, as her dog slunk his way toward her with Matthew a few hobbled paces behind.

He tottered past her and eased himself back down onto the brim of a keg of nails. He pointed the staff at the trunk. "You going somewhere?"

She lifted the tallow candle from the ground and rested it on the trunk lid. "I have to go to Stockton." She turned and went to reach for the candle.

"Who are you...really? You're not just some itinerant merchant."

She sat there in the shadows quite aware of what she was about to say. "I'm part of the Union underground. I was sent here to report on seditious organizations. And wherever or whenever possible, to not only gather intelligence, but create financial havoc."

"I see," said Matthew. "And the Mexican. He is part of that 'financial havoc.'"

"When Whitehorse built the original mine, there were Indians living in the hills. Whitehorse wanted them cleared out. He put a bounty on them, and an army of muckmen went hunting. Joaquim's family was among them."

Matthew looked at the trunk. "How did you and he...?"

"Early on, they'd send gold out on a burro with only two men to guard it. I followed them a few times. Once I brought my wagon along as if I were going to pick up supplies. I stopped where the men camped by the road. They knew me from here. I made them coffee and dinner, and while they slept...I shot them."

Matthew, staring at Hetty, muttered, "Jesus Christ."

"There is a little village of Mexicans in the hills. I told them what I'd done, that I wanted to meet the man fighting the mine. I gave them gold...and I waited. I waited for months. Then one night in the rain, he came here."

• • •

After nightfall an encampment was established on a promontory protected from the wind by a wood of pines that jagged toward the stars. Jason sat alone at the edge of the camp as no man there now would have any part of him.

"You should have stayed behind, Pork Eater."

He glanced up at Tess, who was carrying a water pouch to a

creek that mewed through the grove of pines forty yards back.

"You and the paper man," she said, "if I ever saw a pair."

"You were a fool to do what you did today in that village."

She laughed and slung the water bag over her shoulder and soon was gone in the woods.

Jason was woken by St. Lowe, who was hollering for Tess and marching from bedroll to bedroll to roust up the men.

Search parties filed through the timbers past where she was last seen after talking with Jason. They reached the creek where the moon stared up cold out of the darkling stream. An hour before dawn Jason discovered the water bag near the markings of a struggle. By dawn the column was advancing at a quick trot through stoked lava mantels. The trail for them to follow was clear, as it was meant to be. They knew there was killing up ahead, and Jason was ordered to rabbit for the pack. They followed behind him through the full bore of the sun with rifles cocked and ready across their saddles.

As Jason led them around a broken wing of trail, they came upon a confusion of black plumed vultures clinging to a naked corpse hung upside down over the bent branch of a dwarf pine. A carrion infested human flag draped above the roadway. The condors hung from that cadaver. Their skinless pink and orange heads burrowed and gnawed into the putty flesh, then rolled viciously.

Jason was the first there as the men rallied forward. He raised his rifle and fired to drive the vultures off. They flocked out. Their wings whistled, lifting them onto the thermals where they hovered in safety.

St. Lowe leaped from his saddle and the stovepipe flew off his head. He was stricken, staring up at Tess. She hung there, gutted by a machete from her cunney to her chestbone. Her neckerchief had been stuffed into her pouting mouth.

St. Lowe looked down at the ground. A neat pyre of stones had been set there by the Mexican in a telling reminder of revenge for the old woman at the village.

• • •

A flatbed wagon hauled by two mules was passing through a dark crease in the trees along the bare scratchings of ox carts. The flatbed jugged its way into the sunlight with Matthew struggling over the leads.

He spotted Ed Candles squatting on the mud lip of Dulcimera Creek wearing only boots, stammeled longjohns and a pistol. A cold pipe was clenched up in his teeth. One of the Chinese with Ed was shoveling the sandy river bottom into the funneled bark channel of a long tom while another, who was rocking the hopper cradle, called to Ed and pointed upstream toward the flatbed Matthew drove.

The ox cart path fell away in a wash of sloping gravel, and Matthew had to rein in the mules. He sat there looking out over the camp. There were brush huts and stretches of canvas hung across four puncheon willow poles constructed atop small burrs on both sides of the riverbank.

Matthew saw Ed had walked away from the creek and was sitting on the sluiced half-moon of a barrel in front of his hut. Matthew reached for a gunnysack lying on the bed of the wagon and climbed from the box.

Matthew worked his way along the creek bed, fighting to balance his crutch against the mud. He passed the open face of a hut. Here the old priest sat cross-legged on a blanket in the shade. The pungent smell of galbanum burned up from scored brass bowls.

"Are you the one who helped me?"

The old one's head leaned quizzically.

Matthew pointed to his leg. "Do you understand English?"

A couple of Chinese formed up around Matthew and there was the barest try at communication. The young cleric squatted beside the old man and fell into a stumbling of ill formed sentences trying to make it clear it was the priest who had helped him. Matthew raised his hand in understanding and opened the gunnysack. He removed tins of oysters and sardines, canned fruit and meats. He reached into his pocket and pulled out a neckerchief weighted with silver dollars. These he spread before the priest.

The cleric shaped an awkward dialogue between Matthew and the old man. The old man nodded thoughtfully and Matthew looked over his shoulder at Ed, sitting on that old barrel and staring down at him.

"The priest said he's glad you're getting well," said Ed. "And he can see from your gracious gift, you are an honorable man. He blessed you. Says you're now a protected child of some ridiculous pigtail god."

Matthew bowed humbly, then looked over at Ed, but he had already started into his hut.

Matthew worked his way toward Ed. "At first I thought I dreamed that old Celestial. And you…"

Ed looked at the young man before him, and a whole life came back. "You were always a clever thing, Matthew." A huff rose from his larynx. "Following us around everywhere with your notebook and your questions."

Matthew reached into the gunnysack and brought out a bottle of whiskey and offered it to Ed. "Go on. Take it, Neville."

"Don't ever call me that. Not ever. Now leave me to my world."

• • •

The fiddler hymned up Barbara Allen. St. Lowe sat beside the shallow grave. "She's walking the other side now, and I'll bet she's hell in the hunt."

Bayard came and sat beside him. He was carrying a clay jug of tequila stolen from the village.

"Here. Let's toast to her soul."

"Aye, Brother Bayard. And to the lost family of us all."

He spent himself on the drink.

Bayard leaned over and whispered, "It's time to put the knife in the pork eater's hand."

St. Lowe eyed with disgust Jason, who sat just outside the circle of men. "Aye, Brother. And what I should have done yesterday I'll do one day late." He set his stovepipe upside down on the ground. He stood and held out the jug. "Brothers, I want you to take a frank pledge. Every man. Bitter and sweet. That we see this to the end. Whatever that end is. Even if we're here for a hundred summers. For it's Christian against Moor. And whatever hope you have for your children rests on how you comport yourselves in this calling. It's time for an oath. So drink down."

He took the bottle and passed it. One by one the men drank as if that clay chalice held the blood of their beliefs. St. Lowe followed the jug floating from mouth to mouth where it ended last with Jason.

"Not you, Pork Eater. You'll not drink."

Jason sat there holding the jug.

"You stood against us at the village. And why, I wonder? Maybe there's more greaser in you than you care to admit."

Jason rested the jug on his knee, freeing one hand.

"We're done with you, you dark skinned bastard. Now find the road and be quick."

Jason lay the jug on the stone balancing it gingerly. He stood and walked to the grulla, giving his back to the heathens. He rose up in his saddle and looped the reins through his left hand, and while turning his horse, pulled the Walker from his belt and fired.

The clay jug shattered, sending a swill of shards and tequila.

"To your health, sheep."

He drove his pony up through the black tracings of lava.

"He's got the knife in his hand now," said Bayard.

"That he does." St. Lowe went and got his stovepipe and topped it on his head. "Hennet, you take two men and you follow the pork eater. But give him his distance, so he don't let on. He knows a lot more than he's been willing to tell us. And my guess is, he'll go after that greaser."

He started shoving the men toward their mounts. "We'll stay on like we were predisposed. But Hennet, you send one man back and forth between us each day to keep in contact. We'll trap that Mex now, and we'll use the pork eater as a rabbit."

• • •

Ed drank the whiskey Matthew had given him while he paced about the murk of his cabin. Matthew had not left as was demanded of him.

"The Tills run the 'castle' in this county for the Knights," said Ed.

He stood in the doorway and looked out upon the river. "There was only about fifty of them to start with. Just a lot of noise and a lot of drinkin' and an All Hallows Eve's ride or two. But since the war, since everyone has come to realize California is richer than the rest of this stinkin' country, since they got religion..."

Matthew sat at a scrapped together table and watched Ed thoughtfully.

"I stumbled on them one night out in the hills. Just west of where the road to Los Angeles follows the Bed of the Ton Tache. I saw the fires. They burn fires, you know, and have secret meetings."

"Could you show me this place? Do they still meet there?"

"What are you gonna do, lie in wait and slay them copperheads like Saint George? Christ, half them muckmen at the mine are members of the 'castle.'"

Ed stood and looked out over the encampment. The Celestials were hunkered down around their huts. Outlines now in the trials of survival.

"The river ain't gonna get much older with us. Chinaman got to pay a foreigner tax to work their claims. And Serranus wants us out of here."

Matthew, changing the subject, asked suddenly, "What happened to you, Ed? How did you get to be who you are now?"

• • •

Jason stood looking out on a hogback chain of granite that ridged a line from San Lorenzo to Penache Pass. It was there he'd spotted the smoke that night along the ridge. He slipped his arms up under his Navy cape then across his chest.

What reason could the old man have to constantly retreat toward the papery line of juts? Could a slender trail thread its mark through San Lorenzo to Peneche Pass? Maybe one as yet unknown? This would stand him in a guerrilla war for months until he would have to execute his escape.

As Jason followed the path high into the hills he saw where gusts had blown up from the south and torn at the heart of the stone. He felt about the north side of the rock. He squatted down and fingered the tailings of white crystal. He put a thumbprint's worth to his tongue and tasted the sea salt carried here on coastal scuds. He looked up that long anchory chain of rocks and knew there must be a clear line of march from the sea to the other side, for the currents to shape out such signs.

He rechecked the load in his pistol and walked the path he believed would transverse the mountain. Farther on, he came upon a stream hidden by a thicket. He knifed through the branches to fill his water bag, and kneeling, discovered the remains of a miner lying face down near the water's edge. The weeds had grown up through the trellis of his bones but a rusty pick and flaking, leather back pannier were strapped around the birdcage of his chest.

Later that afternoon, Jason led his grulla across the slag table that was cradled between the east and west rim of the mountain. The miner's pannier and rusty pick were now slung over Jason's pack-saddle. His Navy coat was tucked up under the back of his rigging and his sleeves were rolled to the shoulders. One of his pistols had been lodged up into the cinch between saddle and blanket. Another pistol had been wedged into his rolled Navy cape. Both were butt end out. Both were primed.

He followed the creek meandering through a stand of nut pines. The runoff of the spring rain had torn up the sandy benchland. Jason's boots slumped and swayed and staggered. Where the corridor of the creek turned, Jason went to cross over to the other side when he came upon the old Mexican sitting hunched on a stone.

There was a stack of nut cones at his feet, and he was breaking off the chocolate brown scales to get at the seeds. His head came up slowly, his face shaded by his hat. The two men stood not thirty yards apart with that bourn rushing between them.

Jason did not come forward. Instead he called to the old man, "Are you panning this river?"

There was not a touch of wind.

"There is no gold here," said the Mexican. "The only gold is in these pine nuts."

Jason smiled and nodded as his eyes stole a glance at the Percheron picketed just this side of the creek. Jason sighted up the worn stock of a rifle slung through the saddle ring.

"I'm out of tobacco," said Jason. "Could I buy some tobacco from you... trade for some? I have canned fruit here to trade."

The old Mexican's hat turned in a sparse half arc. "I have punche to trade," he said.

Then that shadowed face finished its slight turn first to the Percheron, then toward a rucksack on the back side of the stone where he was sitting. Jason let the grulla come forward a step. As the old man reached for his rucksack, Jason could make out the beginnings of a lion's mane woven onto the back of his white wool coat.

Jason's boots cracked through the grainy sand and he slipped a bit. He gathered himself. As the burlap pouch holding the punche came up clean and clear, Jason saw that old man's hand. It was not missing a finger. A desperate sigh rushed up out of his lungs, Jason knew he had made a fatal mistake.

He half turned and jumped, kicking his boot through the iron stirrup. The grulla swept to one side and he rose onto his saddle in a forward rush across the creek toward the cover of the far shore. His fingers curled over and through hammer and trigger but before he could clear the pistol from the saddle, there was a crush of thunder from somewhere in that stand of trees.

CHAPTER TWENTY-ONE

In the half light of the cabin, Ed, who had kept on drinking, said to Matthew. "You want to know how I became who I am now… it affects you directly, Matthew. So be warned."

I don't see how I can't know… now."

Resigned, Ed began, "When your brother and I left Philadelphia with the 4th Artillery for Mexico we were much the same kind of simpleton as you. Bound up with flag and honor. It took the march across that hell they'd christened Texas to start to change all that. We faced lack of water and heat you couldn't imagine. We faced hunger. We faced typhus and dysentery. We watched men die every mile. And there were beatin's. Beatin's for any minor infraction of the law.

"By the time we reached Fort Brown and began the campaign against Matamoros, we saw how war really was. No honorable cause, Matthew. Nothin' as stirrin' as those essays in your notebook. It was about our killin' off the nativism of a country. It was about our killin' off their Catholic ideas. The hatred in our ranks for their religion was rampant, except for the Irish troops, who themselves were in conflict. And you should have seen how our own officers went after *them.*

"And we didn't just kill troops. We killed lepers. We killed peasants in filthy rags. We killed peon mendicants. We killed mestizos who stared down the face of our muskets with sticks and shields. And we killed 'em for one reason. They took up the road."

Ed did not look to see if Matthew was shocked by what he had so far heard. "You don't know how confused we became. Half our officers brought their own slaves. Baggage trains of 'em. Slaves who would have been better served fighting with the Mexicans."

"Protests began in the ranks. Especially the Irish who were Catholic. I can't tell you how many were beatin for their protests. Pamphlets against the war began to circulate. One the officers particularly hated was called *'Civil Disobedience'* written by that man Thoreau.

"We'd had our share of desertions crossing Texas, but at the border, it was like a fever. General Taylor set up sentries along the Rio Grande with orders to shoot any man who crossed. And they did.

"Once a Corporal in the company was caught by our Lieutenant with a copy of *'Civil Disobedience.'* The Corporal was Irish and the Lieutenant was a well known mick hater and he ordered Charlie to flog him. Charlie wouldn't do it as he was still of a belief we had the right to read what we liked. So the Lieutenant ordered him stripped and gagged for three days. Matthew, you have no idea what a punishment like that is, survivin' in the scorched Texas sun.

"After that, our decision was made. We'd seen enough. Charlie and I bought some clothes from a peddler, and we stripped off our uniforms and swam the Rio Grande. We deserted, Matthew."

Here Ed paused, then, uncertain voiced, he went on. "But that wasn't the end of it. We made our way south to Monterrey. A notorious artillery company of mostly Irish American deserters was there known as the San Patricios, who had taken up arms with the

Mexicans. So we joined them. We fought under their shamrock flag against the flag of our home.

"I will not speak of our two years in Mexico. At the battle of Churubusco, our company of San Patricios defended a convent along the road. That's where Charlie was taken prisoner…Where against the convent wall, he was put before a firing squad."

Ed finished abruptly. Matthew, too numb to speak, got up and walked out.

• • •

Jason lay on his stomach at the creek's edge. His eyes opened. His head rolled feebly to one side, and there, sitting on the croup of the dead grulla, was Joaquim. A shotgun was cribbed across his lap. And in that face reigned the heart of dark recourse.

"You read sign well, whore," he said, "but not well enough, heh."

The old man who had been sitting on the stone wearing Joaquim's coat trotted by out of breath. Jason listened as the old man rattled off in Spanish of three riders coming on, some hours back up through the canyon.

Jason tried to fathom if what he heard was possible. If part or all of the expedition had tracked on behind him.

Joaquim stood and in Spanish said, "Strip the whore."

The old man hauled Jason up by the hair. His clothes were cut to paupery and the knife that hung from a lanyard down his back was discovered and sheared loose.

Joaquim squatted down. He began to scrap through the disheveled pile of Jason's belongings. On Jason's belt, Joaquim found Coco's pouch of magic. He ripped it loose, searched through it, then held it up.

"Your soul is mine now, whore." He slipped the pouch into his pocket. "Bind his hands behind him."

The old man roped Jason's wrists with the lanyard tight enough so it tore into the flesh.

Joaquim found some Union currency and coins in Jason's pockets. He fingered through the vest and found the watch. He lifted it dangling by the chain, then snapped it up into his palm. He looked the watch over then pressed open the clasp.

The Mexican cursed to himself in Spanish then stood. He stared down at his adversary, naked and barefoot in the waning half light of the mountains. A straw man now marked. "The other whores I understood. They march behind their white god and use our color to destroy us. But you. Who turns against his own."

He slipped the watch into his pocket. "You came to kill a slave, heh? Before you die you will know what it's like to be a slave." Joaquim looked at the old man. "Get a rope and leash him."

The old man trotted over to the Percheron and loosened the horn strings around the coiled hemp. Joaquim went through Jason's saddle packs, stealing ammunition and food and his rifle. Jason was kneeling on the ground as the old man dog looped his neck, pulling the hemp rope till he choked.

Joaquim climbed up onto the Percheron and the old man handed him the end of the line and he tethered it around the wooden saddle horn.

Joaquim spoke to the old man. "Go back to the village and bury your family."

He reined the Percheron around and stared at Jason. He pointed toward a black crevasse through the mountains' teeth. "It will be a long walk to lead your friends to where they will die." He pulled the rope hard. "Now get up."

• • •

Matthew was by the creek when Ed came up behind him.

"If I've made you ashamed of Charlie…"

"I don't think I could ever be ashamed of Charlie."

"That's good. It's just… You're such a goddamn radical chasing honor."

"We were deserters. We took up arms against this nation because of a war we thought unjust. A man can't be much more despised for that act, with the exception of maybe pissing on the bones of Christ."

Matthew smoked and listened to the creek bubbling under all that gray, and far up in the canyon the mist played tricks with a piece of flickering starlight that seemed to move through the damp fir trees, and then disappear.

"My father. Did he know?"

"He knew." Ed swigged down a drink. "This is about the closest I've been to American soil since the war. Hope to get no closer either."

"I wonder if my mother knows." Matthew shook his head. "The newspapers listed the Army's record of deserters. There was nothing ever about my brother."

"Matthew, you're too naïve for your station. Your family is the landed aristocracy of this country. They make out, while the rest make do. Your father is an influential patrician attorney, well versed in the currency of favors."

Matthew stood there brooding. He did not like to see himself as the heir to duplicity. He looked back upstream past the quiet huts and over where the creek rounded some high rocks and swam along in the mist.

"Looks beautiful, doesn't it?"

Ed looked up the creek. Saw the light. Matthew noticed some change in him. Ed stared farther up the creek then along the wooded hillside where a line of torches fireflyed down the mistswept slope.

"Jesus Christ." He dropped the bottle and rushed back to the cabin.

Matthew chased after him. Ed spilled out of the hut, "The Knights…" He fired two warning shots to rouse the camp. He rammed the rifle against Matthew's back. "Make for the brush."

They ran down through the slop mud of the creek bench. A cry rallied up from a battlement of trees where scarlet horsemen stagged out across the clearing. Hooded riders carrying pyred splints. Ed and Matthew were chest high in the current as they made for the far shore. Upstream a breastwork of horsemen swept out across the rocks and charged into the creek. Game legged and great chested mounts high stepping the gray eddy. Matthew stumbled and disappeared beneath the current. The mist spilled and shivered and he came back up gagging and soaked and staggered into the high reeds along the far bank. He ducked down low and looked for Ed, but he was gone.

• • •

St Lowe circled Jason's dead grulla and watched as the men ransacked his belongings. Perty rat scrambled up Jason's boots, tugging off his own patched relics.

"Well, Brother Bayard, the pork eater knew more than he was telling." St. Lowe turned to Hennet, who was trying to work his thick frame into Jason's trousers.

"Hennet, how far ahead are your men?"

"Too far to catch them before dark."

As they made toward their mounts a cockscomb of dust drew up through the ribs of the canón. The shapes of two horsemen darkened as the clouds around their hooves were ragged off by the wind. The men could make out Leon waving his hat and the black prisoner harnessed up in his saddle with hands tied to the horn.

"Well, St. Lowe, your boy found the nigger."

• • •

The two riders that Hennet had sent forth while he waited at the creek were within reckoning distance of Joaquim. He studied their slow gaited approach as they leaned out of their saddles to read the carven niches in the earth.

He pulled on Jason's leash and tapped the barrel of his Sharps against the stone where he wanted Jason to kneel. He stood behind him, prodding his pistol against the stump of Jason's brain. He untied Jason's hands, so he could fire the Sharps.

"You are my gunhand now. My eyes. You miss your first shot, you won't ever hear the second."

Jason took up the rifle, first checking to see if the charges were dry and properly capped, then he checked the hammer and the action and the sight. His back was badly burned from the sun. That and his chest were covered with dried cat claws of blood. He moved with an aching stiffness.

The pistol nudged Jason's skullbone. "You take the back rider first so you can try for the other with a second shot."

Jason cleaned the sweat and grease from his hands by burying them in dirt, then brushing them together. He laid the rifle across the backbreaker stone. The riders moved out onto a trace of blue larkspur. Jason read the drift of the wind in a stormbent stand of pines. He eased the hammer back. He could feel his heart beating against the arid stone. He could hear his timepiece in the Mexican's pocket turning out the seconds as he waited for the wind to settle.

By the time the powder charge's thunder crossed a thousand yards the rider had crumpled onto the withers and his spurs gouged the horse's underbelly. His horse panicked and jousted forward ramming headlong into the other rider who was trying to rowel his mount toward cover and they both toppled.

The Mexican retreated farther into the hills toward San Lorenzo Pass. Joaquim pulled hard on the leash and Jason's throat was scored and scored again. His skin was cracked and burned, and he remembered the black bound behind the coach wheels in the dust of a slave's march.

Nightfall came with cold dispositions where the Mexican set his camp upon an esker overlooking the long channel of the Cañón de los Reyes. A slim haze drifted across the crest from the sea. Joaquim opened his canvas pannier and began to lay out an ordinal of his dwindling ammunition.

Jason could see his thorny anger give way to a solemn passing, "It will be a hard day tomorrow," he said, "but I will fill the chalice."

Jason sat there shivering. "You can't outfight them."

Joaquim did not even bother to look at this naked thing before him. Instead, he carefully prepared fulminate for each cap. "And why not... I have you, don't I?"

With each tentative pour Jason saw the sandy line of powder drift and miss the cap as Joaquim's failing eyes did not afford him any luxuries.

Jason snaked himself up to his knees. "How bad are your eyes?"

The old man looked up and stared him down. "Not so bad I

cannot see the truth."

Now Jason understood why the Mexican did not try to run and come back months later. He was becoming sandblind. And time he did not have.

"At dusk," said Jason, "I looked to the pass ahead. The ground is open and made for a straight fight. That Percheron can't outrun 'em, and no one shot is good enough to hold them back. Especially when one's on foot. I know those men back there. On open ground they'll ride straight down on you no matter how many they lose."

"Gracias… compadre," the old man mocked.

"Let me buy my life back."

Joaquim held up the empty pistol cartridge and blew out the dust. "You are worth nothing."

"If you left tonight you could sneak past their camp and make your escape to the south. You leave me here alive, I'll tell them you went on to the north up into Peneche."

"You will be what you need to be at the moment, heh? Just like any whore. You are a mask. Holes for eyes and holes for a mouth. Nothing to see, nothing to say."

CHAPTER TWENTY-TWO

There are horrors to speak of and tragedies to tell.

The Knights of the Golden Circle went about their destruction with as much of a drunken swagger as vengeful precision. Their heads bound up in stitched cloths with holes cut for eyes and a knife slit for a mouth. Pathetic sacks that held the flour of their heads.

In the confusion of the moment, with a moonless sky and the mist, many of the Chinese made their escape into the woods or to the river and the high tule reeds up and downstream. But the others were shot down as they ran. Slain as if they were nothing more than rag bag targets for the amusement of Saturday afternoon bullyboys.

This night I myself have been ordained. And, as in all things, I'll have to live with the consequences, however frightful. For this night I killed a man. And I killed him with impunity —

The Knights loaded up their few dead and howled their way to the far end of camp then up the incline where they shot all the mules and then were lost to the trees. But one turned about and came splashing back toward camp. That great sack head angling slowly one way and then another. He was searching the creek for the old priest who he found beached among some branches not twenty feet from where I hid. He climbed out of the saddle and hauled up that long white pigtail and was about to cut it, when I stood and fired the pepperbox. This time that rusty piece of ironwork didn't fail me. The shot tore a hole in his gut and he fell back onto his ass in the creek tules.

He sagged drunkenly, tried to stand, but didn't have the strength. I could have shot him again. I could have left him to time's reward. But I did neither. Instead I threw my gun on shore and went about the business of strangling him to death. Just to see it written here — just those words — punctuates the grim finality of it. But it neither defines the rage, nor the horrific sense of exhilaration, as I saw that gray sack of a head fill with water and a trail of bubbly pleas rush desperate up out of the eye wells.

I strangled him for the atrocities he had inflicted upon the encampment. I strangled him for trying to kill the old mystas who helped blow life back into my body. And maybe I could convince myself, or you, there was honor in my act, if there was only that for a reason. But it wasn't so. I saw in that gasping hood every humiliation I had been slave to. I saw the beating Arlen gave me. I saw the insults I took from Demerest and St. Lowe, and I saw Jason's pistol fire down on me. I saw my father's face when he walked unexpectedly into my room at Harvard and found me with the man who shared my bed. I saw that look on a thousand faces since. I saw my father spit on me. I saw him condemn me with his silence. I saw myself cast out on the road. I saw my father's lie in Ed's confession. I saw how a nation's stately promise comes ill conceived from a sense of family honor. And all those bubbles of breath that slipped up from that hood's slit mouth can cry out voiceless all they want for mercy. But at this moment there is none. I can send them all to perdition with an irony entrusted to my fingertips.

• • •

St. Lowe had beaten the black so badly his eyes could barely open. The side of his head was misshapen and distended like some fetal deformity. He could no longer speak, no longer walk.

St. Lowe looked up the canyon past where the men were saddling their mounts. The ground was still blue and damp, and a few birds had begun to call up the day. Bayard shambled down the hill leading his mount and he walked over to St. Lowe.

"He's still draggin' the pork eater and moving none too fast," he said, then spit. "He means to fight this all the way out."

"We'll see whose means outlast the other."

Bayard looked over at the men. They were ragged and filthy. The horses were spotted with sores, and their ribs boned against the hides. Those who had lost their mounts were riding pack mules.

St. Lowe squatted and took out his knife. He filed the blade against a stone. "Leon, cut us two willow branches. One six feet, one five. Skin the bark and shark the tips. Thin as teeth."

Leon looked over at the black. He knew his father meant to crucify him. "Aye."

Bayard squatted down beside St. Lowe. "What are you thinking?"

"You'll follow his markings. I'll split from the column and flank you to the leeward so I have the sun with me. Then I'll swing west come afternoon. But first I'm gonna crucify that nigger. I'm gonna slit his flesh just at the ass and slide that willow right up his spine till it comes out at the neck. Then I'll crossbeam his arms the same way, and we'll prop him up in the saddle and let him head out the column." He looked up the canyon to where the soft light was filling out the rim of the hogback. "He'll make for some show I promise you that."

St. Lowe stood. The wind was running the last of the mist off the hills. "Let's beat the board today, Brother Bayard."

• • •

The Mexican leaned over the ledge of the mantlerock. He looked down through the gap of the Cañón de los Reyes, where to the south, augmented against the sandy rubblestone hills, veiling dust approached unfolding upon itself like smoke drawn in by a fire and out of which a single cross, serifed and black as iron, illumed up from the plains' surface.

Joaquim squinted and kept watching, bewildered for the moment by what he saw, and then as the cross angled into the sun, he could make out beyond it the spanning plume of riders. As they arced away from the sun the phasm of the cross became apparent in the crucified shape of the black.

Joaquim turned away and slid back down the mantlerock where Jason sat bound. He lifted him up and dragged Jason to a spall in the rocks where he could see down the canón, then pointed.

"Is that the black from the coach?"

The wind had taken to blowing across the pass. Jason blinked heavily to clear his eyes. He waited as the wind settled out, and there about a half mile away he could make out, faintly at first, and then more clearly, the black crucified up on the saddle. Overwhelmed, Jason said, "Yes, it's the black from the coach."

Joaquim let Jason go and he fell to the ground.

Jason watched as Joaquim looked north toward the hills. In Spanish Joaquim said, "Soon to see. Soon to know." He then walked over to the Percheron and opened the saddle pack and pulled out another pistol strung from a lanyard and swung that over his neck. The old man checked his rifle, then slid it back into the saddle scabbard beside a broad blade ax. Once done, he walked over to Jason and slipped his fingers under the rope around his neck and tugged him up onto his feet.

Jason tried to speak as the rope tightened around his larynx. "You can't…ride…among them."

Joaquim unsheathed his knife and bladed it against the boneplate of Jason's jaw. "I won't need your eyes anymore, heh."

Jason's breath came up short.

"It is too bad that God gave you the heart of a liar instead of the heart of a lion."

Like Abraham, that old Mexican jacked up the blade to where it slated against the sun. As the arm came hacking toward his throat, Jason shut his eyes, preparing for the deathblow. But the blade stabbed down past his throat as the old man shanked out a piece of flesh above Jason's heart, earmarking him like any beast of burden.

Jason cried out in agony. He crumbled to his knees. His bound arms were yanked up, pressing against his shoulder bones, and he could feel the knife cut free his bonds.

The Mexican climbed into the saddle and roweled the Percheron then plunged up, a spall of rocks, and charged out across the canón. Jason staggered to his feet, blood straining through fingers pressed against his chest. At the rim of the mantle, he could see below and to the south. The bedlam had begun.

The column sighted the old man bullfrogging through the outcrops and up the long grassy flume of the pass. They charged forward with hoots and cries and there came the quick pops of rifle fire. The crucified black was still well in the lead of the column, and in the mad onslaught of that pack of thugs, he was herded forward. As they passed below rushing north Jason could see that stovepipe hat was nowhere among their number. He scrabbled over a heave of plaited stone slipping down a sandy incline and searched out that mob for St. Lowe. And what he did not see. Somewhere ahead, a snare had been set for the old man. He was suddenly caught by a shameful need to warn the Mexican, but he was faced with only the waning dust and a fierce volley of rifle fire.

He gathered himself up and lumbered out into the canyon naked, following where the riders had trampled through the high grass. The volley fire had become more ferocious and a riderless horse sprinted out of the canyon and past him with stirrups bucking and the saddle tainted with blood. Farther up the pass, he came upon the rider lying white eyed on his back.

The rocky straights angled hard up to the east and here the ground was spotted with the dead and mortally wounded. One of the riders was looped over his fallen horse. Another lay where he fell and was trampled by the roughs charging up behind him. A horse circled aimless and whinnying in the middle of the canyon floor.

And there, atop a knoll of fissured iron, Joaquim rode among the knotted band of mercenaries. A pistol in one hand, an ax in the other. The ground was a carnage with the slain and ashen reefs were churned up by the swirling hooves. Blue metal barrels burst with red fire and the men lay scattered across the incline and the horses snapped at each other all wild eyed and seething. The Mexican drove his Percheron into a horseman whose mount tumbled backward and they were crushed under their own weight against the jagged rocks.

He then turned and cleaved his ax through Bayard's chest as his lathered horse stampeded past and the ax handle splintered. They all swirled together in fiendish bands of spiraling dust and light and powdersmoke, and their images the brutal retelling of some parabled hecatomb where neither truth nor blood nor honor might carry its weight in the final outcome. Soon no one man could be singled out from the other, and no one man might be separated from the other, and the black's horse wheeled and charged and the cross rose up in the coffin boned dust that bound them all together.

Along the edge of the escarpment, Jason spied St. Lowe weaving along a brittle trail to where he might find a piece of ground to make a clean shot at the Mexican.

Jason looked over the shambles of the battlefield for a rifle and rushed toward a mount sprawled out in a swale of wildflowers but the rifle scabbard came up empty. He wheeled, struggling up slopy ground toward a blood bay whose knee had been shattered and hobbled three legged, with its shank grueling along the stones. He reached for the butt stock of a Sharps carbine lipping over the saddle fender. He pulled it clean and quick checked to see if it was loaded then backed up and away from the faltering horse.

Passing over that treacherous loose shale, St. Lowe wedged his horse on a bald plate where the escarpment fell away in a sheer drop. He slung the great octagonal barrel over his shoulder and it came to rest on the pinion of his elbow, aiming where that lion's head coat rode mammoth among the butchered ranks, trampling over the dead and firing coup de grâce shots from his pistols into the wounded, who lurched and stuttered and fell away. The Percheron wrenched back on its hind legs in the final sheen of death wails, then bolted forward through the lowering dust.

Jason lifted the Sharps, cropping the grip just below the forend on his open palm. He cocked the hammer and framed St. Lowe against the sun, and as Jason fired, a burst of smoke shot out from the barrel of St. Lowe's gun.

Blood spurted from the Mexican's stomach and his lion's head pitched forward in the saddle as St. Lowe's mount jerked sideways into the shelf wall as it was shot. It went splay footed along the ledge, tottering at the void. St. Lowe tried to leap clear of the saddle but his feet noosed in the tangled stirrups. The pistol fell from the Mexican's left hand and he grabbed hold of the pommel just as St. Lowe and his mount were carried headlong down the flat clifffacing into a pool of silent daylight, man and stovepipe hat and beast and rifle and spillage from his saddle packs down into the crooked rocks. The Mexican weaved and gaited the Percheron and the pistol in his right hand fired wild then he sagged backward, and he too fell.

• • •

The Mexican sat leaning against a stone near the hilltop where the others had fallen. His shirt sopped up the blood.

Jason had taken a serape from one of the dead and this alone covered him as he walked barefoot toward the Mexican with a water bag. He squatted down and offered him a drink. Joaquim pushed the water bag away.

Jason looked at the wound that would kill the old man and then back up into his eyes. "Why did you let me live?"

Joaquim took a slow breath and looked up. The black's horse loped past and whinnied. The old man sat beneath the grim sight and pulled a knife from his belt, "Cut him down."

Jason took the knife and stood and the horse backed away. He grabbed at the dangling leads. He cut loose the rope that had bound the black to the saddle and that carcass slipped heavily onto his arms, pushing Jason to his knees. The willow shaft jabbed into the earth and the corpse lumbered backward falling prone in a flush of dust.

Joaquim's head slipped back against the stone. Along the promontory to the west the wind sent up a wall of dust around the gilding sun. The crest there seemed aflame and vapored.

He looked back at Jason, who had asked him again, "Why didn't you kill me?"

The face of the man before him was marked with dirt and blood. "Why?"

The old Mexican steadied himself. "For one moment…back at the river…you helped the child cross."

He turned away. Jason squatted there silently. The dust silled across the slope where the dead lay. It burned his eyes.

The old man welled inward, to a stream at violent dusk. Where a wind came suddenly from the footlands. Where his mother and father laughed and walked hand in hand. Where the tree crickets called, and he chased shallow prints in the sandbar that marked his parents' steps. How he tried to match their steps as the world about him hung by threads of light. Where green and mossy clear water passed on toward endless promise. Where in that endless moment, his eyes became two black suns with no light before them, and joined the black shroud that bore the best of us with its beauty, before any heaven was thought of to lie about.

Jason sat back on the ground. His head rested stiffly upon his knees. Blood still seeped from his wounds. The wind fluttered the clothes of the dead about them like markers. Their hats wheeled and tumbled like tailless kites down through the rocky canyon. He sat a long hour. Indifferent to life, indifferent to himself.

Dusk was falling away by the time the grave was dug. He used his hands and a rifle stock to frame the sod deep enough against the coming of wolves. Before he lay the old man away, he took back his watch and the pouch Coco had given him. He slipped the old man's arms out of the African coat and lay it across the Percheron's saddle. Then he closed up the earth.

Arlen would have been waiting a week now at the Rancho de Aguirre for a report on the expedition. He glanced at the grave and then at the Percheron and old man's coat. The ox had been gored as promised. Freedom's price was paid. They needed to know nothing more than that. His wounds could back up any lie, as people always believe there is truth to blood.

He took two pistols and went about the killing of the wounded and lame horses. Vultures ringed the escarpada like spectators to some sorry drama and waited for his work to be done. He stripped off his serape and walked naked among the dead. Stealing bits of raiment. A shirt of blue cotton. Canvas breeches the color of sand. A broad brim slouch hat with frayed rims. His father's boots were tugged loose from Perty's corpse.

Where the dead lay the thickest on the knoll, he found Hennet. One of the huge Volcanic pistols was still braced up in his belt, his fingers locked around the other. His face was covered with flies. Jason undid the holster belt and tied it up around his waist, then he broke Hennet's fingers loose with a stone and slipped the other Volcanic into his belt.

He loaded the Percheron down with a water pouch and food and a burlap bag of cartridges.

Jason turned and made his way back over the rocks.

And in June of that year, he started for the vast Rancho de Aguirre, up along the trace known as Wild Horses.

BOOK THREE

CHAPTER TWENTY-THREE

Hetty stood in the breezeway looking out toward Peneche Pass, lost behind the rain. A thunderhead left its mark across the sky and the long shank of the Pass was lit, then gone. She prayed that he was safe. She looked back up the breezeway. She stopped by the door to the common room where Matthew slept. She glanced in. He sat on the edge of the bed. A single candle tin flickered from the sill. He was writing in his notebook.

She knocked lightly.

He looked up.

"Am I interrupting you?"

He shook his head no and quietly invited her in. She walked over and sat on the bed. He slipped the pencil into his notebook and closed it.

She looked back at the door creaking under the wind. "One of the riders who was sent back for more supplies and horses said some of those clochards had been killed already. There's a rumor that a village of mesteneros up in the hills was wiped out. Oh, Matthew. They mean to have us all."

The room was heavy with the smell of wet.

"We have to start making plans," she said.

"For what?"

"How we might go about taking an ore wagon."

He leaned back against the bed and it creaked thinly. He thought on the implausibility of it all.

Thunder came out of the darkness and charged the earth around the cabin. Blue shocks of light brightened out the doorway and the edges around the oilskin shades.

Matthew watched as she ran her hand along the gray blanket smoothing out the folds.

"Goddamn it all."

"What's the matter, Matthew?"

He waved off an answer.

She reached out and took his hand. "What?"

"I was thinking of Jason."

She stiffened.

"He could have been of help."

She let go of his hand.

"Like the day at the river. Damn him."

She had thought of all that. And other things.

"I didn't mean to upset you."

"It's all right, Matthew. I fell prey to good faith. I believed Jason was the man I had seen in that boat back during the flood." She looked out into the rain. She listened.

"I can stand being made a fool of, Matthew, it's just…"

There was something in that scarred face that was feminine and delicate and sad.

"I hope it's raining hard up in the hills," she said.

Matthew reached for the laudanum. Time passed. She leaned

over the bed and blew out the candle. The room fell away to the rain.

"Why did you blow out the candle?"

She did not answer, and he did not ask again. They just sat, as the thunder worked its way across the valley.

"I want to ask you something else," she said, "and it's easier for me to ask you in the dark."

The oilskin shade lifted with the wind and droplets sprinkled in along the sill.

"Have you had relations with many women?"

The bed creaked. "A few. All prostitutes. Usually when I was drunk or I'd had opium. But I was always lonely."

"I see."

"But I...I prefer men. I have always preferred men."

He sat back and looked at her, trying to see in her manner or her silence how he would be judged. After a time he remarked with a sarcastic flair, "I wrote once that the future is yours, if you can just crawl your way to it."

He could feel her hand across the gray blanket as broken sounds sifted up from her throat.

"Are you crying?"

"Yes."

"I'm sorry if I've made you cry."

"I'm crying for a lot of reasons, Matthew."

"That only makes me all the more sorry."

Her hand reached his. "Matthew."

"Yes."

"I have had relations with a number of men. I know I was just an excuse for a woman they think about, or dream about, or have lost or haven't met. I am what becomes them, but even that leaves them disappointed. So I have a feeling for these matters. I cannot go back to my room. I am worried sick, and I cannot be so unhappy alone."

Her head lifted slightly, and her hair fell about her sweater's frayed woolen collar and the wet raven black moon of her eyes were lost in the black of the room.

"Pretend I'm just one of those prostitutes. Or see me as you want."

CHAPTER TWENTY-FOUR

Upon the morning of the third day Jason rose up out of a gill teeming with high grass. He rode in the shadow of Mount Oso toward the shore of the great slough south of Stockton. Before him was the trace known as "Wild Horses." There, architected out of the heart of the valley, stood the fifty thousand acre Rancho de Aguirre.

He worked the Percheron down toward a rutted cartway, and the adobe walls of the campo flushed up distant in the sun. Its tile roof ran a squared red road upon three wings of the compound. Stretching out in each direction from the campo for half a mile were the tents and stalls of traders and farmers come for the week long summer festival, now in its last days.

By the campo gate, a mozo groomed a fine looking dun that Jason recognized as one of Arlen's mounts. His wounds had gutted his strength, and he was forced to rest a moment holding onto the pommel. He asked the mozo in Spanish where he might find Arlen. The man looked up into Jason's blood nicked face. He explained that Arlen and his father had ridden into the hills with three wolfers to shoot a mountain cat that had been wounded and gone mad, and was killing off the cattle. They were not expected back until nightfall.

Jason bought a beer and a shank of roasted venison, and moved through the throng of people. He passed slough hands bent under their crated portage, sellers of sateen clothes, bastoneros hawking up nickels for the freaks of nature waiting in the shadow of their carnival tents.

He wandered toward the brass of bassoons and a string of violas. He stepped over the thill of a flatbed and there a half ring of wagons had been framed beyond the orchestra stand and he was greeted with the remains of a canvas sky over battered sections of the Lord's Italian walnut bar that read, "THE TRAVELING BIG BLUE HEAVEN BAR AND ORCHESTRA". He made his way past the crowded betting tables, and there, by the orchestra, in a black velvet frock coat over a ruffled silk pearly shirt, was Lord Goose.

His eyes swam larcenous through the crowd. He turned and when he spotted Jason pushing his way past the bettors, he flashed a jaw full of ivory bone teeth.

Stepping down from the orchestra stand, he went to put his arms around Jason, but he brushed them away. Jason looked out over the orchestra and bar. Hanging between two wagons on a laundry line was a singed section of that tarp cathedral ceiling filled with the sky and constellations.

"I see you're not Mayor of the Presidio yet."

"Ahhh, that. Well, my boy. Not long after you departed, there was a bit of a recall because of some uncalled for infuriation over that war hero and his apprentice you so neatly shivved. It's a shame you weren't there for the torchlight processional some of our devoted citizenry culled up from their imaginations to help light my way."

Jason took a quick step at the Lord. "I ought to kick that fish jaw right out of your mouth for not..."

A shotgun gated his path. He looked around. Coco smiled from the far end of the belly of that gun and nudged Jason back.

Jason looked at the Lord. "You're just shit for leaving me stranded with those…"

The Lord bellowed, "And Job rails against the perfect government of the universe." His voice softened. "Did you expect some moral imperative from me? I only designed that little world we lived in. I am not responsible for your actions, or what becomes of them. Remember, the knife was in your hands."

Jason went to walk away. Coco grabbed hold of Jason's shoulder, then pointed to Jason's shirt. Jason looked down to see the blue cloth around his breast dampening with blood. He walked wearily to the edge of the orchestra stand and sat. He began to undo the top buttons of his shirt when the Lord squatted down beside him.

"Let a better eye have a look."

The Lord began to undo each button. His bone teeth ground together on first seeing the wounds. "Coco, get him into my wagon and we'll stitch him up."

In the wagon, Jason sat at the edge of a cot with his shirt off. The Lord lipped the wound tailoring up a seam. He closed the sorry flesh with a fibril of Chinese silk.

"My angel here," said the Lord, "has been worrying for you the whole time. Whining with his fingers."

Coco knelt down and fingered the pouch on Jason's belt.

"Yeah, I guess it did serve me well. I'm alive."

"Jason, we do very nicely with these rubes along the road. The Army won't hunt for—"

"Nothing is forgotten."

• • •

Jason weaved his way through the stalls and wagons back toward the campo when he came upon a picket wall ring of spiked pines, ten feet high and rimmed most of the way around with slat hewn bleachers. They were packed with men and boys and a spotting of women. They were all edged over the teeth of the ring and were cheering and screaming at a fanlight of dust.

Jason passed the ring wall, when something drove against it. It shuddered and he heard a bellow and a cry, and those in the bleachers screamed out. He leaned in close and peered through a crack in the pine boughs, and there in the ring, he could see an ox, its horned head was wreathed in blood and not twenty feet away the hull of a grizzly, all black gray, rose up on its hind legs, with the great moon head frothing white at the mouth.

The ox backed off and the grizzly lumbered forward and swiped at the fading light with cleated paws. The ox dropped its head and rushed forward and tunneled its horns into the belly of the bear, lifting him up, and the bear's claws tore into the humped spine, scoring it. Like Goliaths, they twisted and stumbled in the dust as the spectators' hands charged the sky.

Jason saw the bear come up with entrails dangling. The bull had lost an eye but stood ready to go again. The bear cupped its ears, and the bull rocked on its flanks, and they assaulted each other over stoups of hoof and claw marks and fonts of blood in the creases of the earth. Again the bear's belly was torn apart by the bull's horns and again the bull's flanks were shredded and an ear was carved away. Again they somersaulted over into the flaying dirt. Again the spectators' hands charged the sky.

And as he watched these two beasts raffle off their lives, he came to realize who and what he really was… and what he'd done.

• • •

Arlen, his father, and Emmit Till sat at a long plank table, their evening meal fully commenced. Arlen saw Jason being led through the great oak gate. He stood. He was about to clasp the silhouetted shoulders, when he noticed the cuts on Jason's face and the bloody shirt.

"God, man. What happened?"

"The expedition has been wiped out."

Whitehorse stared grimly. "All of them?"

"All of them, Mr. Whitehorse."

"And my brother, Bayard?" asked Emmit.

"Bayard too."

Emmit set down his drink.

"It happened in a small pass that connects San Lorenzo and Peneche."

"There isn't a pass between the two," said Emmit.

Jason eyed Emmit. "There is. I discovered it when…"

"Is he dead?" asked Whitehorse. "The Mexican. If that's what he is. Was he taken down?"

Jason hung on the moment. He looked at Whitehorse. "He wasn't taken down."

Whitehorse's eyebrows jerked. "Twenty men spent and it's all for the furnace. Good picking, boy."

Emmit stood and grabbed his hat.

"And where are you going?" Whitehorse asked.

Emmit walked around the table and passed Jason, then he stopped short and slapped his hat across Jason's face. He sallied a pistol up against his back.

Arlen shouted, "Emmit!"

"You must think we're niggers, coming on sincere like that. But I see you for the scapegrace you are."

Jason's arms spread out palms up.

"Mr. Whitehorse," said Emmit. "Maybe you'd like to ask this ragpicker how come he's got blood on his shirt but no hole or powdersmoke to go with it. And maybe you'd like to ask him why he's got that Volcanic stuck up in his belt when I'll bet five pounds of silver to a fact, he reaved it off a man named Hennet who I hired for this expedition myself. Maybe you'd ask him that, Mr. Whitehorse."

"Emmit," said Arlen. "I've known this man for…"

"Hold on a minute, Arlen." Whitehorse came around in his chair. He stared at the blood spot on Jason's shirt. "Show me the magistrate here is wrong. Open up your shirt."

Jason worked open the buttons and peeled back the blouse. The wounds spoke for themselves. He pulled his shirt closed and buttoned it.

Whitehorse took some whiskey. He drank. "How many did that greaser or whatever he is have with him?"

"Enough to take that column of yours."

Whitehorse set the glass back down. His scarred chin wrinkled. "Get up out of that chair and go wait over by the gate."

Jason smoked by the great oak gate alone. A long hour's passing. Arlen came out through the open gate and stood beside him.

"Till says you're a counterfeit who needs to be put down. My father isn't sure. But he believes in the power of desperation. And a man hunted by the United States Army is desperate and could well use the favor of an influential man who has business with the army.

Jason saw the Percheron was being led up from the stable.

"You're going to ride point on the next expedition, Jason. And the one after that if necessary. I put my faith in you."

Arlen reached into his pocket and pulled out a handful of yellowing pages clipped from a newspaper. He handed these to Jason. "This is another bastard downriver that you could help us deal with. Of course…you may just run."

CHAPTER TWENTY-FIVE

Matthew felt something move across his bed. He dreamed, or had a sense of dreaming it. His eyes opened. The room was black and still until a chair creaked.

"Hetty?"

A match was struck on the table and hoisted toward a cigarette. Jason's face was lit.

"You."

The match was blown out.

"How's the leg, Matthew?"

Matthew tried to clear the sleep from his head and recall where he'd laid his pistol away.

"What do you want here now?"

"In part I came to warn you."

Matthew rubbed his eyes. He got up and walked over to the table and sat. He pushed the candle tin toward Jason.

"Put up some light."

The cigarette tipped the wick and sent a run of light up under their faces and the chinks cut out of Jason's cheeks left dark pitholes.

"Looks like you were kicked around some."

"Some."

Matthew glanced at his coat draped over the raw pine bedpost. "Did the expedition give up on the old man, or have they come home to pageant their trophy?"

"I'm all that's left of the expedition."

"St. Lowe? Bayard?"

"Tess. Leon. They've all blown away by now."

"I think I'll have a drink as it's only proper to toast good news." He walked over to the bed. "Of course, it's not completely good news, now is it? After all, you're still alive."

"Matthew."

He turned. Jason held out the pepperbox. "In case you were planning on making it a formal toast."

Matthew grabbed hold of his coat and flung it at Jason and he swiped it away. Matthew thumped down on the edge of the bed.

"Sit here at the table, Matthew."

"Go frig yourself."

"There's things you need to see. And things I want to say. When I'm done, I want to ask you a favor and if you say no, well...that will be what it is. I'll give you back your pistol, and you can shoot me with it."

Matthew eyed him incredulously. Jason lay the pistol down and gestured him over then took from his pocket the yellowing clipped pages from a newspaper that Arlen had shown him.

Matthew stared at the clippings. He took his makings and laudanum from the sill and came over to the table and slid out a chair.

"Is he dead? The old man? Did you earn your blood money?"

Jason reached for his cigarette. "He's dead."

"Damn you all."

"I know this won't stand for much. But...I took nothing. I just left Arlen and his father and Emmit Till up at Wild Horses. I told them the expedition had been wiped out. But I didn't tell them the old man was dead."

"And why was that? Is there more profit in the lie?"

Jason sighed to clear his throat and began to lay out for Matthew the past month in the hills.

• • •

Hetty woke as always in these hours and took to wandering her room. She was filled with restless details. From down beyond the breezeway she heard a whinny and she stepped out into a star filled night. She looked toward the warehouse and listened, but the whinnying had stopped. She folded her arms across her chest and waited, and soon heard the slow swinging of harness metal and hooves, step by step growing closer, and then framed under the eave beams of the breezeway was the old man's Percheron, its nose poking at grass tufts.

• • •

In the telling Jason spared nothing of the truth. Neither in his intent nor conduct. He rooted himself squarely in the midst of fools and frauds, as much of the one as of the other. Not just part of some vicious tragedy, but a black mark at the very heart of that tragedy. For unlike the others, he was a lie unto himself. Matthew neither rolled a cigarette nor took a drink. Instead he remained fixed upon a man who was gutting himself with quiet fury. Leaving nothing of himself to hide behind or to live with afterward.

Matthew pulled the stopper from his bottle and sat there thoughtfully, then he took a drink. "Why didn't you tell them about the old man?"

Jason's hands fell away from his face and he looked past Matthew into the darkness.

"When Till returns here, he will put together another expedition. I'm to meet three Confederate officers at Torrey's Station out on the toll road. They're to work with the Tills, or what's left of the Tills. Whitehorse has made some kind of alliance with the Knights to protect the ore wagons and this mine. I think a man named Demerest has seen to it. You see, the Whitehorses have come to believe that old man wasn't just some thief. That he may be part of something else going on here. And maybe that money is finding its way into the coffers of another idea. If the Knights ever intend to take this state and keep it, they better have a firm hold on the treasuries. They're going to make a stand here, Matthew."

"You still haven't answered my question."

Jason rolled his cigarette between two fingers. "Arlen thinks you came downriver to Tulare. Thinks you might even be here at the mine."

Matthew eyed Jason suspiciously. "And who helped him get to that idea?"

Jason pushed the yellowing pages across the table. "You did, Matthew."

Matthew looked over the articles clipped from the *Flag* and recognized his work praising the old man and calling down the Tills for what they are, and issuing up warnings about the Knights and their dream for the 'keep' of California. A crooked smile crossed his face.

"Wilcox has been publishing copies of what I wrote and sent him." His eyebrows stiffened, and he stared at Jason. "I only signed them 'Letters From The West.' How did Arlen come to know it was me?"

"It was a certain flair to the insults against the Whitehorses that Arlen took particular note of. And the fact you'd disappeared after the beating he gave you."

Matthew lay the articles neatly one atop the other.

"If you're found here, you're to be killed."

Matthew sat back and stared at the pepperbox. "Is that it then?"

Jason scooped up the pistol with one hand and tossed it to Matthew. Fumbling to catch it, he dropped the bottle, and the laudanum slurped out into the dirt.

"Cock the hammer, Matthew."

He sat with both hands locked around the barrel.

"Cock the hammer!"

Matthew cocked back the hammer. Jason rested his hands on the table palms down. "You want to shoot me for what I've done?"

Matthew's eyes quickly looked down at Jason's hands then back up into his face.

"There's no tricks here, Matthew. I'm going to do nothing to fight back. Nothing. I just wish you'd hear me out and then…"

Jason looked down into the candle where specks of light formed a ring along the tin face around the flame.

"Matthew, I want to tell you…no…I need to…tell you…how sorry I am for what I did. How ashamed I am. The night we argued here. I am everything you thought I was. And worse. I want to tell Hetty how sorry I am. And the Mexican…I wish I could tell him. I've hurt everyone of consequence. I deserve no better than…"

His fingers plodded out an apprehensive line on the plank table face.

"I wish you could find it in your heart to forgive me. That's what

I wanted to ask you. Forgive me…"

Matthew's mouth went dry, and he could feel the empty room press on the back of his shoulders. He looked down at the pepper-box, but could only see his hands.

"You cunning charlatan." Then he looked up angrily. "We needed you."

Jason could barely nod.

Matthew felt his chest rattle and constrict.

"Shoot him!"

Both men turned. Hetty stood in the doorway. She stepped into the room. Her eyes hawked Jason's.

"You killed him!"

"I didn't kill him, but I had my part."

She looked at Matthew. "Shoot him before he hurts someone else."

Matthew's hand squeezed the barrel of the gun, and he looked between the two of them. He lay the pistol down in the sallow light of the table and shook his head. "No. I don't think I will."

She rushed the table. Before she could reach the pistol Matthew pulled it away. Her arms snaked through his. He stepped back and flung the pistol into the murk of the room. The trigger sprung. There was a charge of smoke and a shot that took out a clapboard.

Hetty turned on Jason. "You worked your magic again."

She slapped the candle tin at him and the oil spatter burned his shirt and face.

Matthew grabbed hold of her. "Get out!"

Hetty tried to lurch across the room as Jason backed through the doorway.

"Thank you, Matthew," he said.

• • •

To see you there in the path — to hear you now in your room — the voice of your broken heart becomes my voice. You and I, Hetty, we are both so much a part of all that keeps us apart at this moment. We are children of an afflicted house, you and I.

I think of your suffering. To be born crippled and treated like a pariah. To have your cousin turn you out of her house and her life. And now — the old man — to know that he is dead. How much of us is left after so much is lost?

I forgave him, Hetty, because I must. Because he, too, is the child of an afflicted house. Because he, too, like us, stands unforgiven. For things we have done which are wrong, for things we have done which are right, and for things we have done which are. Because we live, we hurt. Is our only purpose in life then our defense against each other? If I cannot forgive him, then I am my father. And if you cannot forgive him then you might as well change your name to Sarah. Is that the paradise we are struggling for? Or does that paradise come closer to the truth of what the word paradise originally meant, a garden for kings and queens. A pastime for the privileged. The home of divine rule and righteous indignation. I could tell you things I know about Jason in his own defense. I could remind you of Sacramento and the flood. I could quote to you my own mother's favorite passage from the Bible, and you know how little I think of the Bible: *Where sin abounds, grace much more abounds.* I could whisper to you of that night we lay together and we were both thinking of the same man.

But I would ask you to think about one thing. Think back to that day at the river. That morning we crossed the coach, against gun and stone. Against flag and drum. Against all mockery. That was who we were when we were at our best. That one moment, stranded around that rattling box torn with the current. Hanging on from axle to harness metal. With the very wheels of things breaking under us. At that moment we were who we always were. With all our strengths and failings. But we pulled together. And though it was never spoken of, I believe whatever we were was forgiven by the others. And in some small way, that enables us to forgive ourselves certain secrets sealed within us. But not one of us alone — not one alone — could have pulled that coach across. For me, this is another coach to cross.

Matthew.

• • •

Come morning Matthew stood in the doorway of his common room. Hetty sat against the cabin wall, knees pulled up against her chest. He sat beside her. Neither spoke as they watched the sky turn shell pink over the edge of the pines.

The muckmen began their weary line up the hill slope toward the founders' shaft. Ed was now among their number, since the burning of his camp on Dulcimera Creek. Shovel and pickax scythed across his shoulder. Matthew's letter fluttered between Hetty's fingers. She looked at him.

"Your mother named you well, Matthew."

CHAPTER TWENTY-SIX

The toll road to Los Angeles forded Weeping Creek at a bridge nine miles south of the Whitehorse Mine and two miles north of Torrey Station. The creek ran west, from the bridge, into the sloping yellow grasslands, and to the east, just beside it, drained into the slough known as the Bed of the Ton Tache. Lore has it that the creek was named as such in the year of the drought and the great plague of grasshoppers.

The day was hot and dry, and the air hung with the salt smell of slough water as Jason reached the edge of the bridge. Its flat board planks were wagon wide and tarred, the truss railings scarred and sun brittle.

As he tied off the Percheron to a scored post, he noticed a mulero squatting by a fire frying up a breakfast of atol and coffee. His mules, burdened under the weight of their aparejos, hitched and hawed in the frail shade.

Jason leaned against the saddle and looked across Weeping Creek where great willows guarded the roadside. Beyond the trees the road curled then chevroned up into the high grass foothills. He reached across his rig and undid the cordage that bound the old man's coat up behind the cantle. He pulled it loose and shook out the dust. He slipped one arm through a sleeve and then the other. He rolled the woolen cuffs up to clear the edge of his wrists and then reached into his saddle pack for the Volcanic's butt stock. He bolted it to the pistol grip. He slipped a lanyard through the stock ring, tied it off, and worked the lanyard over his neck and slid the rifle length repeating pistol under his coat.

The mestizo was watching him quietly from the brush, shaking the corn gruel across the face of an iron pan. When Jason turned, the mestizo's eyes creased on seeing the lion's head woven into the back of the coat.

Jason checked the load on the other Volcanic as he crossed the powdery gravel road and approached the man. He squatted beside him and in Spanish said, "Good morning."

The brown and sweating face stayed angled toward the business of the pan.

"If you've got some coffee to spare...I'll pay you for a cup."

The man looked up. He grabbed up a rag and shook the tin of coffee sitting on the fired kindling.

"I have enough coffee. And you don't have to pay."

Jason nodded then looked back up the road to where it joisted the ridgeline, for any sign of the officers. The man glanced at Jason's coat. The heavy caliber chink of frayed hole up near the back of the shoulder. The rusty print of blood. That black and scarlet maned head looming up out of the wool.

"Are you him?" asked the mulero in Spanish.

Jason turned to that brown face glancing at the coat and then up into his eyes.

"Are you him?"

Jason looked away slowly. He went back to staring at the bridge.

"No one could be him."

The mulero filled a tin with coffee and handed it to him. Jason stood. "After breakfast," said Jason, "you might consider finding a more quiet spot up the road."

Jason surveyed the bridge and the terrain along both sides of the creek as he sipped his coffee. He set the coffee tin on the flat sawed head of a support truss. He leaned down and rested his forearms on the railing and looked out over the standing water of the slough.

It was clear on into the horizon with long reefs of tule grass. Great flocks of egrets, white as winter clouds, fed. Suddenly small bands rose up on the chase. Their wings formed a great sail against the pale blue of the reach. They arced and circled and then just as quick descended, their calls guttural and echoing across the cienega. Looking over the slough it was as if the earth and sky had merged into one fluid presence, and all that was material and finite had become immaterial and infinite. He let everything just pass away for a time and merge with that before him, until the moment was broken by boots clodding along the plank boards.

He turned. Matthew rode up on an old plow horse. He was wiping the sweat and grime from his exhausted face as he dismounted and walked up beside Jason. "How did you get to be here?" asked Jason.

Matthew huffed erratically. He eyed the coat. "Hetty told me about the old man's coat. That belonged to him, didn't it?"

"It still does. How did you know I'd be here?"

"I sat up all night. I was thinking about why you didn't tell them the old man was dead. You lie, but come back. It puts a limit on the possibilities." He stared at Jason, "You mean to fight them."

Jason lifted the tin cup and drank.

"She said you could come back, Jason. It wasn't easy for her, but…"

Jason's eyes tightened.

Matthew let the rest of what he was going to say just trail off.

Jason noticed dust beyond where the road hollowed out the ridgeline. The wind came up from the east and breathed, then stilled, and the dust fell away.

"I want to ask you something," said Matthew.

Jason's eyes stayed vigilant on the road.

"The night before the expedition left. The black escaped. Was it you who helped him? Cause it wasn't Hetty."

Pockets of high grass seemed to blink at the sun, and three riders friezed up in the haze where the road crested.

"You better get off the bridge, Matthew."

"What?"

"Get off the bridge."

Matthew looked around and saw three riders make a slow approach against the heat.

"Get off the bridge."

"Jesus."

As Jason turned Matthew saw the stocked Volcanic slung under the frock coat. He grabbed hold of Jason's arm. "I'm not afraid."

The riders were lost to where the road curled into the arc of the willows just across the creek. Jason looked at Matthew again. "Get off the bridge."

"I killed a man, Jason. At Chinese Camp. I can do this."

"What you can do for me is get off the bridge. Please."

Matthew looked across Weeping Creek where a trident of riders advanced against the dust.

"Go on now," Jason whispered.

Matthew backed up and wound his way around the truss support at the near end of the bridge. The mulero watched Matthew squirrel down into the rocks then he stretched up and saw the riders coming. He lay his frying pan aside and grabbed up his willow whip and drove the mules off into the brush.

Matthew checked the load on his pepperbox as he watched Jason leaning against a pine truss. The riders reached the far end of the bridge. They slowed when they saw him and one of the men held out an arm and they drew in their mounts.

They were gaunt men all. With faces etched out of scabbard metal and beards timeless with dust. A ragged portage of belted Army Colts and rumpled flat crown hats. Their mounts were all alather and their legs speckled up to the haunches with road dirt. The leader eased his mount forward. Its hooves cobbled over the shaky planks. He called out to Jason, "Emmit Till?"

Jason did not answer.

The leader eased warily back in his saddle. "Did Mr. Whitehorse send you here to meet us?"

Jason did not answer.

"Are you deaf, man?"

Jason did not answer. He saw the leader begin to scan the brush, then he looked back at his men and said something that Jason could not make out. The smaller of the other two stepped down out of his saddle.

"Sir, will you back off the bridge and give us the road?"

• • •

Weeping Creek Bridge
Tulare County
June — 1862

The name of that well known bridge was brought to bear on the outcome of a gunfight this reporter bore witness to on the 27th of June, this year. Three Confederate officers sent under secret orders into the keep of Tulare County to help organize the Knights of the Golden Circle in their protection of the Whitehorse Mine and the eventual overthrow of the county were confronted on that very same bridge by the outlaw known as Greatheart.

He is the same man for whom the Whitehorse Mining Company not one month ago put together an expedition of twenty mercenaries to proceed into the hills with one mandate — hunt him down and kill him. It has been reported here that the expedition was wiped out to the last in the passes above San Lorenzo. Among the dead was one of the local magistrate's brothers, Bayard Till. A man known locally for his mendacity against the law, his hatred of local minorities and his personal sloth.

The gunfight at the bridge lasted less than half a minute. The volley fire from the officers' heavy caliber Colts swarmed the bridge in a pungent gray smoke as they rushed across, two on horseback and one afoot. But these shots were met head-on by a fusillade just as fierce from the belly of a huge repeating pistol bolted to a butt stock and wedged against the outlaw's hip.

With the very first shot, flocks of white egrets that had been feeding in the slough took to flight. The blue sky became a white banner from horizon to horizon. In the bedlam that was those first seconds, the lead officer's mount was hit, and as its forelegs crumpled, the hooves caught in the plank boards and man and mount turned headlong over. The mount's neck was broken as it fell atop the officer, crushing him. The sheer weight and velocity of the charge carried them straight into the outlaw. Man and beast and man were side-spilled into the support railings which shattered. The horse was avalanched into the creek twenty feet below. The officer's arm got caught in between two pine support beams, and he was left dangling from the bridge.

The outlaw had been thrown down on his back but was kept from being cast into the creek by a heavily corded anchor of pines that formed the center support truss for the bridge.

What happened next culminated in a matter of seconds. I am remiss to fill in all the details, for with the sun squarely behind the bridge pouring light through a wall of powdersmoke, the participants were no longer men but mere phantasms of men, fighting a war today for the promise of tomorrow.

This much I do know. The outlaw continued the fight from a sitting position, his back rooted against the stanchion post. The officer afoot had been hit a number of times as I could later verify from having seen the body. He had collapsed and died less than an arm's grasp from the outlaw. The other officer, he on horseback, made a complete pass of the outlaw and reached the far side of the bridge. Had he continued on, he might well have survived. But he made a second pass through that hazy tunnel of gunfire and at some point was hit with two rounds in the lung.

I did not know the fight was even over until I saw that frock coat with the lion's head stand. The outlaw approached the officer hanging from the support posts. He unsheathed an Arkansas toothpick and cut away at the coat of the caught arm that was reaching toward heaven. But heaven is a long way from Tulare County, isn't it Mr. Whitehorse?

— "Letters From The West"

CHAPTER TWENTY-SEVEN

Hetty poured kerosene from a bateo hewn out of cottonwood bark into five gallon tins. Once full she plugged the stopper hole with wadding then began on the flasks made of sheep and goat bellies, and then onto a double keg wallet slung over the back of a mule. She considered, there was enough now to burn the ground for miles but not so much you couldn't travel quickly.

As she made her way up from the storehouse to the cabin she saw Serranus out ahead of a wagon threading its way through the mining camp. What struck her wrong was the flock of muckmen crowding alongside and behind the Dearborn.

Crossing the bridge, she picked out snippets of conversation about the bore size and placement of the corpses' wounds. She pushed through a wall of muckmen, their heads perched over the wagon's sideboards. She toed up on the edge of her boots to find the bodies of the three strangers lying tailorwise.

"Is it anybody I'd be glad to see dead?" a man asked.

Hetty turned, there stood Ed Candles. "The war has finally come to Tulare," he said.

She took Ed aside, "You don't have to pickax for the White-horses. You might rather work for me."

• • •

When Hetty returned to the cabin, Matthew was there. He explained to her about that morning at the bridge. She sat at the table and listened with unusual reserve. When he was done, she asked him to wait at the cabin while she spoke with Jason alone. She made her way down the path to where he was kneeling by the river, washing his face with a neckerchief.

He was unbuttoning his shirt when he saw her struggling over the rocks. He stood.

"It's very hard for me, Jason, to stand across from someone who on the one hand I cared for, and the other hand, I hated."

Jason squatted beside his saddle pack. "Maybe I'm too much the poisoned well."

He looked down and opened his saddle pack. He took out a folded rag and in the rag was a fletching of tin, cut from the face of a can.

"Matthew told me about the bridge."

Jason nodded silently.

He wrapped the rag around the shank of tin. "Things will happen fast now. The Tills are quick. It won't be long before Emmit confronts me about this morning. And they already know about Matthew from what he wrote."

"Yes. He told me all that."

Jason glanced up at her cabin. He could see Matthew in the shadow of the breezeway. "They'll come to your door at some point."

"When they do, they won't find a light waits for them."

"You won't get many more ore wagons. They'll see to it."

"Yes. But Matthew and I have a plan. They stay out in open country now." She leaned forward. "We've seen them camp in these small stands of trees where the grass is waist high. I've loaded three mules with kerosene. If we could get close enough to their camp, we could burn the ground around them. I haven't thought it all out, but we could try. We could follow them and try."

He rubbed his jawbone and watched her closely. He lay the rag down. He finished unbuttoning his shirt and took it off. She saw the long streak of wounds and sunburn down his back and the scabbed mouth of an earmark stitched across his chest. He picked up the bound tin shank.

"What happened there?"

"I had to be taught a lesson."

She watched as he puckered the skin along the scar and began to fleck at the silk sutures with the tin's edge.

"I know I failed you," he said. "I know I hurt you. And it can't be changed. That I'll live with, and all what goes with it. But I swear... I'll walk with you the last mile of the way."

• • •

It was past midnight when they led the mules packed with kerosene into the foothills. Hetty was riding her thick plowhorse, Matthew a gray faced mule. Jason stepped out the trail ahead.

At dawn they reached the grasslands. Within the hour they came upon the treads of the ore wagon and guards where they had drubbed a roadway through the brakes. The trail led north along Lake Tulare. The day became rancorous with heat. By afternoon the ground dust had eaten into their clothes and eyes. They passed a band of wild ponies grazing between them and the lake. They were strung out for a quarter of a mile. Ponies of every color and size imaginable. From a whittled down á Pelouse to a rangy zebra dun.

The air was thick with the scent of their hides. The herd caught the smell of their mounts and mules, and they began to follow along their flank. This went on for mile after mile with cries and whinnies passing from one clade to another. Hetty, Jason and Matthew watched this armada trail north with them through a sea foam of yellow dust. Matthew began to imagine that by some sublime divination or clairvoyance, the wild horses understood they were on a calling, and like those mounts at the center of the solar wheel, they marched along to offer guidance and strength.

Jason rode on ahead after spotting an oar of brushfire against the ruddled plates of sunset. He took with him paper and pencil. Hetty and Matthew waited with the mules in a gully treed with buckeye. The heat was still bad, everything dry. Perfect for burning.

• • •

The Percheron slogged its way down through the briars of the trough. Jason climbed out of the saddle. "They're less than a half mile from here, forted up in a thicket."

He knelt down and unfolded the paper detailing what he'd seen. "They got one of the wheels off the axle and are trying to solder a crack in the casement iron, so I think they're parked for the night."

Hetty saw where he had marked spotters at each end of the thicket and the horses tied to a runner beyond the wagon.

"Can we burn them out of there?"

"You can't burn the ground fast enough so they can't ride out and fight us. And we can't meet that fight. We have to root those mounts out of that thicket. On foot, when that ground starts to burn, they'll be no better off than quail."

He looked down toward the lake where that mottled haze of wild ponies worked their way along a drifting surf. "How well can you ride, Hetty?"

She looked to where he was looking. "Are you going to try and drive those horses through them?"

"I see no other way."

"I can stay aboard."

"What'll I be doing?" said Matthew.

"Sorry, Matthew, but you can't ride worth a crap so you're left to bring up the mules and all that kerosene."

Matthew stared at those gin faced brutes, sniffing for pitcher plants through the waist high jaundiced weeds. "Well if that isn't the way of it, me and the ass end of things."

"You better start off now, Matthew. And stay on the turnpike. When you see us, whip up those mules."

By the time Matthew reached a short rise at the edge of the lea, he could make out Jason, now wearing the old man's coat, and Hetty as they worked their mounts down a sandy berm. They were waving blankets and turning the ponies back upon the breakwater and driving them upshore.

Ahead, Matthew saw a black holt of junipers skewbald where the grassland had settled out. He put the whip to the mules and they jaunted up the turnpike braying like old men. The ponies cleared the edge of the lea farther to the east. They were still dust, beyond the reach of sound. But they were moving swiftly and their manes and tails hackled a slender feathered wing and the ground seemed to break away beneath them.

One of the guards observed the dust and eased his way past the jacked ore wagon. At first glance it was nothing more than beauty itself, and he called out to the others and they ceased their welding and the making of coffee and their lazy conversation to watch the mustangs turn apart the dusky earth.

Another of the guards noticed Matthew crossing the vega as he flayed his mules. The men talked amongst themselves then one of the guards climbed up onto the back of the wagon from where he saw Jason swing out from the tail of the band and quirt his carbine up and over and between the ears of the Percheron.

A sparked thunderclap. The men rushed to rifle and mount. But the mustangs had thrashed their way too close, tearing a vast roadway through the windwheeled brush. And Hetty, chasing after them with her shotgun, drove those ponies down into the sinkhole of that thicket in a wail of dust.

Matthew jumped from his saddle and hammered iron ring spikes into the ground to tie off the mules' leads. Jason swung downwind of the thicket to cut off any line of escape. In the fleeing dust, all he saw were the wheelers' and guards' mounts scatter in a flock, all tethered to one line and trampling one of the guards who was caught up by the snake of that leather thong. He swung the Percheron around and waited for anyone to clear that scarp of dust, but none did.

They had taken to the trees, shimmying and clawing up the spine bark, or jumping into the bed of the wagon as if the ore itself was enough ballast to keep hold of the shaking ground.

Matthew was spilling out the belly bags of kerosene in a fire line when Hetty jerked in the plowhorse. She eeled out of the saddle and stumbled and came up crawling, and she grabbed two tins of kerosene and rattled up a curving fire line in the opposite direction from Matthew.

The horses deltaed through the thicket and a duskling wave settled out. Jason heard the first quick tings of rifle fire. He saw guards running for position among the trees, and he jerked the Percheron around and up to a mule's back of stone, where he could watch every quarter of the copse.

A foray of riflemen plucked through the welter grass toward Hetty and Matthew, and the ground before them began to spit with dust. Hetty rushed over to a mule and grabbed a torch from a bow bag slung across its pack saddle. A rifle ball seared past her. The mule was hit in the chest and sunk forward on its knees. She hid behind the convulsing belly and lit the torch.

The ground startled up red. The wind driven fire devoured the brush that shriveled up in black smoke. The riflemen retreated before the flames into the holt.

Hetty and Matthew led the crying mules along the length of the line and spilled out more kegs of kerosene. Within minutes the thicket was engulfed with an ashen snowy soot. The guards were left to gasp on their desperation as they argued on how best to try and make a stand.

Jason waited, his Sharps carbine resting on his hip. He could make out those human figures against a lead glass gray smoke pincered between the bent tree trunks. And then a large man with wild gray hair came forward waving a rifle. His white shirt a truce tie knotted to the barrel. He could be heard, ceding their position and the ore.

Whether this was the truth or not, Jason understood that to leave them alive was to leave themselves vulnerable. He let that withering white flag judge the fall of the wind. And then he fired.

Later they walked among the smoldering dead. Their faces masked against the incendiaried air, carefully stepping through pockets of flame as they stole away with the orr, and leaving the rest to the wind.

CHAPTER TWENTY-EIGHT

Whitehorse sat at his campaign desk in the den. He listened to the rain fall across the roof.

"I don't think you should go, Pop. I have a sense something isn't right with this."

Whitehorse looked across the room to Arlen, who sat at the octagonal poker table putting the final turn to a cigarette. Arlen looked down at the *Flag* and the article he was certain Christman had written about the three officers killed at Weeping Creek Bridge.

"You can be sure Demerest read this."

"I'm sure he has."

"Well, something must be wrong or why does he send you a note to ride down to Hunter's Point in the middle of a storm to one of his graving docks."

Whitehorse sat listening to the dull hum of the rain along the eaves and he could almost smell the taste of Baltimore tidewater. He looked at the brick sitting on his desk, there to remind him of what he was from.

"I'm sorry, Pop."

"For what?"

"For bringing Jason Clay into this." Arlen struck a match against the brimstone. "Everything in that article is what we spoke of."

Whitehorse's jaw whaled. "Christman, I can understand. But Clay? What could the Mexican have offered? What persuasion is it?"

Whitehorse saw the mozo bring his mount up the flooding ghat of a hillside from the barn, "You better make plans, Arlen. I need you to go down into Tulare to take charge there."

"Well, it's about time. I'll bury them both in the same box."

Whitehorse took a flask from his desk drawer, then a hooded oilskin from the coatrack.

"Are you bringing a gun?"

Whitehorse slipped a revolver out of the pocket of the oilskin.

Arlen followed his father out onto the veranda. Below, the city was nothing more than a faint articulation of rooftops foundering in the mist.

"Arlen, if something should ever happen to me, you burn my body."

"What?"

"I won't be put in the earth. I won't be boxed and buried with common men. I won't be held down by the ground. You burn the body. You hear?"

Arlen stood there uncomfortably as his father climbed into the saddle.

"Son. We have foundries under the eye of one government. And a mine under the eye of the other. If we don't manifest our own course between the two, we'll be blinded by both. For Thomas Jefferson is as much the whore as Jefferson Davis."

• • •

A boot kicked Ed's back as he slept. He cried out. He was yanked upright. A burlap sack was tied around his head and bound. He was hauled to his feet and taken from the storage barn to the woods. "If you mean to kill me —" He was flung to the ground somewhere near the creek.

"You work for the North woman now?"

Ed recognized Emmit's voice. "Yeah. She hired me for the storehouse."

"Too good for the mine?"

"The pay here was better is all. And I don't have to spend so much time...in the dark."

Ed's head tilted up slightly.

"Do you know a man named Jason Clay?" asked Emmit.

"No. I don't."

"Tall man. Black hair. Dark skin. Likes to say he's French."

"I don't know this man."

"You do know a man named Christman? Matthew Christman?"

Ed's head came around slightly as he recognized Serranus' voice passing alongside him.

"I do. Yeah."

Emmit asked, "Is he a friend of yours?"

"I knew his family back east. I haven't been home in years. He was passing through so he stopped to give me news, is all."

"Do you know where he is now?"

"No."

"Where is the North woman?" asked Emmit.

"Went up to San Lorenzo for supplies."

"He's no goddamn help," said Serranus. "Not John Chinaman's best friend."

Emmit took Ed and dragged him back to the edge of the woods.

He yanked the sack from his head. The two men, alone now, stood face to face in darkness.

"Listen to me, Chinaman," said Emmit. "If you hand over either of those men, there'll be a reward in it. I know too, that you hate us in principle. And that you might try and outslick us. Everything is in play here. Blood and moon are on the rise. What's to stop me from killing you? Nothing. I just don't ride too far out ahead of good reason. You do the same, now."

· · ·

Whitehorse stood by the capstan looking down into the mud where the boy's body lay. He was probably not any older than Arlen. He was just a great patch of boiled drying blood.

"Do you recognize him?" asked Demerest.

Whitehorse did not, and shook his head.

"He's a Union officer."

The hard drizzle ran in pin lines across the boy's stippled skin.

"What happened to him?"

"We put him in the steam box that's for shaping timbers."

Whitehorse looked over at the thirty foot long coffin. Steam was drifting up like spirits off the edges of the damp wood.

"Shaped him pretty good," said Demerest.

Whitehorse glanced at Demerest. "What were you trying to get from him?"

"The names of infiltrators, of course." Demerest pushed his jaw out. "Come with me."

Whitehorse followed him past a half a dozen mismatched sheds that looked like they had spilled up with the breakers.

"Whitehorse, I hold you responsible for the three officers I sent to the mine."

"I'm sending Arlen down country to see to things. We'll run these fellas down."

Demerest gave him a hard look. "So you say."

Whitehorse hung on the remark, remembering the story Demerest had told him about the slave.

They made their way past a revenue cutter that had been shored up in a graving dock and came to a row of greaseways where a steamer sat in the mud, cut in half, and was in the process of being elongated. Demerest led Whitehorse up a gangway and into the black aft hull of the steamer.

"Some of ours don't trust you, Whitehorse." Demerest looked down into the hull and called out. A lantern flared across the skin of the black iron boiler, and there Whitehorse saw two men standing over a bound and gagged Union officer.

"Come on," said Demerest.

Whitehorse followed Demerest through the dank underbelly of the steamer. Past crate and shoring. To where they were standing over the officer who lay amidst rusting dismantled cleats.

"Do you know this man?" Demerest asked.

Whitehorse stared at Colonel Madsen as long as it took to make the lie believable. "No. I don't know him."

Demerest looked at one of his men. "Take the gag off of him."

The man knelt and pulled the gag away from Madsen's mouth.

"I want to know the names of the men who have tried to infiltrate our 'castle.' I know that's why you're here in San Francisco."

The officer's eyes warily drifted from Demerest to Whitehorse.

"If you don't speak up, I'll have you shot."

The officer looked down into the black well of the boiler.

Demerest put out his hand, and one of his men slipped him

a Grapeshot. Demerest took the revolver and handed the grip to Whitehorse.

"Recent events have raised certain questions," said Demerest. "Some suggest you might have made an arrangement with men like this officer to infiltrate our ranks and pass along the identities of our hierarchy. And that as part of the "arrangement" they would turn a blind eye to the Knights protecting your mine in Tulare."

"It's a matter of blood then," said Whitehorse.

"It's a matter of faith."

Whitehorse took the revolver.

"Long live the nation," said the boy officer.

"Which nation?" added Demerest.

Whitehorse aimed the revolver at the boy's heart.

For one moment the boy wondered what it was like to die for a cause at the hand of a man who couldn't care less. Who was neither friend nor enemy. Just a face behind the gun. And he found himself fearful and praying for some chance not to die for his beliefs. But that was not to be. Buckshot tore a smoking hole out of his uniform. His chest heaved once, shuddered, stilled.

Whitehorse handed the revolver to Demerest. "Are you rectified now?"

"I am."

Whitehorse's wrath seemed to keep him standing where he was. "It's Baltimore all over again," said Whitehorse.

"What?" said Demerest.

"Do you remember how I told you when I was in the mills, I came upon those surveyors planning for a Navy shipyard?"

"Yes."

"And how I went and stole the plans and borrowed the money?"

"Yes."

"I borrowed nothing. No one would lend a raw foundryman like me anything. No lenders. For they're all thieves and couldn't be trusted any better than me. And no dilettante anywhere would. No one of your class would."

Whitehorse could see that night again, and he could hear it in the rain up along the hurricane deck. "I knew from the maids, who slept with the owner of the foundry, where he kept his money. Maids are like blooded hounds when it comes to that. So I went to the owner's house one night and waited till he slept. I broke in. As big as I was, I was quiet. Desperation makes you that quiet. I slunk up beside that bed, and I beat that old man with an iron chain. I beat that old bastard to death. I whipped him so hard and so long that chain caromed off the bedpost and tore a piece of my chin out. And I didn't just whip him to death for the money. I whipped him to death for being a stinkin' dilettante."

He slipped a hand into the pocket of his oilskin.

"And what is all this to me? An insult? A warning? When it's you who—"

"Did you think you could Lord me with this killing? That I was a field hand like your daddy's niggers?"

"Well, now we get to it," said Demerest. "I have something else for you to consider. Might the likes of that trash lying there be behind the robbing of your mine? That while you made a deal with them, they were exploiting you all the while. Think of what it says if it were true. What is the definition of a field hand? And remember the adage...'As a whore, is a whore.'"

Whitehorse wasn't sure if it was his temper or his judgment that pulled the trigger. But he fired right through the pocket of the oilskin and the charge flashed a white hole all the way to deliverance. Then he turned the gun on the others who were there with Demerest.

Later he stood in the rain a long time between the two halved steamer hulls on planks strewn across the mud.

CHAPTER TWENTY-NINE

For two days Ed loaded wagons and kept an apprehensive eye toward the road. Each night he could not sleep as he worried about whether he should stay long enough to even warn them.

While Ed was kindling up a dinner fire in the kitchen shed, he saw Hetty framed in the owllight of the window leading a party of bedraggled mules out of the woods. They labored slowly, hitching and stopping, and he saw Matthew walking with a cane switch at the rear of this motley troupe. Then lastly a man riding a deep chested old Percheron.

It was Hetty who first saw him shouting for them to stay where they were.

• • •

They circled up in a small open plat among the trees. Ed looked at Jason. "Are you the other one they're looking for?"

"Yes."

"They claim you're wanted for a murder in San Francisco of a

Union soldier."

"It's not a claim."

Ed jabbed black tobacco into his pipe with a dirty thumb. "Do you know what troubles you've brought me to?"

Hetty went over to one of the mules. She loosened up the cincha, and from the aparejo took a small sugar sack and handed it to Ed. "This is to keep you out of the mine. And away from the Tills."

He let the weight of the bag buoy against his palm. He untied the string loop and poured out a jigger full of gold nuggets. His eyes floated from one to the other. He noticed the nuggets were covered with soot and ash. He ran his thumb along the powdery black and then licked it.

"Charred wood. Talk about an unusual circumstance. You're to be congratulated. You seem to be the first who have panned hearths and found gold."

Jason walked past Ed to the edge of the woods. He looked across the river to that wooden glacier of a mine hunkered along the hillside. Through the turrets of the shelf house, scalded black, came a dark strain of men. Immigrants of the iron world, changing shifts. Moving through the battle smoke and fire of the ball mill and chemical tank.

Ed gave the loop on the sugar sack a tug. He walked over to the mules and looked inside the aparejo. It was a filled belly of pouches and burlap pokes. He gave the whole of it a shake and it sounded like a mountain's worth of talus on the loose. "Why you goddamn skeullums. You're blacker than this mule."

Hetty walked over to Jason. "You keep staring at the mine? Why?"

Jason hovered around a thought. "My father was an officer with Napoleon's army. A sound officer, too. When he took me hunting up along the Hudson River, he would talk of the military and how their plans were laid out. When you fight one man, you must eventually strike him down. But when you fight an army, you need only to strike at their pride. Strike at that which gives them strength."

Matthew turned to listen to Jason.

"We don't have many fights in us. How many ore wagons could we get? Not a mine full, I'll tell you that."

Hetty looked across the river where a stria of campfires and chemical tanks traced a burning altered hillside.

"The mine?"

"What does it mean to Whitehorse?" said Jason. "And to the Knights?"

She stared through the trees. Her eyes were black with the thought of it. "It's only so much wood," she said. "It would burn like anything else."

"And we ain't bad burners," said Matthew as he took a drink. He then wiped his mouth and looked up at Ed. "It could be blown out of the ground. That rat maze of tunnels under the hillface would probably cave in like so much salt under the sheer weight of it."

Ed listened and watched them all without discrimination. Just so much a pound for madmen escaped from some lunatic asylum. "Well, you people are a feast. You want to dismantle that mine. Burn it. Blow it. It's all the same. You have a better chance of flying to heaven on moths' wings."

Jason glanced at Matthew. "And heaven's a long way from here, isn't it Monsieur Purloin?"

Matthew smiled at his own words.

Jason walked over to Ed. "You mined that pit, right?"

"I dug beside the rats, yeah."

"How much to draw us a map of that place? Where everything

is. Above ground and below."

"I want no part of it."

"How much?"

"What good would it do you? They got shifts that come and go with the clock. Pauper sun, meets pauper moon. And between the men working the heavy crushers and the ball mill and the vats, and the loafers and drunks sleeping off a bum's rush by the headframe, it's a damn anthill up there. You'd need a cholera epidemic to clean out them people, so you had time to charge the place so it burns."

Matthew explained to Jason, "Ed is skilled with explosives and charges and the like." A moment of bleak reckoning. "Ed has a background with artillery. Isn't that right, Ed?"

With a look of misgivings, Ed answered, "My skill went with my nobility."

• • •

We sat up most of the night there in that plat. What Ed had told us was true. We watched from the trees and there was never a time there wasn't enough muckmen at that slatted anthill to go around.

I sat listening to us talk and I wondered...Can two men and a woman form a line that can be seen for miles? Is this just folly. Isn't folly always the first word in describing an insurrection?

For that is what we are now. We are insurrectionists. We are part of no army. We have sworn no sacred oath before our fathers in the city square. We wear no hauberk of Church or State. We have no legal court to scapegoat our deeds. We have no medals; we are paid no scrip. But what a soldier is, we are, or will become. And what a murderer is we are, or will become.

And what is necessary or horrifying we are, or will become. And what may be worthwhile, we are, or will become. And what will happen...will. And what will not...we will be left with. If we are left at all.

• • •

In the morning Hetty came to us. She remembered that on Christmas Day, Election Day, and Independence Day, the mine had shut down. That between the drinking and the fireworks and festivities the mine was an empty shell. And we began to see a way. Independence Day, which is but eleven days from now, became set in our minds. It would be the day we attempted to give the Whitehorse Mine back to the earth.

CHAPTER THIRTY

Jason rode northeast for a day. He stayed well windward of the flats where the remains of the ore wagon lay flaking in the sun. Jason had read over the itinerary the Lord gave him for the Blue Heaven Traveling Bar and Orchestra. If he rode all night, he might still be able to catch him at Solomon's Hill.

It was the nooning hour when Jason walked his Percheron into the flash mining town of Solomon's Hill. Originally it was just a Mexican settlement along the Mariposa River called Azulear de Calderon for the blue copper hills that formed its western windbreak. There had been then only the small plaza with a faceless adobe church, brush ramadas and a mud hole well. Now, over three thousand miners picked at the hills. There were joss houses and public bake ovens and dozens of mercantiles who were in the midst of a price gouging war that was setting a standard in the sorceries of business.

As Jason moved through the filthy streets, his mood darkened. He passed a platoon of Union troops bivouacked alongside a farrier. He passed a motley handful of Privates trying to impress some black-eyed girls into a pulqueria. Then up an alley, more Union troops were circled around two cocks tearing at each other in a flurry of caws and feathers.

He was sure he'd be recognized in a face here, or glance there. The sweat wilted against his neck, when a voice called out, "Jason Clay."

Jason neither stopped nor turned. The voice called out again and his name carried through the crowded street. It was the old man who had bunked in the room next to his in San Francisco.

"Goddamn, Langston."

"Alive and brand new, right down to my daisy roots, boy." He weaved up beside Jason with bourboned breath. "Are things all right with you now?"

"They are not."

The old man stared at the troops, ringside the flaying cocks in the alley. Jason took him by the arm. They headed up onto a porch and behind a trellis of crimson bougainvillea where they could watch the troops pass. "Why are the troops here?"

"Why? The smelter half a mile east of town. The Solomon Hill Company. There's been a copper run here, boy. This town supplies most of the blue metal for the Union Army. And they brought in all these bog trotters to protect the place against attack or sabotage from the red hats and the Golden Circle."

Jason leaned against a stub of rail. He looked the old man over. Langston was wearing a fine silk derby and a new haberdashed black linen suit, and there was barely a few weeks of dust on him.

"Looks like you've done alright."

"Me and the Dane caught the elephant by the boke and man-handled his bunghole. Boy, we hit copper. And there's nothing like a good war to drive up the price of copper."

He shook Jason's hand. "I owe you, Jason. If it wasn't for you…"

Jason looked across the street, there was a Union Jacket looking their way. Jason turned. "The Blue Heaven is set up here. Do you know where?"

• • •

Jason came upon the Lord's wagons and tables within the ring of a stone corral. He passed under a vast sheet of painted sky that arched the gateway. The orchestra played from a dusty stand and this well of a corral was so packed with bettors they were perched along the rim of the stone abutment.

When the Lord saw Jason he cocked up a smile that just as swiftly withered. "Glad to see you, son. But I would have bet there's a little too much hint of blue around this 'homeric' settlement for your taste."

"I took my chances just to tempt you."

They sat under the flowing limbs of an el roble that had been skirted with sheets against the dust. While they talked Coco sat on the stone fence nearby and listened, as he kept an eye to order over the betting tables.

Jason lay out the canvas of an imposing, but deadly shill. He used a hand drawn map of the broken valley and mine. "The orchestra should be set up along the river here, just east of the bridge. There's plenty of room for your game tables and bar. Keep a group of mouths working the pack, make sure none of them muckmen drift up toward the mine."

The Lord studied the map. Jason smoked.

"How far is it from the mine to the river?"

"Four to six hundred yards."

"What is that ground between them?"

"Slopefront. Tents, huts, squabble grass."

"There'll be fire."

"That there will. You could lose your tables and bar in the panic, or in the fire after we blow in the mine. So you get to name your fee." He offered the map to the Lord. "Will you, is the question? I know you can."

The Lord sat back. He stared at the map. "I've always said the shill is a beautiful thing to watch. A man takes another man's money and humiliates him in the process, and he goes home poorer on two accounts." His head ticked then tocked from one side to the other. "I've already lost one temple of chance to fire."

"Will you do it, Miguel?"

The Lord leaned forward and rested his hand on Jason's. His eyes were coolly troubled and his cheek wrinkled.

"They don't deserve it, son."

"I'll pay you your price."

"And if I don't come?"

"We go short the fairbank."

"Of course. We are little more than our limitations, it seems."

"Miguel…"

"What brought you to this?" asked the Lord.

Coco half turned.

"Is it because of your blood? Or the blood around you?"

Coco watched as the Lord asked Jason again. And he watched as Jason didn't answer. But if he had his voice, he could tell why a good burning might be in order.

Coco sat on that stone wall beneath the sun, and he remembered his princess mother walking down the sand of Whyteete to greet the missionaries, only to be shunned, for all she wore were shoes and an umbrella. He could see his family become evangelized so they might be used as oxen to pull the Protestant disciples in carts along Fort Street in Hanaroora. And their skin was such a disgraceful sight to the ladies' good Christian conscience, they were made to wear shirts while they yoked their wheeled sleds through mud. He watched Fair Heaven become home to measles and venereal disease and white merchant ways. And when he fought against the yoke, he was made to live on water and poha jam in a coral stone prison at the end of Fort Street. Yes, he would have a dozen reasons why a good burning was in order.

Before the Lord decided, Coco noticed a platoon of Union troops spreading out along the street. A few swung up toward the joss houses and opium den. A few made their way down tavern row. Coco stood. He started toward the tent. He saw a Master Sergeant and two troops approaching the stone corral. He pushed back the sheet.

The Lord and Jason looked up. Coco chevroned three fingers across his arm. Both men stood.

"Where?" asked Jason.

Coco pointed toward the far end of the corral where the three soldiers were just pressing through the crowd at the gate. Coco reached for a shotgun he kept resting against the tree.

Jason turned. "I need an answer, Miguel."

"In my own time. Now get out of here."

Jason sneaked out along the stone ring, staying within reach of the trees. He saw one of the troopers moving among the monte tables searching out faces. He saw another stand up on the wall and watch. Jason slid down a scarp and through the brush and followed a cobble dry creek bed to a spinney of cottonwoods past the far end of the corral where the Percheron was tied off with half a dozen others.

He looked out through a drape of leaves into the clearing. The horses lazed. A spool of dust from a scraping hoof lifted. The distant voice of bettors. But nothing more. He moved out of the dark length of shadow across the sand. He sided up along the Percheron and slipped one boot into the oxbows, when a hollow faced hammer locked.

"Just keep the way you are now."

A figure moved like a clock hand into half view. Eyes snagged out from under a rippled kepi's brim. The bore of a Joslyn not five feet from Jason's heart.

The trooper asked, "Your name Clay?"

"No."

"We'll see." His tinny Maine voice shouted out for the Sergeant. It carried well enough so the trooper on the stone wall weeded up and listened, and the next shout he returned as he jumped down and shoved his way through the pack line of miners.

Men were shouting down to the trooper now from somewhere up in the trees. The trooper answered back, but his eyes never left Jason, and in those moments, a form hulled out of the trees beyond the trooper. Jason saw Coco raise a shotgun and fire.

The trooper grabbed at his back as he was thrown forward.

Jason swung up into the saddle.

The shot had rattled up past the panicked voices.

Jason racked the Percheron forward and Coco tossed him the shotgun as he rushed by.

• • •

"We'll be leaving here in the morning," said the Lord. "I'm sure Tulare County is particularly mundane this time of year and in need of a good fleecing."

The Lord went back to studying the map Jason had left him. But Coco, instead of going about his duties, just stood by the table.

The Lord looked back up at him. "What?"

His thick round forehead wrinkled above the broken nose. He ran a fist into one palm, then pointed at the map Jason left, then at himself, then he ran his fingers across his palm and out toward the map.

"You should never take the time of your slavery to heart." He then pointed at Coco's shoulder where the dates of the death of the kings of his island were a lineage of tattooed ink. "You want to go with him? Are you looking to add your date to that arm?"

Coco caught the wind in his hand and cast it aside.

"From firefly to fire eater, I'm to lose them all." Disgusted, he waved both arms at this bull of a man. "Go wait outside."

CHAPTER THIRTY-ONE

Within the cold gothic walls of the First Church of Christ, Charles Julius Whitehorse was always struck by the odd feeling of serenity he saw on the faces around him.

As was his custom, he sat inconspicuously toward the rear of the church, for he held to the adage it is best to downplay one's wealth and position before God's eyes on earth, for they are both jealous and hungry, in the name of the Lord.

As the priest chanted the names of the saints out in order, Whitehorse weighed the options before him. The morning after he had killed Demerest, he'd gone directly to Misters Latham and Holmes at their Chandlery and Ship Builders Offices on Market Street. They were both friends of Demerest and members of the same secret caste.

The three men sat in a cramped second story office lined with drafting tables and a rolltop desk. The air ran musty with ink and damp, and they uncomfortably listened as Whitehorse told them he'd shot Demerest and the Union officer. He explained he would not be coerced by any man, or group of men, into killing as an act of faith. If, indeed, that's what it was. He'd killed the officer because it became necessary, once he could be identified, to protect himself and his ambitions with the Knights. But he would not stand for it afterward. If Demerest had in any way suspected that he might be part of some sabotage against their cause, and that he could be made to come to heel, then he'd deserved no better than any Union pig. Whitehorse also told them he was prepared to walk away from the organization at any time. And Misters Latham and Holmes could convey this to the proper officers of the San Francisco "castle."

When he was done, he probed their faces for any signs of character. But they were merchants, and they had long since learned the secret of a placid face in negotiating their lives.

Now, as he sat watching the congregation and choir chant "ora pro nobis" after each fallen Saint, what he'd seen in those merchants' faces he saw too now in the faces around him. It was some strange lean toward a lifeless hold on fealty and forgiveness. Somehow in a short passing of time, a whole generation had become absorbed into this one state. It was not that they believed in fealty and forgiveness. It was not that this was some spiritual transfiguration. It was only that they did not believe in themselves without fealty and forgiveness. And while they listened to the New Testament lorded down on them from the pulpit, a newer, darker testament was spoken from their hearts and for a time Whitehorse became unsettled.

He saw the country had become a nation of merchants and ministries. There would never be again a world view or grand vision. There would never be a Caesar, or a Christ for that matter. All that was left were vestrymen. All bowed plumage to the throne of God or to what God had thrown across the merchants' table. They had become some knitted investiture of families, and each was one weak pass of wool through the loom. They were a national mourning shawl.

The business of man and God's business had now become part of some trite merchant's face. For the first time merchants and ministries stood together as part of a class so ignoble, so tied to their daily bread, so much in need of each other's complicity in defense of their paltry dreams and pathetic rituals, they would, of course, be willing to forgive freely. For by forgiving others, they bought their alliance here on earth, as they hoped to buy their alliance with heaven. Forgiveness had become the ultimate act of weakness.

This knowledge, in some way, gave him advantage in his dealings with them. He saw better why Holmes and Latham and the Knights had been willing to understand the situation he'd been in, and even though there was animosity and he'd made certain enemies within their rank, he was still in good stead. But it was not because he had outsmarted them, or because they feared him and so would not try for retribution, and it was not because they wanted the mine, or his cunning or his leadership. What they wanted was his complicity in agreeing to be like them.

As he sat there in that church, in that pew, he came to see that a part of himself had been chipped away in the process. But was it their doing, or his own undoing that had caused it?

• • •

At the appointed hour Whitehorse made his way across town and out toward Golden Gate. The shore there was covered with a bracken of driftwood. Miles of it stretching down the coast. The dry kindling of a thousand floods and the rushing tide of spring rains all washed up together in a graying miasma.

He walked along the sand, his hands folded behind his back. There were two islands just outside the bay. They were covered with sea lions that barked and tumbled into the ocean. Great growling faces with noses to the sun.

Within an hour, four Union officers in civilian clothes showed up on horseback. One was the Captain with a withered arm who Whitehorse had met with Colonel Madsen. He believed his name was Firebaugh.

The men walked together out past the rim of the peninsula poisoned with a thick salt carried on the wind. Whitehorse explained to them about Demerest and how he had been forced to kill Colonel Madsen. They listened silently. The Captain pinioned his withered arm between the buttoned brass of his coat.

The officers were disgusted and angry, and they swore revenge against those responsible. And although they didn't have the faces of a merchant, they had a merchant's heart, for that is what they would be after the war, and any shard of doubt about the truth of Whitehorse's words was outweighed by their need for his complicity in their future.

It was then Whitehorse understood that confronting them over what Demerest had said about a secret Union operation behind the robbing of his mine was pointless. These were the merchants of tomorrow, and they would hand him the same answer, whether it was true or not. As it was the price of doing business.

CHAPTER THIRTY-TWO

June 26

Hetty went across the river to the magistrate's office. She was appropriately shocked at the news she had rented a room to two men with such base character and criminal background. She relayed to Emmit and Serranus every possible lie about our desires and destinations. She show'd notes I supposedly left behind. Hetty even went so far as to worry for her own safety should Jason and I return.

No sign of Jason.

• • •

June 27

Bad luck has arrived. Arlen Whitehorse rode in today with twenty men.

Still no sign of Jason.

• • •

June 28

Arlen crossed the river this afternoon and spent hours with Hetty. He said that if Jason returned he wanted to make some arrangement to talk with him.

Arlen worries her. He's not like the Tills, which I could have told her.

Still no sign of Jason.

• • •

Hetty lay in bed unable to sleep. She was fearful about why Jason had yet to return. She tried to remember that fear also was a testament to God's resources within us. It told us how deep was the well of all emotions that we might draw strength or comfort or honor or faith from.

There was a turn of rock somewhere. She sat up quietly and peeled back the canvas curtain. She looked out the window. Tree branches moved in the wind like great black birds. And there, a man she didn't recognize slid up out of the rutted ground and moved toward the side of the cabin.

Hetty rose and reached for her shotgun. She came up the dark black breezeway.

"Don't go firing it, Hetty."

"Jason." The gun eased back. "Arlen is here."

"I know," he said. "We got back this afternoon. We've been watching from the hills."

"We?" she said.

He stepped around her and called out, "Come on."

She turned. Coco slipped around the wall and down through the breezeway.

"This is the woman I told you about."

He nodded. He tapped his hands together and lay them open like he was holding a book.

"Yeah. Make your way to the mine."

Coco headed down the breezeway toward the river.

"Who is he?" asked Hetty.

"A bummer I used to travel with." Jason called out again, "And draw a map of those buildings like when you ink that flesh of yours."

Coco slipped past the moonlight.

"What happened to his voice?"

Jason kept watching till Coco was moving up out of the tules and onto the bridge.

"Back home on Sandwich Island, he stabbed a missionary and the English caned him in a prison there. He wouldn't come to heel well enough, so they made a furnace out of his throat. They burned his vocal cords."

Hetty stared up at Jason who watched Coco slip into that harbor of tents along the hillside.

"I'm glad you're safe," she whispered.

• • •

With only a rille of light from a tallow candle tin, they crouched around handsewn bags of gunpowder in the rear of the storeroom shed. Jason and Hetty stitched fuses along the inside seam of the sacks, letting the tips thill, and then they passed the sacks to Matthew who held them open while Coco balanced a small keg in his arms and poured out black powder till the sacks brimmed. They worked quietly and quick and with every sound they froze, leaving only bits of powder to quiver out of the tipped bag.

They were back at the business at hand when the shed door kicked open. Before they could reach rifle or pistol, Ed swaggered drunk through the doorway with a short lurch. He smiled contentiously, "Well, it's a goddamn good thing those rust eaters ain't quiet like me." He looked them over like they were so much useless cratage. "Emmit ain't but fifty yards down the path playing Red and Black with a couple of shovel stiffs."

Matthew swung the shed doors closed and peered out a thin rift between planks.

Ed tottered a bit as he stood over the sacked powder the others were crouched around. "Fools on a journey," he said as he stuffed the clay jug and tequila bottle up under his armpits. He unbuttoned his trousers clumsily.

"Fine needlework. And neatly stacked." He took out his pizzle and began to urinate on the neat stacks. The spray chased them all back.

"But useless…" When he was done, he gave his pizzle a good shaking and slipped it back into his trousers, smiling at them all. "You know how many of those bags you'd need for that tomb up there? And what about those fuses. How you gonna go from one to the other before those muckmen down below are on you. And what about the mine shaft? Ahhhhh…"

He poured tequila into the tin cup. He took a drink. "Miss North, I hate to steal you away from your sabotage, but go get me a gravel pan. And you, Mr. Clay, I hate to interrupt your needlepoint, but reach the hell over there and get me that ax." He stared down at Matthew. "Roll me a cigarette and keep your mouth shut." He handed the bottle to Coco. "Hold this as carefully as you would your pizzle."

Ed went and grabbed a barrel and rolled it back into the light and stood it up. He pointed at the lettering stamped across its belly.

"For those of you who can't read, it says: CALICUT RAW-BONE. SUPERPHOSPHATES. For those of you who are just plain ignorant, it's fertilizer."

Jason slapped the ax into Ed's hand. He swung it up onto his shoulder.

"You know the English are some of the finest merchandisers of rawbone in the world. And you know why?"

Hetty came back with a gravel pan. Ed pointed the ax to where she should place the pan by the sacks of black powder.

"They send these dour looking, pale faced women to the battle-fields. To Austerlitz and Waterloo. They send them to the Crimea. They even send the stinkin' vampires to the catacombs of Sicily. They dig up the dead then grind them down so they can fertilize their soil with good rawbone. Vampires is what they are. Ahhh…what am I saying? We're all vampires."

He sank the broad blade into the keg plate and wrenched it apart. He swilled down a mouthful of tequila and scooped up a handful of rawbone. He squatted down and formed a neat mound of bone at one end of the pan.

"Look at the label on that damn barrel. One hundred percent rawbone." He ran the powder through his fingers. "That's so much crap. They charge for pure rawbone but this is part nitrogen and potash and part phosphate rock and charcoal, even phosphoguano. The stinkin' American companies, they charge you for what they advertise, but what they advertise you ain't paying for. Well, the farmers' bad luck is our good fortune."

He sank the ax blade into the heart of a stitched sack and scooped out a handful of black powder and made a second mound at the other end of the miner's pan. Then he scooped out another handful of black powder and ran a thin road from one mound to the other. He mixed what was left with the rawbone. The others watched him silently spread some of the mottled powder across his palm. It was as if he were studying the elements' journey through the hand of time. From dust to dust and back again.

"When I was in Saltillo, Mexico, some years back, I watched these zapadores, they're Mexican military engineers, using this stone shed for a powder magazine. Along one outside wall, they'd stacked up some kegs of fertilizer and wood so they'd have more space inside."

He poured the remaining dust out of his hand. "Miss North, that clay pot there, get it for me." He eyed Matthew. "You through rolling that cigarette, boy?"

Matthew held it up.

Ed took a bound cloth from the clay pot. He untied the knot. It was filled with the residue of charred alder which he mixed into the mound of rawbone and black powder.

"Mr. Clay, break a handful of pine shards off that barrel face."

Ed held out the tin cup. Coco poured him more tequila. He took another drink. Jason handed him the shards and Ed speared them in the rawbone.

"Down there in Saltillo, a shell burst right along that stone wall touching off the bags of powder near the fertilizer."

He reached into his shirt pocket and took out some gun wadding and nested the cured cotton into the pile of black powder. He took the cigarettes from Matthew.

"Mr. Clay, strike me a light."

Jason lit up a match but was careful not to let a spark hit the powder. Ed drew in the flame.

"When the dust settled out, I noticed on the shed's stone wall, there was a difference where the powder had blown and where the powder, fertilizer and wood had blown together."

Before they realized it Ed needled the burning tip of the cigarette into the gun wadding and stepped back fast. There was a sharp pop and the powder combusted. The others cleared away. A snake hiss of phosphor veined the powder along the pan into a black spitting scar and when it mated with the mottled bone there was an incendiaried blast twice as raw that threw the blue fired pine shards like shrapnel singeing the shadows where they all stood.

Just then as quick, the flash fell away.

"This is what I saw down in Saltillo. This is what happened when black powder and fertilizer and charcoal got mixed. I keep up with the trade papers on explosives. There's men playing with a mix of nitrate and ammonia and carbon with black powder for a new type of explosive."

Ed twirled the tequila around the rim of the cup. "I should have been a scientist instead of a fool." He squatted down by the smoldering shield of the miner's pan. "There's a way to go for that mine. Those sacks of yours aren't the answer. Fire is the answer."

He grabbed the clay jug. "We'll fill a dozen of these with that mix. Then we'll sheet the top with gun wadding. Then airtight that with paraffin. We'll place a few of these jugs in the lower shells where the ball mill and chemical tanks are. But we won't try and charge them. No time. We'll concentrate on the upper shell, where the heavy crusher is, and the founders' shaft. If this blast works like it should, there'll be a flash fire. And the upper shells, if we place them right, will collapse down onto the lower shell and set those charges. I'll handle the mine shaft myself."

He stared at the barrel of rawbone and his mouth cut bitterly across his beard. "Calicut is a Maryland company. Think of the battlefields and cemeteries they gutted for all that bone."

He looked up into the solemn faces around him. "Any one of you could have a couple of friends ground up in that keg. Or maybe a sweetheart or a mother or a son."

He gave the keg a harsh slap. "You need fire. And Prometheus himself couldn't have given you better kindling."

CHAPTER THIRTY-THREE

Lord Goose set up his tents near the river beyond a labyrinth of betting tables, orchestra stand, and wagons. Hetty stood by the river and watched the first burst of fireworks' star above the mine where the last shift of muckmen streamed out before the holiday. The ground lit above the Lord's packed betting tables, and above the cienega where farmers were setting up camp with their families. Along the ridge where miners tramped in from their claims, and along the creeks in sets of two and three.

Hetty watched as a rush of candled phosphor overhead shined up a man approaching from the river.

"You shouldn't be here," she said.

"I know," Jason said. He walked around her. They watched the orchestra beyond a reach of tule reeds. Neither spoke.

The swell of madness around the betting tables forced them to move farther up the river. There was a hint of pennyroyal to the sky around the moon. They picked at conversation in small bits. Details in the strange dream of their lives. Their words carried them deeper up the hillside where there was only black and the earth's quiet breathing.

They came to a place open to heaven and protected by centurions of knotted bark. They walked no farther. They looked back down from where they had come. A stellar powder burst in the sky along the river and fell away.

They were passion and regret. Compassion and need. *She* felt the old Mexican watching her and was ashamed. *He* tried to hide from his bitterness against himself. She wished she were beautiful. He didn't feel worthy of his desire. But all this would not turn them away. And there would be no more words. Those would be for later. What was profound was to be felt.

• • •

Dawn of the 4th. Matthew looked up from his journal. Coco sat across the morning fire from him, naked, his legs crossed. Matthew watched as Coco pierced the flesh of his thigh near the groin with a hollow awl made from shivved seal bone.

Coco knew that night it would be a hard fight, and to commemorate its honor and importance, he was inking the date into his skin beside a tattoo of the earth rising out of the ocean. The myth of where his flesh was born at the beginning of time, beside the date the myth was born, of the country that bore his flesh.

He smiled at Matthew and stood so that he might glory in the scroll of his life imprinted there. The heart side of his chest was striped like a shark in a coral reef. The other side was painted images from dreams and illustrations in books. One leg was a menagerie of symbols of the island, and the other was a draughts board dyed vermillion and blue. His back was a remembrance of his family and the dates of their deaths and the women he'd loved, and a flock of birds and epigrams and the lurid markings of sailors.

He walked around the fire and knelt beside Matthew. He pointed at Matthew's book, and he pointed at his own flesh.

Matthew smiled then. "Yes. You and me. Yes. I keep the history of my life here." He held up the book. "And you...you wear yours proudly." He gave him a slap on the shoulder. "Can never lose what you wrote, can you?"

• • •

Hetty saw the four of them off as they began the long trek around the rim of the valley to get to the far side of the mine by dusk. There was already a full blush of scrappers around the betting tables. And the campfires of families come for the festivities had filled the open caldera this side of the river. A hand stitched American flag, the length of three wagons, was being hoisted up between two flagpoles sixty feet high above the mudway just up from the bridge on the mine side of the river.

By noon the first pummel of fireworks burst out over the horizon. The men rode behind Jason, silent and apprehensive. A frail echo of the orchestra playing a miner's dirge disturbed the scarred hillface they passed along.

Hetty was selling the quaint plunder of her profession from a stand by the wagon she'd brought across to the mine side of the river. Every kind of tinned specialty and liquor. She was less than thirty yards from another wagon that sat alone, which she and Coco had brought across the night before. The wagon had been weired with stones where the ground inclined, just up past the magistrate's office. The front corners of the wagon had been filled with drums of kerosene stoppered with rags, all of which was covered with a tarp.

Jason and the others stopped at the river where it coursed out of the granite heart of the hills. They filled their hats from a canvas water bag and let the horses drink one last time. They checked their cinches and the clay jugs. They made sure their weapons were primed and loaded. Coco took from his saddle pack a leather pouch the Lord had given him days before. He walked over to Jason and handed him the leather pouch.

"What's this?" Jason opened the leather pouch. He took out a note and a folded piece of canvas.

He unfolded the canvas. It trailed down into a banner. And there painted on that strip of cloth was Jason's one contribution to the Big Blue Heaven's sheeted sky, a comet arcing across the stars. He stared at the comet. He shook open the note and read:

My son,

I bequeath to you one small patch of the heavens that we shared. I give it to you, for you to them, from then on whatever that you may will, be it so.

Comets rise out of the horizon, comets fall. But they change our lives forever.

They are not deserving of what you will attempt, but still. But still.

I will carry my tenting sky to another spot. And if we do not speak again tomorrow, then know that when I am established amidst fools and frauds I will write.

For a swift pair of hands you will always find me wanting.

Miguel Tejara Flores
Lord and Master of the Shill

Jason looked out toward the mine trying to spot the orchestra stand under the firestars, knowing that was where the Lord would be watching over the con. Jason whispered, "You wily old bastard."

He looked back at the others. The light was going softly behind them. He folded the note and carefully slipped it into his pocket. Then he loosened the binding on the Mexican's coat and slipped it on. Without another word, he climbed up into the saddle.

They descended upon the flats and rode four abreast. With the mine less than a thousand yards ahead, shocks of phosphor merloned out of the black wall of night. There were gunshots of reverie and a rusty iron cannon caissoned up from Buena Vista hollowed out a mouth of prideful fire. Through it all the orchestra resounded of Beethoven from the river's rock to the roof of Gull Hill.

Hetty was showing some scowl faced miner the latest calabashes when she spotted Arlen and his gunneys unexpectedly return from San Lorenzo, raddling their exhausted mounts along the crowded path toward the magistrate's.

Jason and the others had begun the long incline up Gull Hill. The rows of huts and tents looked like breastworks beneath a devouring cannonade. Flags emblemed up against the sky from roof, and puncheon, and staff. The great flag near the river, wind framed between the two poles.

Coco leaned toward Jason's saddle and pulled out the canvas banner. He unfurled it above his head with a single snap and swung it over his shoulder, tying off both ends under his arm so the arc of the comet's trail baldriced across his chest. They continued on up Gull Hill. Past the deformed relic bone of the original mine. Then under the still transom. Matthew leaned over the edge of his saddle and looked ahead. He saw they were riding through a graveyard of mud. Plaques of rotting timber flat. Spartan names, long gone, bent at straw angles. Names beneath a rusty solar system of creaking iron ore buckets.

Jason guided them over a crust of stone refuse. The horses slipped some but gathered themselves. Matthew looked up and the mine started to monolith against the moon. One beastly tier upon another. The dark hullhousing of a thousand black dreams, the cauldron of chemical tanks still brewing their magic.

"Jesus Christ," whispered Matthew.

"What?" said Jason.

"I didn't realize…from across the river, it never seemed so goddamn huge."

"That's 'cause you've come to burn it down," said Ed.

They drew up their mounts by the founders' shaft. They waited quietly, then they dismounted. They were like a promised vanguard, slipping out of the night folds of a dream, with those clay jugs hoisted up on their backs.

Coco followed Ed toward the founders' shaft. Matthew went around to the far side of the building where the ball mill was housed. Jason slipped down the plank stepway to the enclosed chemical tanks. They moved slowly, but with some assurance, as each step had been carefully laid out over a map by candle's light.

Ed and Coco dug with granny bars into the penthouse cribbing on both sides of the winze.

Inside the ball mill Matthew, crawled under the jaws of the heavy crusher and placed two charges. He graveled back along the leftover rock, lining up the two charges evenly for one strike of a match after the signal.

Jason made his way around the fuming stench of the amalgamation tanks, then swung down under an ore chute to find the support stanchions for the housing. He grabbed up a miner's anchor and picked away at the floorboards till the hole was big enough to wedge the clay mine up under the rafters.

The sound of iron on stone interrupted a pitman who was clandestinely holed up in one of the founders' sheds with a half Indian jade and bottle of dehorn. He had just about cheated that young whore out of her canvas shirt when the chinking started.

His socks made no sounds up the clapboard passage between the shed and the founders' shaft. He came around the bulkhead and through a dangling gallows frame and he spotted Coco and Ed filling dirt in around a clay pot wedged in the cribbing.

"What in Christ's name are you doing?" brogued the pitman.

Both men turned.

The pitman came forward. "I asked you boys what in Christ's name are you doing here?"

His stockinged foot got a half jigger of a step closer when Coco slammed the crowbar across the side of the pitman's head and laid him out. Blood spurted from the broken socket of eye bone. Coco knelt and was about to bludgeon the pitman when the Indian girl screamed. He looked up but she was already stumbling down the attled hillside toward the river.

He stood. Matthew and Jason came running back through the plank funnel of the upraise in a moment of panic or betrayal. Ed shouted that he needed help with the charge. Coco ran two fingers across his mouth and pointed. Jason could just make out the girl waving her arms as she ran for the torch lane of huts and tents.

Jason hauled up the stocked Volcanic strung from around his shoulder. A spider's web of phosphor threaded up to the stars. He pumped the lever. He aimed at the girl. Black swallowed the light just as he fired.

She was still running, shouting.

"Fuck." He turned to Matthew. "I'm going after her. You take my charges. If those muckmen start for here, I'll hold them back till you blow this place. But goddamn, blow it."

• • •

Arlen walked out onto the veranda of the magistrate's office. He drank a bottle of beer and looked down toward the river where couples waltzed before the river moon. Farmer and bride, immigrant and lady, clumsy boot and crease worn dress. He looked back through the doorway. Emmit and Serranus sat before the fire, and Serranus explained about finding the body of their brother. Just a torn, boned remnant. He could feel the shattered family in their downcast frames. The hollering along the path only made their sorrow all the worse.

He turned away. Shooting tapers flared the hillside, and there Arlen saw a woman running along the stony neve and a horseman in a wool frock coat on a tall Percheron trying to close the hundred yards between them.

"Emmit…Clay's come back!"

• • •

The pitman's eyes opened and not ten feet away Ed and Coco mudded the last clay pot into place by the shaft entrance, as the Percheron lost its feet on the spilling gravel hillface and tumbled, throwing Jason from its back. The pitman dragged his hand toward the sheared face of a hoist bolt, lying crimped in the mud, as the Indian girl plunged into a pack of drunken muckmen, cardplaying outside a tent. She pointed back up at the mine.

Ed and Coco each struck a match, as Arlen climbed into the saddle and Emmit tossed his brother a shotgun while they raced along the porch to their horses. Ed called out to Matthew, "Are you ready?" and the sky burst with another fusillade of colors. Hetty saw

Arlen and the others trying to press clear of the crowd by firing off a warning with their shotguns, and Matthew yelled back, "Ready."

Ed gave the command and the fuses were struck and Jason reined up on the Percheron, as a stream of muckmen began to scale the hillface like footsoldiers to find out what all that firing was up at the mine. The lone cannon howled up a celebration shell and jumped back on its wheels away from a belly of smoke, and Ed and Coco turned to run for their horses when Ed was struck across the jaw with a hoist bolt.

Parts of the crowd swirled back on each other as Hetty pulled a sledge hammer from under the seat boards of her other wagon, and Jason sided the Percheron and started to fire upon the muckmen to slow their approach. The wind blew up and a whirl of flags across the valley tailed toward the sea, and Arlen and his horsemen trampled over a farmer and through a hawking stand, and there were screams.

The fuses rushed up the spindle thread, and the screams and flaring shotguns seemed just so much a part of the festivities, and Matthew clomped his way from the ball mill as the pitman rammed Ed against the heading and clawed him again with the bolt. A wave of panic bled out from the trading stalls nearest the mine and another cascade of Roman candles hued its image in the river all violet and yellow, as Hetty hammered out the stones that wedged the wagon's wheels in place.

Coco vised back the pitman's head and grouted out his neckbone with a shiv as horsemen slurried over the debris on the far side of the mine, and the orchestra strings blended into a languid ottavio. Coco tried to lift Ed, who sat dazed and tottering, with blood frothing around his mouth.

Jason wielded the Percheron, and shot down a pickman rushing at him over the misshapen sandstone bedding, and then he retreated back up the hill and stopped again and charged a wolf pack of shovels and claw hammers and pickaxes. He fired into them and retreated further up the hill and stopped again. The half-Indian jade was on her knees surrounded by muckmen and spewing out a bare bone English about the black souls there to burn the mine, while Matthew screamed for Ed and Coco as he tried to rein all their mounts clear of the founders' shaft. The hilltop was like a battlement under siege with muckmen on the climb and Chinese firewheels burning tracers above the teeth of the trees. The fuses burned up that last inch, and Matthew shouted their names again.

Coco curled back, knowing that he couldn't clear Ed through the tunnel, so he dragged him over into a jack head pit. Hetty grabbed a lantern from an abandoned trader's stall and tossed it into the canvas tarp over the kerosene in the wagon as Matthew was pulled across the landing by the panicked mounts. Hetty put her shoulder to the groaning cart, as the first clay jug ignited. There was a moment of gray smoke and then there was a crushing rattle down through the spine of the earth.

A landslide of men and children and women were stunned silent as the penthouse cracked apart, and some were unsure if this wasn't part of the fireworks as fletchings of the plank founders' shaft exploded wondrous against the moonlight. A second jolt spined the earth for a hundred miles beyond the river, as the ball mill fire-branded above the crown of Gull Hill, and a woman's cry presaged a flash fire and pandemonium.

The wagon creaked toward the magistrate's and Jason saw the three riderless mounts charge through the clouds of black fire that began to wind circle, and there were rifle shots coming from the far side of the mine. Droves of muckmen grabbed buckets of foolish hope and ran to put out the fire. Jason quirted the Percheron up the desiccated slope to see if any of the others were still alive, as the wagon stumped head-on into the porch of the magistrate's office. Flames weeviled up through its canvas skin, and there was a streaming chaos of boots down the mud path.

Serranus saw the frame shanty burning and he called to his brother. Jason weaved up through a tangle of smoke between the fiery remains of the founders' shaft and ball mill, and in that gray hell he looked for the bodies of his friends and called out to Matthew and then Coco and Ed and then Matthew again. The Percheron reared back and around on its hindquarters when a buffalo robed gunney plunged through the flames on an albino stallion. Its head snapped at the Percheron as it charged by, and the Percheron's teeth shimmered white and tore into the beast's muzzle, and Jason fired the Volcanic through the gunney's heart. He sawed back on his saddle and he and his mount fell together into a flaming kettle of clapboard.

Jason yelled out Matthew's name again, over the hissing of board sheets being torn asunder. Jason looked out over the ravaged shell of roofs being sucked in with heat and past the wasteland of mud and strewn quarry rocks and past the welded tuff of tents and huts and traders' stalls. He looked past Serranus and a handful of gunneys trying to save that stencil scrap of shanty, all the way to the betting tables and bar and orchestra that stood abandoned on the flats, and beyond to the river, ribbon thin and sparkling, where miners and traders and settlers and immigrants and frail blighted children and frail women fled from the flames.

Another charge quaked the ground, and the Percheron lurched back, and above Jason the strutted wall face began to break apart and the hill started to come down behind it. He could stay no longer, look no longer, or be swallowed in the backdraft. On one flank the muckmen stormed the hill, and on the other Arlen and his gunneys crept up through the blasted remains of ballast stone. One wall of the ball mill began to waffle then fell into a melting splinter. A cinder and ash ghost maelstrom made Jason gasp and cover his face, and the Percheron cried out, and he had to slap the branding flakes away from around the horse's eyes. The trees that crowned Gull Hill were a funereal of burning, as he looked down through the well chute of the mine where a thin path followed alongside the flaming tiers and between the huts and tents, straight to the river.

Jason slipped the Volcanic across his waist and wrapped the leads tightly around one wrist and summoning a last breath spurred the Percheron down through the slogged earth. Past the yawing walls, past the gunneys trying to pinfire his rippling image that swung up out of the reeking smoke. The pylons that supported the ball mill began to billycord, and the elephantine structure came crumbling down onto the housing of the chemical tanks like some screeching beastly tower and ignited the charges wedged up in the rafters. A holocaustal sun of mercury and powderbone seared up through the night, and from the burning tents by the magistrate's, Hetty could see the Percheron swing up out of a mud chott into clear view of the valley.

Arlen and his gunneys turned about and lay chase, and some of the muckmen scaling the hill turned back and scrabbled down the slope for a clear shot at the rider who seemed to be coming out of the heart of an incendiaried atoll. The wind carried fireironed sparks with hellacious velocity across the sky.

Jason cleared open ground and made a rush down the path between the stalls and tents where the wayfarers scattered before him. Hetty spotted a square jawed immigrant behind a wagon haul up a New Land musket and brace the butt tang as he set his aim on

Jason. She slipped up beside him, took a Patterson from inside her deerskin coat, and put one shot into the bone behind his ear.

Amidst the chaos at the river, Serranus and his crew of keeners tried to sweep in and check Jason's run to the river. When Jason saw them, he swung out of his saddle and scooped up a torch left guttering on the ground. And as he rode beneath the vast tarpaulin strung between two poles he flung the torch up into the flag that seethed and rippled of branded stripes and stars. It was torn loose from its binds as it burned wholly. The horsemen were forced to check their mounts before its conflagrant remains, and the Percheron dunked down into the river thrashing through reeling countrymen, then scrambled up and over a slate gray shingle and left behind that flag draped coffin of earth.

CHAPTER THIRTY-FOUR

The earth burned as it must have with the first breath of creation. Gull Hill was engulfed in smoke. The sky was lost. The tents and huts burned everywhere. Hetty made her way among the scattered and stricken. The mantle shell of the mine collapsed in on itself. A final charge detonated and hurled a searing cautery all the way to the river.

Hetty looked across the valley and saw an ensemble of errant torches fanning out along the hillside. The outriders were on the hunt in the high forest. Suddenly one torch began to firefly as it moved quickly up the slope. Soon afterward others began to converge on that same point.

One of them had been found.

• • •

Matthew had no breath left and his legs burned. The cob coal ground he clawed at gave way. Back down the slope he could see the torches closing in. Closing in so they had voices now. He heard Emmit yell to Arlen, "It's that frig dodsey."

Matthew's bootprints had given him away. He tried to hook his fingers into the hillface. But he was doing no better than a crab in a bowl when a hand got a stranglehold on his collar and dragged him face first up to the crest.

Jason held the boy's head in his hands and looked him over. "Thank hell for something. When I saw those torches chasing after someone, I knew you were alive."

• • •

As the sun rose it had little impact on the day. Exhausted after traveling miles, Jason and Matthew stopped at a standing pool of water and drank. Behind them the sky ran black for miles, as if the ground had opened and a millennium of hellfire and torment had escaped into the atmosphere.

Jason kept a vigil on the ridgeline as he filled the last belly pouch with water. Matthew sat in the hot grassy sand wiping at wounds on his face. Jason nudged him. "They're coming."

"Where?"

Jason posted an arm over the boy's shoulder.

Matthew wiped the dust off his eyeglass lenses. Phantoms corporealed from the smoke.

"Can they see us?"

"They're coming this way, aren't they?"

"Arlen?"

Jason swung around the Percheron. "Arlen."

"I'm surprised the goddamn dilettante can ride so well."

Jason squatted down and lifted each of the Percheron's front legs looking for sandcracks or sidebone.

"Can we outrun them?"

The tendons were strained and swollen pretty bad. Eventually the legs would give. "No. We can't outrun them."

"Will we fight them?"

The ground around them was dry chalk and flat. "This place is more suited for what comes after a fight." Jason looked back at the hills. The horsemen had slowed as they traversed a windgap where the ground was flagged like Spanish masonry.

Jason draped his arms over the saddle. In his mind he could see the old man back up there in the hills wearing that African coat, as he wore it now. He rested his head a moment. "You're probably laughing at me is the bet."

Matthew looked at him oddly. "What?"

Jason lifted his head and shook it. "It's of no importance."

Matthew took the laudanum from his satchel. Jason tied down the cinches and climbed into the saddle.

"You could leave me behind, Jason."

Jason sat there quietly exhausted.

Matthew took a drink and blinked, looking up at the sun behind Jason's head. "It would be alright."

"Monsieur Purloin, you were born and bred for ballast. Now," he stretched out his arm, "climb your ass up here."

• • •

By sunset Jason and Matthew had approached Lake Tulare. At the pitch of a sandy revetment, they saw the husky backroll of the breakers at evening tide.

They could go no farther. Jason let the Percheron walk down to the lake and drink. He sat on a piece of driftwood at the lip of the rise and kept guard. He and Matthew did not speak for a time. In the latten sunlight the sheen on the lake stretched for miles, and in the distance, Matthew could see the sliver of a fishing punt cradled on a lazy seiche. Too far to waste on hope. Too far.

Some leagues back they'd begun to see torches flare up in the paling light, only to be swallowed in some reach, and then appear again on the next stretch of flats. Arlen and his thugs came on slowly, but with unabated assurance.

• • •

No one heard the shot that left Charles Julius Whitehorse lying on the floor by his desk. It was not until a groom, drunk with profit from a friendly game of Euchre, approached the dogs flocked up against the den doors.

Within minutes bearers lifted and lay Whitehorse onto a sofa of burgundy silk. Blood had leafed down the back of his robe. He slipped in and out of consciousness. With the coming of the first light, the veranda and parlor were a war room of overseers and grooms, foremen and field hands. They tried to piece together events that had led to what they saw as an attempt on their master's life.

Amos Edding, Whitehorse's doctor, knelt alongside the den sofa and daubed clean the wound entry below the right ear. Fragments of grapeshot had left the skin peppercorned, and the right eyelid could not be opened from the swelling.

One of the overseers began to question the men as to any strangers who might have been seen on the property the previous night. Most of the men had been celebrating, so no strangers were spotted. There was one hint from the farrier of a man smoking by the gate. A vagrant possibly. Trackers were sent to check for sign. Theft became an issue and two men servants and the squat Mexican cook, all of whom had been with the household the longest, were ordered to go from room to room, because Whitehorse was always fond to mock, "It was the servants' solemn duty to know where any valuables they might want to steal were hidden."

The men drank and a dark morphology began to overtake them. They watched the doctor pry out pieces of iron from the skull bone and neck.

In time other business associates of Whitehorse's who had been notified showed up. Misters Latham and Holmes pulled up in Mr. Latham's silklined shay.

The curtains were drawn to fight off the white sun of noon. The room grew heavy with dust. Men who would never associate by class or character conversed at cross purposes as to motive, circumstance, and reasoning. Atrocious ignorance bulled against incidental specu- lation. Each hoped to find the key in solving the riddle of this fallen man.

A mestenero, whose face was polished with time, asked if Arlen had been notified about his father. A wave of stubborn embarrass- ment worked its way across the men. Riders were quickly dispatched. A businessman with long spartan red gray featherdusters stared into his stovepipe as the riders had off and whispered, "They'd need a horse as quick as heaven itself to reach that boy."

While one of the manservants was looking over Whitehorse's desk, he noticed the silk pouch filled with gold that was always kept beside the first kilned brick from a Whitehorse foundry, was miss- ing. The room was searched. Another servant was sent to White- horse's private rooms to search. These turned up nothing. The over- seer asked if anyone was seen in the den the previous evening.

A mozo recalled seeing the young maid bringing Whitehorse

coffee near midnight. The overseer sent the mozo off to find her, and the men gossiped among themselves. It was common knowledge Whitehorse was fucking the girl.

The doctor observed a surreptitious moment between Misters Holmes and Latham. He tried to decipher the whispering that followed, but a shudder in Whitehorse's chest stole his attention.

Soon after, the girl was led into the den. She could just barely bring herself to glance at the sofa. She was led by the overseer back out into the light. A train of men followed her. The overseer began to question her. Other men interrupted. She was a pathetic creature, lost as one question tumbled into another.

She was shaken hard and she started to cry. She tried to pull away but the overseer slapped her down, and she responded by screaming and trying to break free. They were certain that her act of panic was an indictment of her actions as much as theirs was an indication of character. They held her down unmercifully. She was sprawled about their boots until the doctor cleared a path with his elbows.

"Stand back, you mules. We've got a dying man in there." He cradled the quavering child. "You're better off with the magistrate if you believe this child did such a thing."

"When they can work on their back, they're no child."

"You're so quick with a thought." The doctor helped the girl up. "Do you think she robbed him and—"

"And why not?"

"And shot him?"

"And why not?"

"Then get the magistrate up here," demanded the doctor, "and let him question her." He helped the girl past the men, past Misters Latham and Holmes.

"And you...Misters both...With your secret caste we all know about. I saw you in there." He looked from one to the other then scoured the crowd. "Put your remarks to this trash as the Knights have had their share of night killings."

"What does that mean?" demanded Mister Latham.

"The editor of the *Flag* for one."

"Are you insinuating—?" added Mister Holmes.

"That he was beaten to death with lathe irons by your very own. I am," said the doctor. "Maybe Mr. Whitehorse wouldn't go along with you on some scheme and—"

Mister Latham slapped the doctor across the eyes with his derby.

The doctor spit in his face.

The men flocked in, separating the pair. Mister Latham wiped the spittle from his face while Mister Holmes pointed a deadly finger. "If you want to look for secrets look to the *Flag*. It was one of theirs that was chased off after writing insults against Charles. They're the pharisees in this."

CHAPTER THIRTY-FIVE

Where the great slough drained into Lake Tulare, Jason made a torch of tule reeds wrapped around a switch. Matthew followed behind him through the high grass leading the Percheron. The ground was a fleecy gravel that gave way to mud edges. Their faces were fingered by the spider brush. They struggled deeper into the maze of runny brine, their boots slipslogging. Farther on, Matthew noticed a cut rod six feet high with a white rag tied off at the top. His boots graved a foot down into mire. The Percheron arched back crying. Its hooves tried to suck their way out of the mosquito breeding mire.

"Jason, where could this lead?"

Jason turned and backed farther into the brush. He waved for Matthew to come on. He pushed away drapey straw and pointed. Matthew came forward kneeling under the torch that cracked and spit, and lying there at the edge of the fen was a raft large enough for men and horses.

"Coco and I lashed it together when we came south."

• • •

The raft reached the eastern shore where it was pink and cool with the beginning of day. Jason and Matthew rode the Percheron to the south. They veered away from the lake for safety. To the east, the Sierras imposed themselves like some huge planet cresting over the backward crawl of the plain. From the north, Arlen and his trackers followed boot marks caked in the road dust. From the south, the Knights pressed around the Bed of the Ton Tache, along cart paths and passes. Vagabond groups were left to patrol the shore where fishing boats netted out for their catch. One day begat two. Two bled to four.

It was the eighth day out, when the scrabble hooves of a rider broke camp with word for Arlen. The men waited stoically while he read a dispatch written in the doctor's hand:

Arlen —
    Come home. Be quick. Your father is shot. The wound appears mortal. God's speed!
                                — Amos Eddings

Arlen looked across the bleached latitudes. A cratered land formed by a waste of a sun. Panic seized him as he knew he could not reach across the vastness to touch his father. He felt the words, "Oh, Pop," gravel up out of his stomach. His last order before returning home — stay to the hunt.

• • •

Jason and Matthew spotted the hulls of two scoop wagons. They scavenged the remains for food. Desperate as they were, there weren't no easy pickin's in a meal of dry wood and bolt rust or shanks of a cast iron bed frame. The open crates had seen the hands of beggars before them, and they left only shiny spots in the sand where empty tins of canned meat and fruit had been licked clean and cast off. Sparkling spots that called attention to their misery.

Jason rummaged through a crate of books, and as he searched for some cache of food as yet unfound, he browsed each title: *"The Lays of Many Lands"*, *"Chambers' Encyclopedia of English Literature"*, *"The Life and Loves of Eloise"*, *"The Song of Roland"*.

He looked thatast book over closely, cleaning the rat scurf from the face and binding. He opened the battered shell of a cover and his eyes wandered from passage to passage. How many trips he had taken with his father through the pages of that poem to the battlefield of Roncesvalles. But he was now just a brown, burned face, looking past the feudal truth of a poem into the futile truth of the sand country of his days.

"Find anything over there?" said Matthew.

"Not unless you got a recipe for eatin' paper." Jason stood and gave the crate a disgusted kick.

Matthew reached for one of the volumes as Jason went and sat in the shade cast from the remains of a chest of drawers.

"You read much?" said Matthew.

Jason glanced at the books lying there then closed his eyes. "No."

Matthew eyed him skeptically and then, while he thumbed through *"The Anatomy of Melancholy,"* Jason scanned the surrounding rubble. Beneath a raft of wagon slats postured over the axle, Jason spotted a can peeking out from behind a lump of trash.

Matthew looked up holding his finger to a spot on the page, "Well, it says right here that the whole world is mad."

Jason got up, "I think we both knew that."

"And it also says the cause of all melancholy is love and religion."

Jason squeezed down under the wagon and reached for the can, "I guess the bastard who wrote that book had never been hungry."

As Matthew went to speak, there was a whir of dry bone behind that lump of trash. Jason yelled out and his hand recoiled. His boots dug backward. The book rabbited out of Matthew's hand. Jason jumped away from the slithering crossband of a rattler making for the light. Blood spurted across his middle finger, torn to the vein, as the arrowhead of that yellow ophidian curled back with one fang pronged and the other snapped off into the bone of the wound.

Jason wielded out his knife shouting, "Get a fire up with those goddamn books, so I can cauterize this wound."

Before Matthew could stack the brittle sheets Jason had laid his hand palm down on a shank of stripboard. The knife winged a lofting shadow, and Matthew yelled, "What are you doing?" as Jason drove the blade down through the bone so it split the wood. His blood vomited out from the stump and across the sand and he vised the blade down, shearing away the last of the bony finger.

• • •

Matthew lifted Jason into the saddle. His swathed hand was slung with rope against his chest. The cauterized stub stunk of seared flesh.

"The bastard viper was a full bore, Matthew, and if I got half the poison, I'm in luck." He slumped forward and Matthew caught him. "I'll be gettin' pretty sick, maybe even die. If I get too sick, you just cast me off, heh."

Matthew's glasses were stained with perspiration, and he held onto Jason while he decided upon a course.

Instead of going around the lake as was their plan, Matthew

embarked upon a chance, trying for the granite thunderheads massing across the purple gray hollows of the Sierras.

"Look there, Jason, if we can make the rain, if we can make the rain they can't follow. We'll go to the rocks, Jason, we'll go to the rain."

They stumbled through the dusk of the lower foothills. The rain came dark and foreboding over a landscape of incense pine and cedar devastated from the spring floods. Jason was half delirious, and slipped down into the mud, "I can't fly any further, Monsieur Purloin."

Matthew looked up toward a line of redwoods that blocked out the sky. "Just a little farther. We need cover." He tried to pull Jason up. "Come on. Look…look behind us there." Two dozen miles back it was raining. "Look. They can't find us through that. But we need cover…we need…"

Matthew tried to haul Jason over a decaying trunk, when he first saw this thing watching like some gatekeeper in a portal of trees. It was a filthy thing. A man, or a boy growing queerly, with clothes of bound rags and a festoon of rags for a hat and footing brewed from bits of stitched leather.

At first Matthew, frightened, tried to reach for his pepperbox, but this man, boy, just stayed locked where he was, so Matthew finally chanced a shout, "Hey you. I need help! I got a sick man here!"

The filthy stray hunched a bit like some primate sniffing at the wind of a decision.

"You understand me?! I have a sick man here!"

The slop Matthew stood in slipped away under his boots and he braced Jason and when he looked back through the rain the hermit was gone.

• • •

I found the remains of a giant redwood that had fallen before this country had a name.

The hull of this dinosaur lay corded beneath its fallen brethren, that had for one century germinated and grown up on its sturdy back.

Time and fire had hollowed out the vast cedar trunk leaving a round house for Jason and me and the Percheron. I built a fire and the smoke chimneyed up through a hole in the bark ceiling I'd chopped out. Rain steamed where it landed in the flames. I took the African coat and our clothes and hung them from the parasitic ferns and branches that had trained up through the trunk's redwood heart.

The cave was dark. I made a bed of leaf and branch. We are like animals in a lair.

I have never been responsible for anyone. For anything. No one life has hung in the balance of my being. A sudden ill wave came over me. An impotence. Well, Monsieur Purloin, you still see yourself as Arlen sees you. How much does a person have to stand up to before they can stand up to themselves?

I have one bottle of laudanum left and Jason lying on my right wrapped in a blanket shivering with poison. There is little I can do for him except let him drink some of the opiate so he can at least sleep and not suffer. But I have not gone without, one day in ten years.

Something or someone burst through the twilight brush of the alameda tearing away the brambles Matthew had used to drape the tree's opening. Matthew dropped his notebook and scrambled away from these two feral specimens toward his pepperbox, when the rusting mouth of a big bore barreled up. The filthy losel called out to him in a mixed pigeon English and Spanish to keep where he was.

Matthew eased around, positioning himself between the two of them and Jason. He looked over this filthy clan with their peculiarities of feature and smell. The urchin from the woods peered around the patriarch with the shotgun. He was a wild eyed boy and younger than Matthew had even suspected.

"What do you want here?" said Matthew.

The man's eyes were small and gray like a bird's but in a huge head. He tipped his shotgun at the air just enough so his boy read the sign in it to start searching. He stumbled over Jason as he made for their packs.

"Hey. Be careful. That's a sick man there."

The boy grinned between a couple of ears bent outward like a cockleshell from some defect of birth. His grubby hands ratted through the leather wallets.

The old man stared at Jason. "Sick?"

"Yes. Snake bit."

"Snake? Serpiente?" The man hissed.

"Yes…a rattler. Bit by a rattler." Matthew raised his hand, shaking the bent fingers and brattling like a bone tail.

That soiled turnpiker squatted down and looked Jason over with his fingers but his shotgun kept an eye on Matthew. He looked up and leered grimly. "Presto." He started to dig a grave.

"He's not gonna die. Not unless you toadfaced miscreations…"

The man spiked at the air with the barrel of the shotgun and his brown ignoble skull worked up another hiss.

The boy was tossing every trinket worth stealing into a pile beside the guttering twigs of the fire, when he saw that African coat.

He called to his father and shoved a hand toward the coat hanging from a vine that had grown up through the bough of the trunk.

Matthew watched those bird eyes look past the dying fire and into that lion's mud smeared face as it loomed out of the smoke. A breath appeared to startle its way up from the man's lungs. The hermit pointed at Jason, and in Spanmish said, "Is he the one from the Cañón de los Reyes?"

Matthew held his hand up peacefully and slid forward some, "I don't understand." He shook his head.

"The buscadero…from the canyon of the Kings…the one who fights…crucifixión at river…shoots the mine…"

Matthew hesitated, one answer might turn things to his favor, but the other bore the bad stench of bounty

"He's the one." He lifted Jason's watch from his vest pocket. He pointed at Jason and then at the coat. "Have you seen the smoke? The fires…to the west?"

"Smoke…yes…dos days…smoke…the sky…negro de humo."

"The mine was burned. The Whitehorse Mine. He burned it to the ground…like the fire there."

Matthew pointed at Jason as if he were Prometheus himself.

That highwayman looked for a minute like he was dangling between the impossibility and veracity of such a thing. But a hundred miles of lampblack doesn't lie much.

Matthew held up the watch and opened it. He passed the timepiece over to the man for viewing.

"His mother…and father."

The man ran a flat thumb across the chipped images and then he studied the man lying there unconscious and shivering. He contested the alchemy of the features with his own eyes. His boy leaned over and perched on his father's shoulder.

"Pop-pop…a crow."

"Yes…like you…born of dos birds…diferente."

Matthew slid forward, "My friend needs help, or he will die."

The man looked up. Greedy eyes and all.

"He needs help. Can you ride to the mine? The Whitehorse Mine? We have a friend there. Bring her here. There are men below coming. To hunt him down. To kill him. Please."

The boy looked at his father.

Matthew took the few bills and coins left from his pocket and tossed them into the pile of trinkets. "Take all that. But please, he needs help."

• • •

It's been twenty-four hours since that gad left with a note for Hetty. I gave him the Percheron as he had no mount of his own. He didn't forget to stuff his pockets with all the ballast he could take. He should have reached the mine by now unless he saw the better side of greed. Left alone I'm quickly left with doubt.

• • •

Jason is in such pain I gave him a couple of swigs of laudanum and he fell asleep. Bad fever. His hand is swollen. We're two days in the rabbit hole. The sky cleared, I wish it hadn't.

• • •

I have the jimjams and can't even lace my boots, my hands are trembling so. It has begun to rain. Four days now.

• • •

It went cold tonight. Rain worse...fog worse...and me...worse. Sit bundled with Jason. He got the last taste of laudanum. Slept across my lap. Fever has peaked...maybe breaking? Five days... or is it six now? The bastard left us! I watched my hands...I mean my arms...hold Jason and I imagined that I was one of those redwoods that had germinated on the bole of the tree we're in. That my arms were rootstocks grown down around the heartwood of the fallen cedar that is my friend and...and that I anchored him now, protected and covered him and this was possible only because he had held me on his back long enough so I could live. Whatever form I have will always be shaped in part around him...It is only nature that could have foreseen how we are all entwined together. I lay awake with the thunder, and when I was sure he could not hear me...I whispered...that I loved him.

• • •

Matthew was sure he was asleep, when he heard the cry of a horse. He crawled from one fog to another. A thin tremble of disembodied spirits slipped through a wet mist. It wasn't Hetty or the highwayman. And they carried long guns. They dismounted, and in the mist became a bleak pack of shapes forming and reforming an approach.

Matthew cocked back the hammer on the pepperbox and gathered himself and then he realized he was staring into the faces of ghosts from the grave. The dead walked toward him with a smile.

"Ed? Coco?"

"I see that pepperbox is still your weapon of choice," said Ed.

He heard the wheels of a wagon approach. Then a woman's voice.

"I thought you were both dead."

"We are," mocked Ed, "me and the Hawaiian here. We're dead as five pounds of rawbone." He lifted Matthew off the ground. "And we've come to carry you to the grave, you papery barefoot fool."

CHAPTER THIRTY-SIX

The cemetery ground of Laurel Hill, even with its finely carved markers of Italian red marble and western granite, was a meager defense against the rain that swept its topsoil across Arlen's boots.

Home too late. A lone mourner now, before the mound of earth above the box site. A tumulus of mud epitaph.

Arlen stood away from the protection of Doctor Eddings' umbrella. His beard, two weeks grown, was specked with rain. "He didn't want to be buried. He told me so. I failed him here, Amos. Even in that."

• • •

Arlen stood in the doorway of the den. The room was lit by a fire from the hearth. He stared at the spot his father had been felled and the sofa where he'd died. The doctor brought in two mugs of bumbo made from gin and warmed Cuban sugar. He handed one to Arlen.

"Do you think it was the girl?" the doctor said.

"No."

"But she ran away."

He sat in his father's chair at the desk. His anger began to work its way up through his disbelief. "How do I find out who killed him, Amos?"

The doctor walked over to the sofa and grabbed a stack of newspapers and tossed them onto the desk in front of Arlen.

"Give those papers a look. Go on." Amos pulled up a chair and sat. "Every front page has filled their columns with your father. They itemized what he acquired, and lauded what he achieved. But if you look closer, you'll see something else. The papers for the North claim him as their own hero 'cause they say he was killed by the red hats for not standing with them and this is their way of frightening other men of wealth away from the Union cause. And the red hats say he was killed by the North because he would not come to heel and pass on the gold he took from the hills to help the Union cause, and so he was a true sympatheir of the South and independence. He's a hero to both because they can both use him. So how do you expect to find out the truth?"

Once alone, Arlen sat at the campaign desk that was his father's. He'd closed the den drapes, put out all the lights. The room was just pitch and memories.

And yet, he could not dispel the thought that in no short measure, he was at fault for his father's death. It was he who hired Jason to go down country and kill the old man. It was he who'd driven Christman from San Francisco.

These facts caused him to be cautious, as it was now his own life in the hands of a wrong decision. He tried to find a way to put all those tutored years of knowledge and book reading to the service of answering one thought: Should he go back down country or not? After all, he had no allegiance to anyone, except himself.

CHAPTER THIRTY-SEVEN

The first thing Jason saw was the canvas hood of the wagon turn with the color of the light. He tried to sit, edging his way back up along the sideboards. He could hear somewhere Ed's voice telling Matthew about how he and Coco had survived the blast.

"When I came to, I was sittin' in brown dust, and the side of my head felt like the earth had landed on it. After that hole caved in on us, I saw the Hawaiian trying to dig his way clear of the shaft. Well, good luck, I thought, 'cause that door is shut for good."

Jason looked toward the back of the jostling wagon.

"So what was left. Well, me and Coco crawled from adit to adit and we weren't makin' for the bridal chamber, no sir. I knew there was a jack head pit that our crew had bored out in case of a cave in."

Jason lifted the canvas enough to peek out. Ed and Coco were walking their mounts alongside the wagon.

Ed was waving his hand like some sham actor. "Let me tell you. Those shooflies we crawled through were filled with traprock. But when we got to the vug where that jack hole was, we found it filled with attle. I mean enough hard stone to sink one of those Pacifica

Steamers. We was trapped clean."

Jason twisted around and saw Hetty and Matthew's outlines up on the box seat. Matthew was swigging from a bottle of laudanum Hetty had brought. Jason sat back and took a long breath and filled up his lungs with the cool aurora air.

"The air was gettin' warmer, and the smell of the mine burned my nose," said Ed. "And I knew we'd be choked to death. So what was left? Nothin' but crawlin' from hole to hole. You're living a bad bet down under. We were starting where most things end, and we still had crawling to do and we crawled, didn't we?" Coco paddled with his hands like he was some gopher rutting a tunnel. "Talk about luck. Right there in the dark, I see what I think is an open cut or a plat, and I put up my hand and feel the air and it was cooler there against my palm."

Jason silently questioned how much fight left the five of them had as the wagon jutted and wobbled over a log bridge laced with hop vines. The water below tumbled through the stone sided mill-race of a river that ran the full half mile width of the valley.

"Chance brings you to the right spot sometimes," said Ed. "And sometimes it's just sheer stupidity. But what difference. I struck one of the few matches I had left and started looking into that tunnelway of a hole."

Jason envisioned the country ahead filled with patrols and the ground behind them being closed off by Arlen and Emmit. The old Mexican had understood. There's only so much ground before the will of numbers has its way.

"Me and Coco followed that speck of light through the hole, and what'd I see? Timbers rotted. So rotted you could fleck them apart with your thumb. So rotted the white fungus had eaten through them. So I felt around that salt and pepper granite, and I saw something that started me dancing and stomping my boots like a wild-man."

After crossing that bridge, the wagon trundled up through the trace. Jason looked over the valley as it receded. On both flanks were a succession of low sweeping hills that curled like the backs of two giant nightcrawlers along its four mile length. Downriver, within pistol shot of the bridge, were the remains of a two story stone farm-house and a waterwheel. Battered masonic walls of nubbed field-stone. Looking this valley over, Jason thought of his father, and Egypt, and a plan started to unfold.

"I was a jumping Mad Hatter," said Ed, "and Coco, he stared at me like I'd swallowed too much blackdamp, dragging him like some sheep through that dusted black hole. Then I showed him…some-one had chiseled into that spoiled rock, 'I shat on Whitehorse's name in this spot'. And it was dated 55…55, see. The mine wasn't built then!" Ed did a half turn like he'd just come through the moment and his arms waggled like a drunken bird.

Jason's father had been ordered by Napoleon to lead a scouting party of chasseurs into the desert so he might look upon the plains of Jezreel. From Meggido to a broken tower by a river, the solemn little man had walked ground sacred with war since the time of Ahab's fall. He'd told his officers that if he could trick the armies of the world into fighting them on that spot, he could defeat them all, as the ground was made for secrets.

Jason reached for a water bag and drank, and for the first time in six days, his stomach gnawed for food. He sat back and studied the country. How much fight did we have left…enough to trap them with the trick of Armageddon?

Ed laughed. "We'd given that hill such a fuckin' hard shake, we'd opened up a shaft to the original mine built beside the one we were digging now. Aladdin didn't have it so good. We could just walk through the shafts of that old grave, upright like two fine gents." Ed shouted out, "Thank you, Mr. Whitehorse, for being such a greedy bastard you needed all those holes for your dandies."

• • •

They were nine days traveling back toward the mine, when Jason explained to them the trap he was planning.

Jason, Matthew, Coco and Ed crossed the slough on rafts. Torches heralded the slim passway of their approach. Their horses' muzzles were muffled with shirts and rags.

Hetty continued south toward Buena Vista Lake, then on to the toll road that would lead her to Camp Fitzergerald in the Los Angeles basin. There she would meet with the Union agents she'd worked with to see if she could persuade them that, at the appropriate time, a battalion of Union troops could be brought north to help execute their plan.

Jason and the others reached the western shore of the slough then continued north toward the mine. They traveled by night to avoid the Golden Circle patrols and in the half gray dawn of August 1, they were given their first full view of Whitehorse's valley in almost a month.

Repairs on the mine had begun. Crews of Chinese labor had been brought in to do the dangerous rat work of digging out the rubbled shafts. The torched mine structure was being torn down, and new lumber lay along the hillface squared up in neat piles like shrines. There were rows of freshly patched tents and rows of muckmen along the river, washing and lazing and getting ready for the shifts to come. The charred remains of the huts lay where they were left to darken and blow away. Guards ringed the hills, and the valley looked as much like a Roman marching camp as it did a mining settlement.

Matthew noted:

Pound for pound they're back to pounding out a nation. A slave to enslavement. A white moment.

. . .

The magistrate's office was now a rectangular piece of shade, edged by posts that held up a large canvas tarp. Arlen sat at the desk from his father's den that he had transported down to the mine. He and Emmit discussed another expedition while Serranus lay sleeping on a cot trying to outlast a hangover.

Both men turned as Ed ducked under the edge of the tent. Emmit rested an arm on the back of his chair. "Well, I haven't seen you since the festivities."

"You can thank Miss North for that. She's had my ass strapped to the seat of a freight wagon."

"Maybe you should have stayed working at the mine?"

Ed's boots nervously picked away at the sand. He looked over at Arlen. "You're Mr. Whitehorse?"

Arlen's hand ran along his thickened beard. "Yes."

Ed stood there mute. Emmit prodded him, "You got something to say, Mr. Teacups?"

"I have news of Christman," he said, "and that other one...Clay."

Emmit kicked the cot and his brother's head wrenched around. "You better hear this. He's seen them."

"When?" said Serranus.

"Two days ago," said Ed.

"Where?"

"A place called the Millrace."

Arlen didn't know the country and deferred to Emmit.

"I think it's on the eastern shore of the lake."

"Ahhh." Serranus hauled his legs over the edge of the cot and rubbed the back of his neck with both hands. "You should spend less time on your ass and more on the road and you'd remember it's southwest of Tulare Lake." He got up. "It's a rib of land with this abandoned stone farmhouse and a waterwheel. The river's got some spic name."

Arlen glanced at Ed. "Is that the place?"

"Yeah. Me and the North woman were comin' back from the mining camps in the hills, and we'd stopped for the night by that farm. That's when Christman and Clay rode in, and they were shit for wear, too. But I'll tell you, there's something between them that is all wrong."

Ed squatted down and started running his fingers along the sand. "I don't know what she 'fessed to you, but she fed those men, and gave them whiskey and money, and they talked all night, and it was like they were family."

"And how much of this conversation did you snipe?"

Ed kept working at the ground with his fingers, and he wished he could dig a hole deep enough to bury everything that he was feeling. "Mr. Whitehorse, the magistrate here promised me—"

Serranus struck a match along the side of the desk and it left a trail of smoke, "You stinkin' apple-shaker, where's your sense of cause?"

Arlen took a square of brown paper from a stack. "Have a look here." He slid it across the desk.

Ed stood and looked over the roughly printed sheet.

"It says five thousand dollars reward for Clay, does it not?"

"Yeah."

"That's what you can expect then, for him or Christman."

Serranus flicked the match at Ed's boots, but Ed just looked away.

"They mean to fight you, Mr. Whitehorse. And the Tills here. And the Golden Circle."

Arlen leaned forward and sat there quietly. Ed glanced at Emmit and Serranus who stared at him as if he were lower than any Celestial. "The North woman is putting a cache of arms and munitions together that I'm to cargo out to the Millrace."

"How much munitions?" said Emmit.

"A hundred men could leave the ground pretty ragged behind them."

"We ought to drag that bitch by her paps out into some field and dry bob her with a shotgun," said Serranus.

Arlen waved Serranus to sit and shut up.

Ed reached into his pocket and took out a folded letter. "When the North woman left she gave me some letters to get posted out. I stole this one. It's Christman's."

He passed it to Arlen who looked over the envelope. It was addressed to Randall Wilcox at the *Flag*.

"Wait outside for a few minutes." Arlen opened the envelope. He unfolded the note.

Mr. Wilcox —

Enclosed is another of my "letters" for the paper. Say nothing yet — but the fight is about to start. We've put together a "castle" of our own. Radicals with a proper aim. We ought to shock Whitehorse and his "mules" pretty good by the end of August.

— Matthew

Arlen looked up and passed the note to Emmit. "How many men could you put into the field?"

Emmit considered awhile, "If we stock them with food and cartridge…three hundred. And that's most every Knight in the county."

"And I've now almost thirty hireds."

Serranus drew in the phlegm from the back of his throat and spit out into the sunlight. "He's a bummer Mister Whitehorse. A walking black spot that can't be believed."

"I don't entirely believe him," said Arlen. "But I won't have him know it. Bring him in here. And exude caution."

CHAPTER THIRTY-EIGHT

A whiskey bottle was pushed up against the side of Matthew's head as he wrote in his notebook.

"Gettin' it all down there?"

Matthew looked up. Ed squeezed down beside him. They were both leaning back against the stone wall of the old Mexican's shelter, south of the mine near Dick's Creek.

"I don't like being stared down at by the Tills," said Ed. "Or by Whitehorse. I'm their right proper field hand now...the bastards."

"I know what this is really about."

"Do you?"

"Neville Faire is dead and he can't ruin the reputation of Ed Candles. But now Ed Candles will be called a—"

"Yeah. A traitor once. A whore now."

"Pride," damned Matthew.

"Pride," damned Ed back. He jammed the whiskey bottle against Matthew's notebook and the liquor swilled over the pages. "Are you any different?"

Matthew daubed at the washed over pencil work.

Ed kept on, using that whiskey bottle as a pointer. "You there with your comments and considerations. Will people see events as they really were, or as they were when your pencil got through with them? Don't you call that pride? Is how you see the world how the world is really seen?"

Ed took another drink. When he spoke again there was a slight woe to his voice. "You know, Matthew, there's so many faces to go around, we should at least be entitled to dealer's choice. And the hell with history."

• • •

Hetty arrived tonight, her wagon creaking up the scarred cascade. The horses were so exhausted they could go no farther than halfway, and she herself looked pale and tired but she buoyed us all with good news. Our plan will be executed.

On the 15th of August five companies of Union Dragoons will march north from Los Angeles to an abandoned outpost in the Tejon Pass. From there Hetty will guide them northeast toward Walker Pass where they will begin a circuitous march toward the Millrace so their dust will not be seen. At the same time Ed will earn his Judas wage by letting Arlen and the Tills know he is to deliver a wagonload of arms and munitions to Jason and me and our "imaginary cohort of revolutionaries" on the hills above the Millrace.

It should configure up to be quite a summer, with us playing the rabbit to their Golden Circle of wolves, as they chase us down into the snare we've set.

• • •

The dark tended back from the shelter door as Hetty finished dressing. She slipped on her deerskin coat and stood one minute more, alone, looking down at the blankets where she and Jason had slept. She stepped out into first light.

Jason was by the old stone trail where the tree had been struck by lightning. The last time she'd seen Joaquim alive was at that very spot. Jason was tightening down the newly twined cinches on her drawhorse. He reached into his pant pocket for his watch. Smoke drifted up from a fire beside which Hetty was saying goodbye to the others. Without anyone seeing, Jason slipped his watch into a hand woven maleta that was strung across the saddle and carried her personal belongings.

As she and Matthew said goodbye, she leaned up to his ear and whispered, "Keep a place for me on the other side of the lake." He nodded, and she kissed him on the cheek.

As she turned, Ed held up a pocket Colt. "I carried this with me in a war once, and except for the Pepperbox Kid here's iron monster, this five shot was hell for nasty. If you've got no more vision than Ichabod Crane, it will leave no ground between whoever you fire at and the kingdom of heaven."

Ed holstered it into her belt just beyond the cover of her hide coat.

She thanked Ed then looked over at the Hawaiian who squatted by the fire, milling coffee. She held up a hand. He ran his fingers out fast and straight to the length of his arm, then he brought it back and his two hands clasped together.

Hetty walked over to her horse, coming up alongside Jason. They held each other. She then climbed up into the saddle. She leaned down and kissed him. Then, in slow time, she became part of the landscape.

• • •

By midday of the fifteenth, Hetty reached the abandoned mud and slat structures of Fort Tejon that squared up in a pale valley cut from the intrusive rock. She walked her horse across the weed strewn parade ground. There were no signs of Union Dragoons, as there should have been.

She made up her bedroll on an empty barracks floor. Pieces of torn strut burned inside the hearth. She looked out the tilting frame of the doorway and past the stolid crumbling bunkers.

Morning came to her, alone. She was wobbly and weak and she knelt to vomit in the sand. The sun was now moving time against her. The day filled out and the day withered, and it was only then that she spotted a powdery weal coming up through the colorless gemstone hills.

She labored to the edge of the sunburned camp. It wasn't five companies of Dragoons that cleared the haze but rather a solitary Union officer covered with the scurf of a hard ride.

He dismounted.

"Where are they? You can't be alone."

She recognized him as one of the silent Lieutenants around the Commander's desk when the plan had been laid out.

"They aren't coming."

She had a fleeting sense the earth was turning back on itself.

He took a letter from his coat and handed it to her.

She tore it open.

"We just got word," said the Lieutenant, "that Carlton and the California Column defeated Sibley at the Rio Grande. Our regiment has been ordered east for the drive into Texas."

Her eyes rushed through the Commanding Officer's letter,

which confirmed all that the Lieutenant had said. She threw the letter aside.

"There are men north of here counting on you."

"They'll have to give it up."

"Give it up?" She stepped within striking distance. "They're out in open country. Do you understand? They'll be swarmed."

She hung onto an expectation, but the Lieutenant just pulled a water bag from the saddle and filled his hat with water so that his mount might drink.

"I have orders to issue you a letter for any horses or supplies at the outlying posts that you might need."

She looked back up through the Tejon Pass. "Where is the nearest post?"

"Fort Mojave."

She remembered being in the dark with Jason, wrapped in blankets, their backs against the stone wall in the old man's hut, knowing full well what would happen if—

She turned upon the Lieutenant, who was shaking the last drops of water from his hat. "You have regimental stationery and seal?"

"Yes."

She stepped back and reached inside her coat. "How many men are stationed at Fort Mojave?"

"Eight companies. If you can call niggers men."

She pulled up Ed's pocket Colt and cocked down the hammer with the flat of her hand.

"Ma'am? What are you doing?"

"You'll write me a letter, sir, and sign it with your Commander's name, authorizing the officer at Mojave to spare me the men I need. And you'll seal it."

The blood pulsed up at the edge of the Lieutenant's temples.

"You could hang for this, ma'am."

Her face remained impassive.

"Ma'am, this is an act of treason."

She held up that iron frame Colt. "America was built on treason. Now write the letter, or I will send you on your way."

• • •

Hetty rode up through the Canyon of the Grapes. She had the forged document in her coat. She was riding the officer's mount while her own was tethered to the saddle. She had left the Lieutenant with water and cartridge and a set of legs healthy enough to see him home.

By dusk she whipped the frothing mount down toward the dry basin where rock and brush lay scattered across its moonscape like shards of broken earthenware.

She pushed on through nightfall till the officer's mount, with blood and saliva frothed up around its muzzle, stuttered, then slumped forward. There in the black came a single burst of white powder and the beast crumpled away in the dark. She climbed up onto the back of her drawhorse and continued on.

The sun rose over what appeared as some abhorrence that had foresworn itself against her. Sand the color of dead eyes brined around desert shrubs grown like iron spikes out the earth's dusty flesh. She followed an old miner's trail that was signposted with paltry rot. The day was a puzzle of wells over which the summer had blown the bad luck of alkali. Her mount's head lolled and pitched like a child's broken toy. She cast off extra weight; slicker, blanket, saddlebags, but it would not help where rest and grain were needed.

A day fevered together with another. Her skin blistered, her lips welted, and there was no whip that could drive that horse harder.

By late afternoon she saw a party of travelers pitched up together on a windswept enclave, and she rushed to them, pulling at the reins of her drawhorse and waving her hat and shouting. They waved back with the breeze, and it was only after exhausting herself for a mile did she realize they were the lurid remains of mesquite, standing buckled and blighted black from fire.

She tried to get her mount to continue on, but its hooves were raw and splintered and each coulee had been a more painful passing. It finally just sank down on its belly in the sand, preferring to die than go on suffering. She struggled out of the saddle and tried to implore the beast up, but its tongue could only draw at the rocks as it whimpered to be left where it lay.

She slumped down, and wavering in the heat, tried to count the days. Is it the seventeenth or the eighteenth? How far have I come? How much farther?

She fought the nausea, the dizziness. She crawled over and began to strip the horse of what bare necessities she would need for her walk. She grabbed a canteen. She untied the maleta and shook everything out into the soft gravel. She plucked up a tied kerchief of cartridges and a broken piece of mirror to signal with. It was only then that she saw Jason's watch. The silver case glyphed against the sand.

Her shadow scooped it up. She blew the dust from the finely etched case and pressed open the latch. The faces of the dead smiled out at her.

CHAPTER THIRTY-NINE

"I'd like to know where they are, Matthew. Yes, I damn well would." Ed paced alongside the freight wagon. "I don't like being out in open country arsey-turvy, not at all."

Matthew was lying on a blanket between two junipers that were the lone markers along the ridgetop above the Millrace. He rolled over and sat up. He looked out over the hills to the west. They were bleached with the end of summer, and there was barely a tree for border.

"Jason will be here soon as he's sure Arlen and—"

"Not him, you fool."

He looked to the east where the low grass hills gave way in time to the Millrace. "It's her. She should have been here with the Army last night."

It was a troubling fact, and Matthew reached to his satchel for a drink of laudanum. Ed glanced at Coco who was sitting braced against the wheel of the wagon, shaving down a seven foot section of branch into a slender staff.

"Am I right or not?"

Coco looked out toward the Millrace where a thick morning haze had begun to obscure the ridges. He looked back at Ed and came up like a squat bear. He pointed at himself, then his horse, then at the Millrace. Then he pointed to his eyes and began to wave a hand.

"Good idea."

"But what will you wave from there that we can see?" asked Matthew.

Coco walked over to his saddlebags and took out the stretch of canvas with that painted falling comet from the Big Blue Heaven. He held it against the staff he was whittling like some heraldic banner.

Ed eyed him closely while he climbed into the saddle, "You bastard, you've been shaving that staff all along so you must have had the same damn —"

• • •

The Percheron huffed its way back into camp. Jason pulled himself from the saddle. "They're here."

He squatted down and sanded a spot in the dirt so he could draw what he'd seen. "Where's Coco?"

"That barbarian went to watch for the woman."

Ed and Matthew crouched alongside Jason as he freehanded out their moves.

"Us…the Millrace." He etched a slow line with his thumb and the stub of his middle finger poked at the air, "They came straight on from the slough till they got about here and then they broke off into two packs. One is camped just below there." He made another mark. "The other is camped above us there. Both are about two miles out."

Ed looked over at the scratchings and the two points facing down on their position from the west, like the wide end wings of a V.

"Looks like nothing too complicated from these Cousin Sallys. When the fire signals them, we're all here, they'll come on merry for the pinch. And us with the sun and them straight out of the black."

Matthew closed off the thought. "Then we run them dead end into the Millrace."

"And if the woman and those blue dogs don't show," said Ed, "we'll be swallowed in our own game."

Matthew looked over at Jason to see what he thought, but he was still tied to the map.

"Jason?"

Jason's eyes peeked up, then he stumped his thumb against the northernmost wing of the V. "A small group broke off the pack and kept traveling up and around in a half circle east. They were too far up country for me to see where they were heading."

"That dirties it up," said Ed. "They could be moving all the way around so they can come up through the Millrace from the other side of the river."

"Maybe. But they risk giving themselves away. How many hireds did Arlen have?"

"About thirty by last count."

"Do you think it's him?" asked Matthew.

"Whoever it is, they're making a clever move," said Ed. "They could even be testing the truth of what was told 'em, and they'll probe a little tonight."

Coco returned just past dusk. He carried the staff and banner across his saddle. As he swung his mount around he drove the staked end into a hump of ground.

The others squared up around a blanket, setting out a cold meal. Coco sat with them and not a question was asked as his not waving the flag was answer enough. They ate Indian cornbread and salted fish from tins.

Ed was the first to speak. "Well, since I'm the only one with a mouth full of bad news, I'll say it. What are we gonna do?"

"She'll be here."

"We need more than a wish now, Jason. We have to decide."

Jason stood. "She'll be here. And we'll go in."

Ed swung his head around as Jason passed. "Two days late is not bein' here."

Ed looked at the others. "You know if we get stuck here facing this alone, it's going to be some Nantucket sleighride."

Jason stopped beside the wagon. It creaked restlessly with the wind as he looked out toward the Millrace. The air was heavy with the smell of the earth.

"There's no partnership in tragedy, Jason," Ed told him.

Jason looked inside the wagon, loaded as it was with arms and munitions as part of the ruse.

"How much explosives do you have?"

Ed stood and joined Jason. "I've got enough clay jugs filled with rawbone to scorch a few acres."

"How long a charge can you set?"

"Not long enough for us to get out of the county."

"Tomorrow after we set the signal fire to draw them in as we start to run, you set a charge. So if they rush this hill they—"

Ed cut him off. "You know why I'm saying all this."

Jason's face became drawn. "In the morning—"

"Christ, even if they show up down there, they can't get through to us tonight. In the dark. How would they find us? And in the morning it would be too late."

"Then we set our fire. We draw them in. We run."

"But how will you know if she's there, 'cause if she's not—"

"She knows we're here, and she won't leave us abandoned."

$$\bullet \ \bullet \ \bullet$$

Scouts came and went that night reporting on what they did and did not see in the country of the Millrace. Arlen sat with the Tills at the end of a long draw where he and his hireds were huddled up around their bedrolls. A lone guard watched in the moonlight as the three men conferred on their plans for the following morning.

When Candles set the signal fire, each Till brother would lead one group of Knights over open ground from the west and east while Arlen swept in from the north, crossing the low foothills and descending upon the Millrace from across the river and cutting off all means of escape to whoever survived the charge.

Later when the Tills had gone back to their camp, Arlen considered the plan more stoically. Something had been nagging at him since that day Candles brought in the information. It was at odds with what he saw and what he sensed. This whole expedition was framed by certain considerations that nagged at him and had nagged at him all the more upon their descent toward the Millrace.

He wondered how his father would deal with this. His father was a man of huge emotions, and those emotions demanded huge resolutions. And many times the passion behind those emotions dictated a course of action vastly different from more prudent men. Such was his father's involvement with Demerest, the Knights and the Union. His father had tried to exercise his will upon two opposing forces to further his own personal dynasty, and in the end was destroyed for it. Arlen had privately seen it as a mistake, and yet here he was, with the same men in a not dissimilar configuration.

He looked down through this gulf of men, then up along the windworn crest of the draw where a solitary gunney watched out over the country of the Millrace.

Arlen called the two keeners over who ran his day to day operations. They were ravenlike men who had survived years of bitter rivalries throughout the back country.

"What do you think of the plan?"

They were silent at first, prudent.

"I want the truth now."

"It's a sound plan, Mr. Whitehorse," said the one.

"What do you think of this country?" asked Arlen. "I don't know it at all, and the Tills only fair. The Millrace, it seems to me, is ground that could work against us."

"Mr. Whitehorse," said the second, "most of the men with the Tills are tobacco drizzling crackers, and I doubt the men with those we're going after to be much different. But you're right about one thing, sir, if they knew we were coming and were dug in, they could make a hard fight of it."

"But we'll be fine in a hard fight," said the other, "If that's what's worrying you."

"That's not it." Arlen thought on how best to explain what he was sensing. "When I was a boy, my father made me study with a tutor, and it was a dark day for me."

He reached over and took the cigarette from one of the men's hands. "Greek history…Ovid…Herodotus. My father wanted me educated and every night I had to read to him what I'd learned or face his bear of a hand."

He drew in the smoke and he watched the ground being blown

off with the wind. "There's one story I remember that plagues me now. There was a king named Xerxes and he invaded Greece with his Persian Army. A huge army, bigger than anything this country has ever seen. And he had this uncle…"

He paused a moment. "For the life of me I can't remember his name. But this uncle warned him at every turn about the expedition. And Xerxes kept saying, it's only to those who are willing to act that mostly win the prize, for big things are won through big dangers. My father liked that part of the story best."

A sharp animus surfaced in Arlen's eyes at his father for not having heard the wisdom in the story. He took another long draw on the cigarette and handed it over to the man. He tried not to be hurt or angry at his father.

He continued on. "Now, there were these Greeks who offered to help this Xerxes against their own countrymen. And his uncle warned him that any man scoundrel enough for that, was of no use in a fight, for he would scoundrel you just as quick. But if he was just only playing the scoundrel, then he was more deadly yet, for he was willing to push the gamble."

He looked closely at both keeners. They were bare men, spartan in all things. He felt suddenly awkward even trying to reach them.

"The man we're hunting…I know him well. And he knows the shill better than anybody. He has the smell of it under his fingernails and I don't feel he could be gamehened by a man like Candles."

"I see now where this is goin'," said the first. "You think Clay might know, and he's ready to make a fight of it out there."

"Maybe he's planned a fight. Or maybe I've just read too much in books."

"Well, sir," said the other, "they're just friggin' themselves, or they've taken too much of the bottle to think they can outfight us."

"Just tell us your intention, Mr. Whitehorse, and we'll see it through."

How accurate a measure of the present was the past? He saw how he was different than his father, but not yet how much the same.

• • •

Jason was sitting alone on the wagon seat when Matthew came over and eased down on the thill. Both men looked out into the blackness that in the morning would become the Millrace.

Matthew half turned and looked up at him. "If anything happens to me tomorrow I want you to do me a favor."

Jason looked down from the wagon seat and his voice tried to assure, but Matthew cut him off, "Yes, but if it does," he tapped his satchel, "I want you to take care of my notebook."

Jason tried again to assure, but Matthew parried and cut him off. "See it gets back to Wilcox at the *Flag*. Or at least to someone who might know what to do with it. If there is anything.

"You see, Jason, it's all I've got really." He looked down at the filthy canvas bag marked with months of dirt and blood. The frailty of it all overwhelmed him. "It's all that I am, Jason. And...well...I don't want to be forgotten."

Jason looked at Matthew, caught there in the act of life. He jumped down from the wagon seat and walked up alongside his friend and he rested his hand on his shoulder. Matthew's hand came up and rested on his. The two men together were just feet from where the ground began to gently slip away toward tomorrow.

"Remember that old man on the junk who shepherded us downriver?" said Jason.

"That huge crow," said Matthew,

"Remember how he asked us to piss down country once for him?"

"We never did."

Matthew tinkered up a smile.

Ed watched the two of them unbutton their pants and stand side by side, with their members rinsing the ground around their boots like wolves.

Later, Jason joined Ed, who sat like some shoddy Buddha guarding the bottle. Jason slipped down beside him and held out his porringer for Ed to rinse with another shot.

"You should have told him the truth."

Jason sipped from the cup. "I thought I was."

"Yeah, well, you and the boy can piss all you want, but he'll know the truth when he's washed up on the side of the road."

"What is it, then? Truly?"

"What?" Ed pulled at his beard. "You and I are more alike than you know. Oh, yes. We are. You and I both know that two weeks from now, Whitehorse or the Tills or any of the shit with them will butter their bread and slop down their liquor and they'll squat and shit and frig themselves to sleep, and we'll be so much nightsoil. We both know it. And we both know what this all is. The only difference between us, I don't weave any fringe into it."

"There is some part to what you say. But part's missing." Jason stood.

"And what is that?"

"Does the sun ever come up on you?"

Ed stared at him bitterly. "Ask me tomorrow night."

Under the rustling yaw of the junipers, Matthew looked up from his notebook to see Coco take a pair of pliers and begin to pull out his left front tooth. Blood spurted in thin veins from his mouth and the shank of the tooth ground out through the bone and snapped. Coco did all this silently and without the least emotion. Matthew got up and went to him. Coco held up the tooth for him to see. Then Coco took his knife and began to shave away the weeks of scraggly beard until all that was left was the right half of a moustache that hung like string along his lips.

Matthew asked why he was doing this. Coco explained with the slow precision of his fingers that tomorrow would be an important fight, and he wanted to pay tribute to it in the calendar of his flesh.

Then, with blood still seeping out the corners of his mouth, he unpacked his dyes and fluted needle bones. He removed his shirt and began to engrave an upside down, crescented blue anchor into his chest. When that was done, he needled the initials of each man at the four points of the compass around the blue grappling hook, and then he finished by carving a swath of wind the anchor could sail on.

Coco put his dye and fluted bones aside and borrowed makings from Matthew. He rolled a cigarette, and with his stained fingers proudly showed off his work. He blew smoke through the bloody gap of his teeth and he licked the blood with his tongue. Then he lay down to rest and Matthew was alone.

The moon began to turn to morning, as Matthew turned to a clean page in his notes:

August 19
I believe this may well be my last "Letter from the West"...

CHAPTER FORTY

With first light, the wind came blowing up from the southeast. The ground smoked of dust and scrub and dry grass all the way up through the Millrace.

Ed yelled to Jason, who stood like a sentry along the cutout fold of the hills. "Still nothing from her. And there'll be no message of any movement through that dust, so save your eyes."

It was true. The wind cheated him. But as with all things, there was a double edged blessing, for if Hetty and the troops were coming up through the country of the Millrace, Arlen and the Tills couldn't see their movements either.

"Jason…we could still make it away from here."

Jason looked around him. A steam floated off the earth. The men were solitary as carved pieces on a chessboard. The horses stood by, saddled and ready. Weapons were primed and charged. Coco had lashed the staff from stirrup to saddle. The canvas comet streamed in the wind above the other mounts. Inside the wagon a flash line of powder ran into the womb of a clay jug, pregnant with rawbone. Jason could feel the heat coming on early against the bloodstained face of that coated lion who watched out for the world that hunted him. The bloodlines of the sun pushed up shadows, long and slender and reaching.

Ed asked him again, "We can still quit this?"

Jason did not answer. He looked instead at the wagon, the canvas hood lifting out in the wind like a heart, like a thought forming. The four mules that had pulled the wagon stood loose and grazed. The two junipers together, like a portal to some post where all things were possible.

The two junipers, the wagon, the mules— The flood. The two twisted hulls, torn through the wagon and canvas and horses, bearing down dead through a black scheme of slumgullion to sweep them away. All things were together here.

Coco slapped his billy against his hand and then motioned to Jason that the ground told him the two great horns of the Knights' casque had begun to move slowly for position against their station.

Jason could smell the old man and the months worn on that coat. The sun kept coming. The wind was still against them, the wind was still with them. The sun kept coming. It created flesh across the bones of the faces around him. They were solemn parings, one by one by one, waiting for a command, for they all knew the decision had been made. It was made somewhere in the iron hills of time when the first forge stamped the story we call man, out of wisdom and hate and mud.

There was no other moment now. There was no other time. There was no other history. There was no day. There was no night. There was only this. The closing of all things. The beginning of all things.

"Set the fire," whispered Jason.

Ed grabbed a can of kerosene.

"You think we have enough wood there?" said Matthew.

"Enough wood?" Ed tossed the can to Matthew. "We're looking eye to eye with that pile." He scooped up another can and they began to douse the stacked shred. He tossed the emptied can onto the pyre.

Matthew tossed his can beside Ed's. He scrounged up a match from his satchel.

Ed ran his fingers up through his beard. "Well, we're about to become the rawbone of our own fire. Amen and fuck you."

There was a rush straight up and the flames swooshed and swinged in fluted shapes, coughing up smoke at the dry air.

Ed and Matthew ran for the mounts. Coco came around with his hands tumbling one over the other. Jason followed the line of his billy to where a convergence of men, not yet men but the dust of men that preceded their fury, squalled up in gulfs. Their slim catclaw lines charged over the skinned hills like some plague of vermin.

Ed led his mount over to the wagon. "Should I charge the fuse?"

The hilltop curdled with smoke and Matthew had to wave his hat to hold back from choking. Coco swung up in the saddle and the canvas banner armed out to the wind as he reined around his sorrel.

A mile away, the swarm left its mark from slope to lea, fanning out in packs.

"Did you hear me, Jason?"

Jason stepped through the smoke. Matthew was holding the Percheron alongside his horse. Jason took the stocked Volcanic that was hanging from a lanyard across the saddle horn and swung it over his neck.

Came the first shots now. Riffles of yellow powder. Cats' eyes that burst and vapored and disappeared. More to rouse the blood of the mongrels than to bleed an enemy.

"God damn you, Jason, are we gonna wait till we can trade samplers with those bastards?"

More rifle fire. A hem now, a thousand yards out. And the Millrace still a whirl of unsettled dust. He glanced at Matthew.

"Li reis Marsilie de nos ad fait marchet; Mais as espees l'estuvrat esleger."

"What?"

Jason turned and climbed onto the Percheron. He looked back down at his friend, his face and coat dappled with gray ash.

"Though King Marsilla bought us in a bargain; He still will have to close the deal with swords."

"Why, you gut pulling...you said you never read a—"

"Set the charge, Ed!"

Before the smell of burning sulphur turned the air, the four had begun a slow descent down through a coulee washed with shade. They moved quickly out of view and along a dry bed of soft argil buying themselves some distance. Their weapons were poised as they pushed through the short brush tailorwise. Behind them on the hills, small pockets of men were in movement.

They turned into a swale that would lead them to the south. As they made their way up through the dark lines of early morning along an incline, there was an explosion that rocked them to their bones. On the hilltop a thin shrill of men and horses were thrown out from a scorching wall laced with spears of wood and the two great junipers streaked up in flames like devotional candles set out on the table of the sky.

"They get their first taste of the dead, heh!"

They made straight for open ground now. A clean, wide, yellow run over the arc of native hills toward the dust blown Millrace.

Dark pockets of gunfire erupted as the rabble tribe hunting them was spotted. Yelling along the slope comrade to comrade. A great half circle of men whipped their ponies out from the center of that crescent shaped plateau afire.

Down through a slurry of strewn cake and grass where the slope slipped away into a shallow bottom of round worn gravel and baby tears, then up again to the south, the four pressed on. Here at the edge of a swale, the first two gunneys were come upon, with their rifles staked and sweeping in at a cross angle.

Jason shouted to the others and a wall of shotgun and rifle fire blew out a one bar cadence. The gunneys were torn asunder and trampled underfoot. The four horses' hooves were spotted with blood, and the men's faces started to flush and stain with sweat and powder and filth. Once again they rushed up into a clear face of sun.

Their packs and saddles banged like chimes. The maniples of the Tills maneuvered over the wind formed fingers of ground as pin-pricks of scattershot churned up the sod that girded the riders. They strung out like harts, as they charged across a meadow toward the tawny slanting summit of outcrop that guarded the valley of the Millrace.

They were bent low to the saddle, with the stench of hide and the leather and metal pressed against their faces. The patchquilt keepers of the country, ferine and barbarous, posed their muskets and breechloaders and hackbuts to the wind in full stride. The air was filled with trails of gray yellow stains chasing the tail of a comet painted on a swath of canvas and imprinted on a stretch of sky. Chasing the long shade legs of the horses, their necks and heads stretched and their muzzles bared for breath. Their eyes were all white and furious chasing the scent of the river that lured them all with safety, lured them all with death.

They came upon hard earth and their hands slapped the rein-whips. The four Carolingian horsemen leapt a short raincut gap and thundered down again, as brass cap and mini-ball tore out the air ahead of them in a warning that their time had come. They pressed on in a jumble of shouts and curses, and a bullet tore out a piece of saddle and a water bag. Another bullet shattered Ed's wrist. A mini-ball claw-marked a scar across Matthew's face. The smell of their riders' blood drove the mounts on fiendishly through woven brakes of stone where the sun rimmed out the gray rock like shields. Their black forms swept the crest through one long, racked volley of fire that stung and burned and echoed, but before they cleared, one was thrown.

The tumbling carcass slid down the escarpment like a child's sleigh and was battered up against a nest of stones. The riderless horse rushed on, with only that thin banner left to claim him. The others topped and came around in a tangle of coats and hooves. Coco rolled back on his bullet shattered hips and tried to wave them off as he struggled up a grapeshot pistol from his belt.

The three hung on that rocky slope in a half moment of try-ing to go back to their friend, when an acid line of fire peaked the ledge and damned their mounts to pitch and bolt. Jason could see their flanks were being swept by solitary keeners scrambling for the ground ahead.

Ed shouted, "You both go on." He was winding a scrap of canvas around his bleeding wrist. "I'll see if I can drag the barbarian back up on my saddle."

As he turned away Matthew tried to turn with him, but Ed chested his mount into Matthew's and chased him back.

"You got enough trouble carrying that satchel of yours." His boots rammed along the fender and his bay plunged back over the netted gravel. He hoved up beside the twisted bulk of the Hawaiian, hugging a knot of boulders.

He kneeled down and saw a shank of thighbone driven up through the flesh where it stood out like the longpiece shaft of an arrow. Both pant legs were covered with blood from the groin.

He looked at that moon face twisted up in a grimace. Coco tried to push Ed back to his saddle with a pistol wave as a hedge of men charged down from the crest.

For one instant Ed could see himself and Charlie swimming that river in the twilight of their innocence. As the riders poured over ground stamped wild raw and rutted, Ed swung up and grabbed a clay jug filled with rawbone that was lashed across his saddle. He wanded up his double barreled Chance and fired one round of scattershot into his mount's head. It collapsed. He barricaded himself behind its tremoring corpse. Coco watched as Ed jammed the clay jug between them. He arched back and cocked the second hammer of the shotgun as the banshee line came screaming down upon them, with dusty beards and fists hanked around their firing pistols.

Ed looked at the Hawaiian and whispered, "Close your eyes, Charlie, and I promise…we won't feel a thing this time."

Ed aimed. Bullets tore into the bay's flesh, spattering blood across his neck and face and beard and hands. It wet his eyes. Coco screamed out silently from a hollow throat kilned in a rage by the white Lords who'd stolen his country. He fired pointblank at the riders, who howling whelmed their barricade. With one last chance at civil disobedience, Ed pulled the trigger.

The borderland behind Jason and Matthew and Coco's bannered horse became a rainbow of flaming rawbone and rock. Men and mount were catapulted away. Bits of cloth and hat were firebranded across the chaotic stampede, rushing forth through the dust under a sky turned scarlet.

The open table Jason and Matthew crossed was touched and charged with fowling pieces and muskets hung high across the saddles of roughs and farmers and stiff necked shovelmen. The two broke through a grotto of thickets and crossed a rust colored gulley of mica and hornblende. Jason pointed his Volcanic across that nameless trace to where a hundred short yards away the plateau descended into the long strip of valley that ended at the river and the old wooden wheel.

Matthew went to yell that he saw it, when a lone Cornish bullyboy came slanting up through a swale across their path, flush with pistol fire. Before Matthew could react to the gray barks of powder, he was hit in the lung. His brow lurched up in shock. Jason screamed and hammered down the lever of that Volcanic. It smoked empty and the errant tramp was torn through to the bone. He fell back over the cantle like a shawl.

Matthew sagged and swung out from his saddle and Jason sided up to him in full stride. He held him in place. Blood spurted out onto the canvas satchel. The horses slammed into each other and tipped, their footfalls stuttered. The whoops and cries and curses were closing in on a horrible destruction. Jason leaned over and got a hold of Matthew's reins. Matthew could feel the blood clotting in his throat and the last straight before the Millrace seemed never coming. Never...

His voice coughed out, "Let me go...Jason...let..."

Jason whipped both horses.

"...me go..."

Blood colored Jason's coat as he whipped both mounts again.

"...Jason...Jaso..."

Jason braced up the bloody shell of his friend.

"...Let me go..."

His vision began to wither. "...Jason...I'm..."

"I can't!", said Jason.

The horses slammed together again and almost fell.

Matthew's face hung. Warm blood spilled from his mouth. He tried to slip his hand across the saddle and—

His fingers tipped the reins and—

Soft clay around the hooves was thrown up into his face and—

His fingers numbly curled around the tether—

As a riderless bay and a comet thundered past—

One charge of strength—

Just one—

Just—

Matthew pulled the reins hard. They burned through Jason's fingers. Matthew's horse cranked around. The Percheron ran past the weight of Matthew's falling frame that cartwheeled man and mount down the chafed back of the ridge. Jason tried to rise up in his saddle and come around in a battery of fire.

Matthew was lying on his hands and knees beside his dead mount coughing blood. He tried to focus but the world was spinning on without him.

Jason could feel the ship of himself breaking upon the tide of that rocky esker. He went to kick the Percheron back to his friend when something, something infinite and imperfect and impervious to all sufferings loomed up through the shadowless funnel of the Millrace. His eyes went black as the belly of a cannon, and he knew he must leave Matthew to die.

Leaves blew past Matthew's glasses. His salt colored fingers were flecked with phlegm and dirt and blood. He could feel, barely now, but feel, the drum of hooves rolling up out of the earth upon him.

He tried to stand but wavered, and the pendant of his canvas satchel slung across his shoulder like a baldric almost carried him away. But his boots anchored. He leaned into the slope.

Above the crest a hundred yards back the two Golden Circle maniples converged behind the Tills, as Matthew's fingers snailed across his belt to free the pepperbox.

Against their howling he struggled up a defense behind that iron monster. With both hands he held it out straight, gasping for any breath he could find within himself.

This ragged phalanx of ruffians did not yet see Matthew as they surged toward the edge. He slow thumbed back the hammer and life spared him seconds…but they did not seem to reach him…and the world went white and silent…as he was deaf now and almost blind. A history was being painted in a frail son whose words were the life he scarped out in this temporary apprenticeship for death. And then the rim was stampeded.

The riders became the black shield of a sky, dust colored and pistol born. Eyes marbled in fury and flag and cause. Matthew felt Charlie lean over his shoulder in a wisp and hand hold the gun and promise to help him eye that rusty barrel. The two brothers' souls merged into one rush of rifle fire. The trigger was struck and the iron hydra blew apart, and through the cinerous smoke one of the Tills' saddles swept past, empty.

The ground gave way and there was seven feet of sky beneath the Percheron as it cleared the steeply dipping tuff. The lion coat and winded mountain horse cut a line straight through the grooves and chamfered architecture of an ancient lake that meadowed up an entrance to the Millrace.

Half a mile more and the hills would swell up in a banded stone along his flanks. A mile beyond that, a flat run. A mile more lay the river, and the end all the way around.

Up through a slake of ground, two blood red roans charged across his line of escape. Small pitched men with years under the sights of their long rifles swung up for a stand. There was no getting past, so Jason bore a path straight at them and hauled up his Volcanic. The riders circuited and stopped. One leapt from his saddle and readied up a long barreled Ballard. Jason fired, but the Volcanic was out of rounds.

Each breath now marked a turn. Jason's hand scrambled across the fender for his carbine gun. A Flatriver hat flew off the head of the second man as he jumped from his roan for position. There came a strike of smoke from the Ballard and the Percheron was hit in the chest. Its teeth railed and it stumbled, but held on. Jason cantilevered out from the saddle and the rifle barrel flashed white hot. The small man was thrown back stumbling against the horses. The other man tried to clear himself of the backward crush of hooves.

Jason heard the Percheron's breath come hissing in harsh, wet heaves. He slid the gun away and grabbed for his Jennings, but it got caught up in the rigging ring. The mere strip of ground between them vanished in one surge as the man weaved back behind the horses that skirted and maundered fiendishly. Jason let go of the reins and buckled his knees against that warhorse's flanks. He grabbed a pistol in one hand and a broad blade ax in the other, and drove down on the spinning ponies firing round after round into their soaked flanks. One collapsed away a path toward the man, who steadied, aimed, and fired, but the breech jammed. He was left open in the flats where Jason swapt down that ax with an arc that shattered bone and teeth, and lifted the man off the ground and flung him against the fractured earth.

One more huff carried them over a sandy bench and down into the long, gentle, sloping channel of the Millrace in a fusillade of rifle crack and fire.

The hole rented in the Percheron's chest spumed blood and globs of liquid along the length of its muzzle. It was dying, but wouldn't give way as Jason leaned in currying a call to keep on. To keep on. To keep on.

There was nothing ahead of them now. Nothing save the maul of hooves down through the open sun well of the barranca. Nothing save the silent reefs of dust along the hills that held their flanks. Nothing save the rushing current at the far end of the valley, churning through the cleaved stone vein of the earth. Nothing save the horse and rider who now seemed of one will, one breath, one meaning, one blood. The blood that brought them here, the blood that carried them on, the blood that in time would carry them away.

But in one blush of full stride and half the distance gone, the Percheron's heart burst. Its legs succumbed and the dust of their collapse rolled over them both. Jason staggered to his feet, woozy and choking.

The Percheron struggled to raise up the crown of its head. It struggled to free itself from the dark and bloody earth, where the stench of its voided bladder left a caking mark. It was a desperate and pathetic creature trying to will itself through its suffering, as if it had a sense there was more yet called for. Its muzzle and chin hung open snaring wildly for air. Jason knelt beside it, pulling up a revolver and rested a hand on the Percheron's neck, "No more...no more...you've done yours." He cocked the hammer, a single shudder of a haw. "Rest."

One shot. The Percheron's head slammed against the earth. A rush of dust and powderblack and blood. Jason's eyes burned, his eyes wet.

And then it washed over him. The salt of it flooded over him.

He was alone. The hills stood empty. It seemed he was the last step in a faulted plan.

A manuscript of riders swelled the sandy bench and stopped. The riders did not come forward. He could vaguely make out Emmit Till, hatless, at the ready. His brother's horse sauntered empty along their line. They expected Jason to run. The river was still six hundred yards across open ground.

Jason stood and pulled free of its scabbard the Sharps. He reloaded it. He leaned it against the bloody chest of the Percheron. He freed the Jennings from the rigging ring and stood it beside the other rifle. He pulled a second ax from a saddle loop and drove it into the ground. He scrambled bullets from his pocket and reloaded the stocked Volcanic and swung out the lanyard strung from his neck so the gun hung clear of his coat.

When he was done, he took the Sharps in one hand and the Jennings in the other and followed his trace over the warhorse's fallen hull.

The black smoke from the hill branded a thundercloud to the north, and at the far end of the compass, a white gray ash cloud marked the rawbone of his friends. At their center and farther back were the granite hills where the old Mexican man lay buried. It was all their manes that shaped the lion's head he wore. In his eyes were the torn images of the bull and the bear, in a ring of worn men dying.

He could hear the river run crystal through the creaking wooden wheel, and he came forward a step. Then another. His hands hafted up the rifle barrels to form a cross above his head to tempt them on.

They were a stoic castle behind Brother Till. With crossed Colts and sallet derby and plug hat and Gothic hide gauntlets. A corselet of rifles and pistols that shimmered in the light.

He took another step forward and screamed out for them to charge him away, that this poor beggar owned as much of the ground as they did.

Emmit rose up in his saddle. His brother's empty horse whinnied. A lone hat was swept up with the wind. Another horse bit and snapped at the air. Another dug at the ground. A rider drummed his pistol against a miner's pan strapped to his saddle.

Emmit leaned forward in his saddle. He looked around at the others. "Well, if it's his will and testament for us to run him down."

The vanguard rushed down the sandy bench and into the valley of the Millrace.

Jason crossed the bore of one rifle over the breech of the other to steady up his aim. He fired but the wind carried his shot away. He crossed the bore of the second over the breech of the first. He aimed. The ground between them closed in with dust. He fired. A horse traced out a stumble, and a rider was crushed beneath its weight.

Jason cast both rifles aside and reached for his Volcanic. He hammered down the lever. They were beyond his reach and so he waited. Their fire spit at the ground around him, when he saw a single prick of smoke from the hills and a rider fell.

Another shock of white followed. Then another. And finally, all along the length of the ridge on one flank, and then just as quickly, on the other.

The trap was sprung. Emmit hove up in the saddle. He saw a flag come haunting along the crest. Uniforms rushed alongside it. A company of black Dragoons began a sweep toward the sandy bench. The Knights circled and swirled as their ranks were sheared. Men twisted and wrenched like bits of flag torn apart. Their only hope — the river. That's all that was left to them so they made a desperate flock toward it.

They charged again toward Jason, who fired till the belly of his Volcanic was empty. He pulled up the other Volcanic and fired until that too was empty. He hauled up the old man's pistols from his belt and fired until he was choking in his own smoke.

They rushed down upon him, and he was only an ax now and a knife and a face painted like some savage with the powderblack of his own pistols.

A withering fire erupted along the river and past the rotting wooden waterwheel and past the crumbling stone farmhouse. It tore into the riders like the teeth of wolves and, with whatever magic Jason imagined, came one wish. Let me die today…Let me die.

CHAPTER FORTY-ONE

Hetty made her way among the bodies that lay in clusters behind the carcass barricade of their mounts. Among the dead were a few remaining wounded. Their heads shifted from side to side like sleepwalkers, or they grabbed at the infernal ghost of their wounds pleading for help. Both met the same fate at the hands of black troopers.

Hetty was frail and spent and went from corpse to corpse calling out to Jason. She came upon the bull chested warhorse. The air was speckled with flies that darted and lit across its face. She knelt and tried to brush them away, but could only sit weakly in the face of such a futile chore.

A shiny faced Private shouted out to her, "I think I found him, ma'am."

She looked up to see him kneel amidst a rubble of men.

"Is he alive?"

• • •

On a small rise near that crumbling waterwheel beside the Millrace, Hetty North and Jason Clay lay Matthew Christman down in the hole. She kissed his face. She took one of her mother's rings and cupped it in his hand and they closed him away.

Hetty went and sat by the river. Jason sat beside her, and he opened Matthew's satchel and looked through his few things till he came to the notebook.

In that ledger Jason came upon an entry written the night before:

August 19

I believe this may well be my last "Letter from the West"... Tomorrow, the time may have come for me to hand myself over.

I sit here alone on some dark stretch of the frontier within a handshake of the sky and a shooting star, and I wonder what meager place I have clericed for myself in this life.

I have thought of writing my family, but what could I say as I still remind them of the truth, and the truth of me to them is failure, Christian and otherwise.

But here, in the rugged back country of our nation's youth, I have been able to find another family. A family closer to my own callings. One that has never seen fit to cast me aside for my failings, which are many. They have, it seems, even found strengths in me I could never have had the courage to call upon myself. It would be hard to say goodbye to them, which is something I have not allowed myself to feel until now. Not really feel in some fully frightening sense.

I seem to be always caught between two distinct emotions. My need for peace, for home, and my anger at the peaceless homelessness of it all. I am like the fool who dances for affections to the harsh drum of acrimony. I am not unlike this country that must always be forever wounded by itself.

Of course it is never our ignorance that destroys us, that would be too simple. For ignorant people have gone on mercilessly for years. But it is our belief in our knowledge, or half knowledge, that suffers for us our future. Our only hope may be to betray the system that betrays us all. Otherwise there will be no ruins here. No time for that. Not the way we dig and carve. No statues. Nothing. The only ruins will be the land and, of course, man.

We study dead languages to increase our knowledge of the past when we should invent new languages to meet our future knowledge head-on. The real America will ultimately be built by those who walked away from America, and in so doing, build an America no one would want to walk away from. For every life is a parable; some for better, most for worse, but all are truth.

Of course, a hundred years hence it might well still be a battlefield of thoughts and ideas whose shores we have yet to reach.

And, when this is done, might we be viewed by many as just another parable of wickedness. Insolent losers: murderers, deserters, assassins, heathens, drug addicted dodseys—body plagued and soul dishonored. Whether the moral quest for order or the nightmare warned of for noxious centuries in the great book—we will all meet at the Millrace, in time...

People talk of the times they remember best. When times were good. When times were simpler. When San Francisco went only as far as Water Street. When our fathers took us out into our first snow. Or we saw our first ocean of summer in our mother's hand. With all of that I will always remember the time of insurrection, in our land...in our beings...And my friends here, those true, living "Letters from the West"...for that is what they are, them I will always remember.

No matter how much I were to write, one thing would stand true above the rest. From birth to death, we are just one moment midstream.

— Matthew Christman

CHAPTER FORTY-TWO

The gift of the day was the ground stinking from the carcasses and bodies.

Jason unloosed his gear and saddle from the Percheron. To the west, out of the bare tails of the coming sky, Jason could make out two riders skirting the perilous tuff of the hills. They seemed to linger, and they craned from their saddles in a soft wash of color, and it left him sure they were Arlen's men.

Walking the field Jason realized Arlen had not taken part in it. He must have sensed the plan for what it was, and so let the Tills be sacrificed. But he would come on again after. It would be a long hard winter for both hunters. And what about Hetty, now? Arlen knew about her. What should be done now?

Jason lifted the saddle and leather wallets and he hefted the Sharps carbine and the Jennings across his shoulder and made his way back toward the river through the rot of corpses. He passed Coco's horse, and she saw him stop there. A broken staff lanced up from its carcassed back where that piece of canvas from the Big Blue Heaven swooned a slim way with the breeze and then the life in it died away. Jason put rifles and saddle aside and knelt down. Carefully he undid the stretch of rigging and laid it on the horse's back, and then he folded it neatly as a handmaiden would table lace. He placed it in his saddlebags.

Later, by the bridge, Hetty was with Jason while he saddled up a blood red roan that he'd found snaked up in a thicket after the fight. Neither spoke during these disquieting moments, and Jason's eyes were constantly being drawn back toward the ridge now kindled with sunlight.

"He'll be coming soon?" she asked.

"Soon." Jason looked over at the troops who had only just begun to company up. "But not until they leave."

"Why don't you tell the soldiers Arlen is still out there with men?"

"Because Arlen knows I'm wanted by the army. If the soldiers found out…What do they do about me then?"

That fact had escaped her. Word probably had not even been sent to the black troops in the desert.

"Arlen is waiting because he doesn't want the army to have at me. Arlen is not his father," said Jason. "In fact, he seems much more deadly."

"What makes you say that?"

"He didn't come on with the others."

She looked down into the river. Jason glanced at her and the flush around her cheeks barely concealed her worn pale hue. How do I keep her alive, he wondered.

She looked up at him, and his face edged a bit with the light. She couldn't see how much pain was there. She pointed to the roan. "It's not like that old Percheron, is it?"

His mouth formed a no.

"It's got long spindle legs," she said, "that's for sure. Good for running."

"They're game for that."

There were beads of sweat along the bone beneath her eyes. He took an old kerchief and wiped at them. "There's things we need to decide now."

• • •

One of Arlen's scouts returned to camp at a full run with word the Army had crossed the river leaving the Millrace to the south. He and his gunneys made quick time of it. They approached the Millrace from where the twain of burned junipers stood out against the sky.

Reaching the Millrace, one of the men beside Arlen pointed to movement along the river. He stretched up from his saddle and there, in the old man's coat, was Jason. He and Hetty were leading their horses quickly up onto the bridge.

On the bridge Jason stopped. He reached across the saddle and lifted the loop of Matthew's satchel from the horn. He slipped his head and shoulder through the loop so it swung up along his left hip.

"Jason, here they come."

Hetty backpedaled both horses across the tremoring span. Jason kneeled down and cupped one hand around a line of black powder that seamed the clapboard sheets to a clay jug of rawbone wedged between the strut spans. He struck a match and ran. Arlen and his men were forced to hove up before debris was cannoned out into their pathway.

Arlen ordered his men to find a crossing along the river. He looked up into the hills and the cutout figure of two riders watched from along a draw. He dismounted and came through the smoke and began to scream across the river, "You think this will stop me? Do you? Do you think we can't cross any river you can blow the bridge to?"

Jason watched the men try to step their mounts down into the steep channel, but the current overwhelmed the mounts and they struggled and stumbled, turning back upon themselves. Jason answered Arlen by shouting back, "I only meant this as a warning. So you could spend a little more time with the dead."

Jason said not another word. He and Hetty began a slow crawl into the keep of the hills. His plan was to weave a trail over ground that would take them weeks to follow. Then he would turn back out of the hills. He would turn upon them again.

The ground began to smell of sugar pine and the green moss of creeksides. The Millrace was a flat plain now of unassailable distance. Withering floes of random dust.

They reached a spot high up where there was a watery gorge that flued breast high down through a wilderness of moss. Jason tested his taller mount first in the crossing. His roan shied and backed away and almost was lost in the current.

On the other side he dismounted and tied off a lair rope to the stand of a tree. He tossed the braided manila back across the chasm, so Hetty could secure the loop around a rock and use it as a sure line to keep her smaller mount from being dragged over the rocks.

She reached out for the rope. All the way up from the Millrace she had been host to the jealous contradictions between longing and judgment. Not the least of which was her act of treason. She looked across the chasm at Jason and then she threw the rope back.

"What are you doing?"

"I'm not coming with you."

Caught off guard, lost to react, he just stood there with the rope lying at his feet. "What do you mean?"

She stepped back. "I'm too slow, and I'll only get slower with time."

She turned and began to walk to her horse. He tried to speak but she cut him off. "See the better of it."

He took the leads to guide the roan down to the edge of the rocks so he could cross back.

"Don't. Don't come back across. Please, Jason. Please."

He could hear the plaintive in her voice and stopped. He watched her there in a small patch of sunlight the trees let through. A hundred questions came down to one. "Where will you go?"

"I'll make my way back to Sacramento. There are people there to help. I'll even try to see my cousin again."

"How do we keep in contact?"

She went to answer, but could not. She noticed her image in the water being turned by the current and knew he could hear her answer before she could say it.

"We won't."

His head shifted and he sighed. "Hetty—"

"Don't, Jason." She took another step back. "We're not finished yet. You know that. We both know."

He made a silent nod.

"In the end, when it's over. When this war is all over. I'll find you there." She pointed down to the valley of the Millrace. "Where the bridge was, Jason. Where the grave is."

He looked toward the Millrace then back at her, "I'll find you..."

He turned away and climbed onto that red running horse. There were worlds of feelings as he put a hand out, but she could see all of that.

"Go. Do you hear me?"

He reined the horse around and followed a graveled path that edged the gorge. There were waves of mist coming off the stones in the thunder rush of the stream. She followed, laboring over rocks, walking parallel to watch a little longer. His path began to veer back from the shelf, rising. He stopped again, and she could hear his voice above the rumble of wreathing foam.

"I was broken once. Before—"

"Just go!"

He moved quickly now. The long spider legs of the blood roan arching up a sand landslip, arching up through a thin spilt of trail.

She felt the life stirring within her. Maybe she should have told him about the child. Maybe in some way it would have helped him, maybe in some way given him something if he were lost. But maybe it was wiser to have nothing said, maybe it would have changed him in some way, some other way that might have slowed him down, made him choose caution and cheated him. Maybe.

She walked back to her horse. She went to pull herself up in the saddle, but stopped. She was shaking and sick, and she was alone with her decision. Her head rested against the leather. "Please, don't let him die. Please. And don't cheat him of everything but that coat. Don't leave him with only that."

She looked back up toward the crest. She could barely see him now weaving his way on through the gnarled stalks of bristletoe. A fanlight of sun stole his image. She took a step to one side to steal it back. She cupped a hand over her eyes. She caught sight of him where the crestline touched the sky. Then he was gone.